The Mockingbird Drive

A.C. Fuller

SERIES LIST

To my brother, Noah Brand, who helped create this story.

A.C. FULLER

THE MOCKINGBIRD DRIVE

PART ONE

CHAPTER 1

Payoff Plaza Strip Mall, Las Vegas, Nevada
Tuesday, June 13, 2017

Twelve years ago, Greta tiptoed up behind me in our tiny kitchenette in New York City, wrapped an arm around my waist, and asked me to marry her. Even at nine months pregnant, she moved elegantly and spoke poetically. "We have this one life," she said. "Let's use it to walk each other home."

Her only demand was truth. She knew that we'd both change over time, and someday one of us was bound to change in a way that would fracture our marriage, at least temporarily. But as long as we were completely honest, we could work through anything.

I promised her that day that I'd never lie to her, and I never did.

About a hundred years before I met Greta, Joseph Pulitzer

wrote three words on the newsroom wall of *The New York World*, his flagship newspaper. *Accuracy. Accuracy. Accuracy.* The founding principle of journalism. Above all, get the damn facts straight. I learned this on my first day of journalism school, and I've never had to retract an article. I haven't once made up a detail to enhance a story.

But Greta kicked me out eight months ago, and I haven't been a real journalist in years, so I guess truth and accuracy aren't enough. At least, not anymore.

So here's what *probably* happened:

James Stacy stepped out of his bright blue MINI Cooper, glanced left and right, then slowly rotated three-hundred-sixty degrees, eyes shifting from car to car, hands tight around the handle of an old leather backpack. He was pretty sure he hadn't been followed.

He spotted the office of *The Las Vegas Gazette* between a Chinese restaurant and a liquor store, and huffed across the parking lot in the already oppressive heat. James had lost and regained the same twenty pounds ten times in the last ten years, but recently he'd regained the twenty, plus a few extra, so his jeans and blazer were too tight. His face quickly became slick and blotchy. The sun was hot on his back, and his shirt clung to his damp skin as he paused to read the paper's credo on the glass door: IF YOU DON'T WANT IT PRINTED, DON'T LET IT HAPPEN.

He scanned the parking lot again. There were about a half-dozen cars in the lot, and none had come in after him. Traffic was light along South Rainbow Boulevard, and most of the businesses in the area wouldn't open for another hour or two. Everything was quiet, which was how James liked it. It wasn't that he'd expected to be followed—not exactly, anyway—but he was always a little anxious. And the stolen hard drive in his backpack wasn't helping.

He stepped into *The Gazette* office and stopped at the receptionist's desk. A young woman looked up from her smartphone and smiled. "Mr. Stacy?"

"Yes, I'm a little early. I'm here to meet—"

"Ben is expecting you. I'm his assistant, Esperanza. Let me check to see if he's ready for you."

James took a seat on a threadbare sofa against the far wall and watched Esperanza walk down a dark hall and disappear through a doorway.

The lobby was a dump. Two clashing armchairs faced the sofa, and between them sat a low coffee table littered with old magazines. In a corner, a small rock fountain buzzed quietly, out of water. The hallway looked to be only about thirty feet long, with two doors on each side and one in the back, which James figured led to a back alley. That was it. The newsroom and corporate headquarters of *The Las Vegas Gazette*. The fourth-largest weekly in Las Vegas, and there were only four. The whole place couldn't have measured more than eight-hundred square feet.

Even without much of a sense of humor, the irony of the situation wasn't lost on James. He was sweaty and nervous, but he was one of the most influential journalists on earth. And there he was, sitting in the office of a half-assed newspaper, waiting to meet its half-assed editor, Benjamin Huang.

In the mid-nineties, when he was an up-and-coming tech reporter at *The New York Times*, Huang had been caught inventing sources. Desperate to stay in print, he'd spiraled downward from *The Dallas Morning News* to *The Boise Register* to *The Albany Free Times*, until he finally bottomed out at *The Gazette*, a paper that only existed so its casino-mogul owner could use it to smear his competitors.

James, on the other hand, was part of the two-person team known as NUM, Next Underground Media. Fifteen years earlier, he had gotten his first newspaper internship and figured out within five minutes that he'd never be a regular reporter. He believed that the journalism of the future would be done by data leakers and computer hackers, the people who operated outside the media. The ones who could get to the bank statements, memos, and emails that were *supposed* to be private. And, like most young people in the early 2000s, he knew that newspapers were dying anyway. People weren't going to keep paying a dollar a day to have someone throw yesterday's news in the bushes when today's news was available online for free.

So, three years later, he'd co-founded NUM with Innerva Shah, already a notorious hacker. Their plan was simple. James would figure out what information the world needed, Innerva would figure out how to hack it, then James would leak it to teams of reporters throughout the US and Europe. Over the last twelve years, they'd done more for journalism— for genuine transparency between government, business, and people—than most newspapers do in fifty.

Esperanza was back at the desk. "Okay, Ben is ready for you."

He thanked her and walked down the narrow hallway, casually drying his sweaty hands on his jeans, hoping no one would notice—not that there were many people around *to* notice. The only staff in the office were Esperanza, who was already chuckling at something on her phone, Deirdre Bancroft, the paper's tech-guru, Eric Kaczynski, an ad guy, and Huang, who was now standing in front of him.

Even thinner than James remembered, Huang looked like he'd been up for days. He wore an old polyester suit in hideous green, and his face was sunken and leathery, like a Korean Keith Richards. He extended a cold, shaky hand, which James shook as they stepped into a ten-by-ten office with a single window facing into the hallway. Huang slid into a chair behind his desk and lit an unfiltered Camel, then waved at a busted-up recliner across from him.

James sat down, the backpack on his lap. "Innerva told you why I was coming, right?"

Huang took a long drag from his cigarette, as if he were trying to smoke the whole thing at once. When he exhaled, a gray cloud filled the space between them, and he tapped the ash into an empty Budweiser can on his desk. "Something about an antique hard drive, right?"

James eased the drive out of his backpack, cradling it in

both hands. It weighed over ten pounds and looked like a rounded case of old vinyl records enclosed in clear plastic.

"Where the *hell* did you get that?" Huang asked.

After setting it carefully on the desk, James slid it toward Huang. "From a guy."

"And you want to know if I can extract the data?"

"I've heard that's something you're good at."

Huang popped a piece of Nicorette gum into his mouth, then folded the foil wrapper over the tip of his half-smoked cigarette, extinguishing it in the process. He picked up the drive and turned it over in his hands. "It's IBM, obviously. Double-sided magnetics. Probably from the late sixties."

"Is it possible to access the data?"

"It's possible, but the data could be damaged. And even if the data is fine, extracting it won't be easy. What's on it?"

"I don't know."

"But you have a *hunch*, right?"

James blinked, and a drop of sweat rolled off his eyelid, down his cheek, and onto his jeans. The smoke in the room was burning his eyes and he was growing more uncomfortable by the second. "Look, can you help us or not?"

Huang set the drive back down on the desk, unwrapped and relit his cigarette, then yelled, "Hey, Bancroft! Come check this out!"

James relaxed a little when Deirdre Bancroft appeared in the doorway because she looked like the kind of tech-hipster he was used to working with. She was in her early thirties and had a bright face and short, spiky hair. An Ewok tattoo poked out from under the sleeve of her vintage Ramones t-shirt. James tried to make eye contact with her to calm himself down, but she locked in on the drive immediately.

"Is that real?" she asked, walking over to Huang's desk and picking up the drive. "It looks like one of those cake protectors my grandma brings to family reunions."

Huang said, "Cool, right?"

Deirdre turned it over in her hands, just like Huang had.

"Late sixties?"

"That's what I thought, too," Huang said, "but there aren't any markings. Looks like they've been either peeled or scratched off."

"Assuming it *is* late sixties," Deirdre said, "there can't be much data on here. Twenty megs, maybe forty."

Huang nodded. "Probably just text files."

James remained silent.

Huang took a long drag, then blew a thin stream of smoke from the side of his mouth. "James, ya gotta give me *something*, okay?"

James crossed his arms and pulled them in tight across his belly. He hated negotiations. He hated confrontations of any kind. "Assuming you can find a way to access the data, and assuming we won't tell you anything about it once you access it, what do you want?"

"I know you and Innerva have a lot of stories you don't use. I want one. And I'm not asking for anything big. Just *something*."

"Can you help me with the drive?"

"I can. It'll take a few days, though. I think I know a guy with the right old hardware."

"Okay. We'll get you a story."

Huang smiled. "And if it happened to shine a negative light on one of my competitors, I wouldn't object."

Deirdre put the drive down where she'd found it. "I don't see what the big deal is," she said. "It's fifty years old. Anything of value would have been backed up decades ago."

"Maybe, but *I* certainly don't have the backup," James said.

Huang lit a new cigarette off the stub of the old one, then crushed the tip of the old one between his thumb and index finger. He dropped it into the beer can and smiled at Deirdre. "And, knowing what I know of James, this drive *might* have been obtained illegally."

James relaxed into his chair and smiled for the first time. "Might have."

And that's when he heard the first shotgun blast.

No words. No footsteps. He hadn't even heard the front door open. Just a single thundering pop, followed by a thud. Esperanza's head hitting her desk. James glanced at Huang, who was already on his knees, crawling under the desk. Deirdre peeked out the door, dove into the corner, and wedged herself behind a drooping potted plant.

James just sat, dripping with sweat and frozen in fear.

The shooter was Baxter Callahan, an unemployed recluse with a long rap sheet of minor crimes—reckless driving, vandalism, a couple disorderly conduct charges—but never anything serious enough to get him more than a month in a county detention center. He was just another angry white guy in his mid-forties—living alone, except for his dog Worf and a collection of guns he thought he might one day need to protect his fringe political beliefs. He was the type of guy the Las Vegas Metropolitan Police Department *kept an eye on*. The type of guy you'd expect to snap some day and shoot up a post office or a movie theater. For some reason, he'd chosen the morning of Tuesday, June 13, 2017. And, for some reason, he'd picked the office of *The Las Vegas Gazette*.

After shooting Esperanza, Baxter locked the front door, scanned the lobby, peered into the empty server room, and stepped into the doorway of Huang's office. Without a word, he murdered James with a shotgun blast to the chest. James's body slumped over in the recliner as Baxter reached into his belt and brought out an old nine-millimeter.

Huang's cigarette had fallen out of his mouth and Baxter ground it into the carpet with the toe of his old work boot. Deirdre was still behind the plant, now screaming and pressing herself into the wall. Baxter shot her twice in the back, and she went still.

Just then, Huang leapt up and tried to slide across his desk toward the door. Baxter caught him with a shot that passed through his right shoulder and spun him onto his side. One large step, and Baxter was next to the desk, pressing the pistol to Huang's forehead. The bullet exploded through Huang's skull and brain, then exited out the back, lodging bits of bone in the faux-wood desk.

Eric Kaczynski was stumbling down the hallway toward the back door when Baxter caught up to him. Kaczynski got two bullets in the back, followed by a shot to the base of his skull. Baxter stepped over the body, checked the bathroom at the rear of the office, and made his way to the back door.

As he entered the alley, he heard the sirens.

Two minutes earlier, an old man had arrived at the front door of *The Gazette* and spotted Esperanza's body through the glass door. He'd come to cancel his subscription because his grandkids had given him his first smartphone for his eightieth birthday, and, as it turned out, he could use it to get all the news and weather he'd ever need. He could also use it to call 911, and that's what he'd done.

The Gazette office sat along the eastern edge of the Spring Valley neighborhood, about a mile west of The Strip, and two miles west of Captain Shonda Payton's favorite Starbucks. She'd been pouring half and half into a Venti dark roast when the call from the dispatcher had come through and, for the last sixty seconds, she'd been speeding down West Charleston Boulevard in her black and white Ford P.I. utility vehicle.

She'd be the first officer on the scene, but she wouldn't make it in time.

Maybe Baxter intended to kill himself all along, or maybe he'd planned to escape. But by the time Captain Payton arrived in the alley behind the Payoff Plaza, Baxter was lying in a pool of his own blood, the shotgun and the nine-millimeter next to him. Like most mass shooters, he'd taken his own life as easily as he'd taken five others. A single shot through the roof of his mouth. Nothing for Captain Payton to do but call it in, secure the building, and sip her coffee until CSI arrived.

Like I said, that's what *probably* happened.

But I wouldn't try to piece together the details for another twenty-four hours. I wouldn't even hear about the shooting for another eight. For me, it was just another bright summer morning in Seattle. The coffee was hot, the Internet was fast, and the office was bustling.

Then my laptop dinged with an email:

Alex,

James has a story for you. Can you get to Vegas tonight?

I.S.

CHAPTER 2

Offices of *The Barker*, Pioneer Square, Seattle

I read the email twice, closed my laptop, and strolled out of my corner office, grinning like a fool as I surveyed the eighteenth floor. My floor. Eight-thousand square feet of digital-media domination.

Damn, it was beautiful.

When I'm about to land a massive story, every detail in life becomes a little sharper, every color a little warmer. Like the feeling after the first puff of my first cigarette of the day, back when I smoked. Or the feeling of tingling anticipation I used to get on the walk home with a date before the first time we had sex, back when I went on dates. Back when I had sex. It's like I've discovered the perfect Instagram filter to transport the picture of my life from decent to extraordinary.

Every nook and cranny of the office was bright and shiny. There were seventy desks in neat rows, stained black, but with purposeful irregularities in the finish that matched the black mesh of the ergonomic chairs. On top of each desk, a beautiful, shimmering iMac. Above each desk, cables of Seahawks green and blue ran along exposed steel beams. Behind each desk, one of seventy writers and coders and social media gurus that made *The Barker* one of the top independent Web sites on earth. We had men and women from twenty states and six countries—every race and religion, gay and straight, jocks and geeks, vegetarians and meat eaters, old and young.

Then there was the space itself, which I'd designed with Greta when I'd moved *The Barker* here ten years earlier, before Greta and I began our long, slow, drift apart.

We had a full floor in the Puget Tower overlooking Pioneer Square, with windows on all sides. Four-foot window after four-foot window, each separated by six feet of wall space. We weren't into walls at *The Barker*, so we'd mounted high-definition flat-screens to cover the blank space. But we weren't showing Netflix. The flat-screens were streaming live video from wide-angle cameras mounted on the outside of the building. As you scanned the room, the windows blurred into the screens and the screens blurred into the windows, creating a panoramic view from the Space Needle and the San Juan Islands in the northwest, all the way to Mount Rainier in the southeast. We even had screens along the western wall showing Pike Place Market and the ferries coming and going in the port. You could practically smell the flying fish.

I soaked it in for a full minute before walking to the other side of the room and into the office of my number two, Wesley Byrd. He was the only person I could tell about the email.

"Morning, Bird."

He didn't look up, so he didn't notice my ridiculous grin. He was typing fast. Even faster than usual.

"Um, sir, may I speak with you about an important matter concerning our shared business venture, *The Barker*?"

No response. He knew he could get away with ignoring me.

I'd promoted Bird to the senior editor job three years earlier, and hadn't regretted it for a second. He'd started as an intern just three years before that, and had worked like a madman ever since, making the site better and smarter without losing sight of the bottom line. And he's a great counterweight to me.

Bird's a millennial, I'm a Gen Xer. He came from a tech background, I came from journalism. He grew up in the South, I grew up in the Pacific Northwest. He's short, gay, and black. I'm tall, straight, and white. I call him Bird, because his name is Byrd, and he looks like a bird. He's small and lightweight, with angular features and a way of darting around—with his eyes if he's sitting, or his whole body if he's not—that reminds me of a hummingbird. I've been told I look like a bear—once a svelte grizzly bear, now one of those out-of-shape pandas at the zoo. Anyway, he's almost as good as I am at figuring out what stories people want to read, but much better than I am at figuring out how to get them to read them. He knows keywords, search algorithms, metadata, and social media like I know how to read sources. We make a perfect team.

He stopped typing, scanned the screen for a minute, and tapped one more time. The laptop let out a whoosh, the departure of an email.

Looking up, he said, "Morning."

"What was that email?"

"Guess."

"Just tell me."

"I thought you could read me, boss."

"I can, but I need to talk to you."

"Oh c'mon, Alex."

"I really need to—"

"Guess!"

"Okay," I said, studying his face, which he was trying to make as blank as possible.

I stared at Bird until he couldn't hold his blank expression anymore, and his face broke out in a devious smile. I said,

"You were serious while writing the email. Focused, but not worried. So, it was something important but not something difficult. Not something personal, because you'd do that by text. Unless it was to your dad, but you emailed him last week."

"How'd you know that?" Bird asked.

"Psychic powers."

"Really. How'd you know?"

"You ate three donuts last Friday. You only do that when you're stressed about Kevin or your dad. You only stress about your dad when you email him, and things with Kevin are good, from what you've been saying."

Bird gave me his screw-you-for-being-right look.

"The email wasn't to anyone here," I continued. "You'd relay that message in person just to have an excuse to walk around the office and burn a dozen calories. You were typing fast, for a full minute after I came in, but judging by how long it took you to scan the email when you finished typing, you'd written a few grafs before I got here. You wouldn't have written a response that long just to accept or reject a pitch. So, it was something important. Something we've been working on for a while."

Bird took a long swig from a can of Red Bull, then smiled.

I knew I'd been right. "Movie Buzz?"

A week earlier, a Stanford student had found a full-resolution screener of International Family Media's next big kids' movie on a bar stool. The student then sold it to Movie Grind, a site we owned down in the Bay Area. The movie was being marketed as *Finding Nemo* set in the world of plants, so, of course, we wanted to have some fun with it. It would be illegal to release the film, and we had no intention of doing that. Instead, we'd planned to do a *Mystery Science Theater 3000* thing. We'd have our snarkiest staff members watch the movie while doing a running commentary, then upload it to YouTube with most of the copyrighted material blurred out. Skirt the law without breaking it. Right in line with our general policy at *The Barker*.

"Big news," he said. "We agreed to give the movie back in exchange for an exclusive with their CEO."

"Dewey Gunstott? On the record?"

"Deep background."

"We're giving up the screener for a deep background interview?"

"With *the* CEO."

"I get that, but—"

"Alex, you always say that journalism is about tradeoffs. A chat with a guy like that could fill out all sorts of stories for the guys at Movie Buzz, point them in a hundred directions that will pay off later. They're flying up Monday for the interview."

I was going to object, but I was trying to dial back my micromanaging, and Bird knew what he was doing. "Fine," I said.

"You look happy, too."

"I am. And that's why I came in here. Let's see if *you* can read *me*."

He usually could. One of the things Greta used to like about me is that I'm pretty transparent. "As good as you are at reading people," she'd say, "you're exactly as bad at hiding things." Bird knew me as well as anyone other than Greta, but he wasn't gonna figure out about the email I'd just received.

He put his elbows on the desk, cradled his chin in his hands, and pressed his fingers to his temple like he was activating his psychic powers. "You won the Seahawks season ticket lottery?"

"Nope." I'd been on that damn list for two years.

"We got an offer?"

"Not that." I had no intention of selling *The Barker*, but I didn't mind the fact that we got offers. Every time a major media company tried to buy us out, we'd leak the story to the business blogs and get a spike in traffic.

"You got a story?"

"Ding-ding-ding. Can you guess from where?"

"Well, all our best sources come to me, these days, so—"

"That stings."

"Who?" he asked.

I smiled.

"Who?"

"Innerva. She said James has a story for me."

He paused a beat, checking to see if I was serious, then leapt up and clapped his hands together once with controlled, violent joy. He sat back down. "I thought he'd ghosted you."

"He *had* ghosted me. Until fifteen minutes ago."

Bird was the only person at *The Barker* who knew that "I.S." was Innerva Shah. Other than Greta, he was the only person I'd told about NUM. And he was the only person who knew my history with James.

We'd met when James was an intern at *The New York Standard*, where I'd been an ambitious court reporter. I broke some big stories back then. The kind that got me on TV and now have their own Wikipedia pages. But that's like saying I was an up-and-coming deckhand on the Titanic. James and I knew the newspaper model was sinking, and we were looking for a life raft.

In 2002, we'd founded News Scoop out of the rubble of the dotcom bust. We were the first investigative journalism site on the Internet, but we only investigated one thing. The media.

We knew about all the behind-the-scenes wrangling that shapes the news America consumes. When an international media company tried to stack the FCC to take control of the broadband Internet market, we were the first to know. When *The New York Times* buried a story on the dangerous side effects of a well-known blood pressure medication, we had sources who told us. When the editor of a national magazine got caught charging shareholders for wild nights at a strip club, we heard about that, too. I was on a first-name basis with half the journalists in New York, and one degree of separation away from the rest. We did real stories. Good stories. And for a couple of years, it was great.

But despite our early successes at News Scoop, James had bigger plans than playing Internet journalist with me. In 2004, he teamed up with Innerva and took off. These days, an email from James or Innerva was like God tapping me on the shoulder and whispering, "Hey, I've got a scoop for you."

Not that *you've* ever heard of them. People like James and Innerva don't take victory laps on CNN when they break a story. Strictly speaking, they don't even break stories. If the wrong people knew who they were, they'd be in jail. Or dead. That's why they leave the breaking—and the victory laps—to guys like me. In the early days, they called me to Vegas several times a year to feed me stories. But I hadn't heard from them in a year.

Until fifteen minutes ago.

Bird said, "What did she say? I mean, did she tell you anything about the story?"

"Just that they had something for me."

"No details?"

"No."

"When are you meeting her?"

"I need a flight. Can you call Mia in?"

Bird texted Mia from his laptop, then gave me his thin, conspiratorial smile, exposing just the bright white bottoms of his top row of teeth. "Best guess. What's the scoop?"

He followed me with his eyes as I made a slow lap around his desk, which was situated in the center of his office. "Maybe they finally cracked the shadow banks in the Caymans," I said. "Last time I saw him, James was talking about that. Said it would be like the Panama Papers times ten."

"They wouldn't give that to *us*, though."

"Probably not." I paused a beat. "They were getting pretty good at hacking the iCloud accounts of corrupt politicians, and it's the kind of thing they don't like to give the big papers. Could be one of those."

"Maybe," Bird said.

Mia Rhodes appeared in the doorway behind us, holding a

stack of paper in one hand and an iPad in the other.

"I like the new hair," Bird said. "Looks like a horse's tail, but in a good way."

Mia changed her hair every week or two. Today it was a black ponytail that hung over her right shoulder and didn't stop until it hit her hip, which wasn't actually all that far, because she was barely five feet tall. But what she lacked in height, she made up for in every other way. She was efficient and smart, sure, but most of all, she was trustworthy.

And she was always in a hurry. "What's up?" she asked quickly.

"Vegas," I said. "I need to get to Vegas. Fast."

She tapped at her iPad for a few seconds, then said, "There's an eleven-thirty-five, but you're not gonna make that. I'll get you on the four-forty."

"Nothing before that?"

"Not on Alaska."

"Can't we use another airline?"

Mia sighed and gave me her *don't-make-me-go-there* look. It was a look she used whenever I tried to do something to upset the immaculate systems that kept the office running smoothly. "Do I need to explain again why we went exclusive with Alaska?"

She didn't. It was something about upgrades, frequent flyer bonus points, and a special reservation system. My policy with Mia was to push a little bit when I wanted something, and if she pushed back, just give in. I'd never told her this, but I lived in constant fear that she'd realize she was too good for this place, and quit. "Okay, four-forty."

"When do you want to come back?"

"Tomorrow, noonish?"

"Okay," she said. "And I'll book you your room at the Wynn."

"Not gonna stay and eat for a few days?" Bird asked. "A few more tasting menus and they'll give you your own cage at the zoo."

I ignored him and nodded to Mia. "Before you go, what's

up with Dexter Park?"

"I emailed you about that."

"Must've missed it," I said.

Half the time I asked Mia about something, she'd already handled it, checked it off her list, and emailed me about it. She sighed and walked to the window. "I've booked his flight for Saturday night. Flight seven out of JFK."

"Is that on United?" Bird asked. "Maybe Delta or JetBlue?"

Mia gave him a look. "Park will be staying in a suite at The Bryant. That's assuming, of course, that he's willing to do it."

"He hasn't confirmed yet?" I asked.

"No, but I'll let you know when I hear back."

"It's T-minus five days," I said. "And everything hinges on him."

Dexter Park was a major piece of my plan to surprise Greta on our anniversary, which was on Sunday, five days away. We'd been separated for eight months, and had barely spoken over the last three. Despite my best efforts, the relationship felt like it was slipping away. Like there was a thin thread of love that still connected us, but it could snap at any moment. This plan was a Hail Mary at the end of the fourth quarter.

"Is that all?" Mia asked.

"Just one more thing," I said. "Honest opinion from both of you. Is this going to work?"

Mia looked at Bird, who looked at the floor. Each was waiting for the other to speak first. "Well," Mia said. "I mean—"

"Hard to say," Bird chimed in, not looking up from the floor.

"Maybe it's an age-gap thing," Mia said, "but I just don't think women respond to grand gestures anymore, if they ever did."

"What should I do instead? Hit her up on Snapchat? Bling her on Insta-Booty?"

"A grand surprise anniversary thing *is* a little old-fashioned," Bird said. "It's like, what's next? Show up at her house with a boom box playing Peter Gabriel?"

"I already tried that."

"Really?" Bird asked.

"No."

Mia said, "Have you tried just *talking* with her?"

"We talked for the first few months, then she went quiet."

"Is she dating?" Mia asked.

"I think so."

"Are you dating?"

"No."

"Not at all since the separation?"

I nodded toward Bird. "Not unless you count my codependent relationship with this guy."

Mia ignored my joke. "You still love her?"

I said nothing and Mia stared at the floor. Up until that moment, the tone of the conversation had been light. A serious topic kept at bay by humor. But I think she knew she'd crossed an invisible line. Not that it was *her* fault. I'd started the conversation, and *I* was the one who wasn't comfortable talking about how I felt. It was like another thing Greta used to say: "You're good at many things, Alex, but facing your emotions isn't one of them."

Bird said, "He loves her more than anything."

He was right, but I couldn't say it out loud.

We just stood there, until Mia gave Bird a *do-something-to-break-the-silence* look.

Bird took a quick sip of his Red Bull, then looked at me awkwardly, flashed a cheesy grin, and said, "Innerva, *amirite?* Get your butt to Vegas and get us that story!"

CHAPTER 3

The flight into Vegas at sunset is the stuff of dreams. You cross mile after mile of black desert, anticipation building as you flip through magazines, play Sudoku, or watch a movie on your iPad. Then, bang.

The city appears out of nowhere. A concentrated radiance like nothing else on earth. The sun dips behind the mountains and casts a gold glow over the valley that somehow makes the millions of sparkling lights even more beautiful. The descent into McCarran Airport at twilight makes you feel like you're about to win money, or have a great meal, or fall in love. It's a blank screen on which to project your dreams.

Other than getting Greta back, I had just one dream. To land a story that would break the Internet.

I took an Uber to the back entrance of The Wynn and stepped into the solarium. My rolling suitcase clicked on the mosaic floor as I dragged it past the koi pond and through the gold door into the private registration area for the Tower Suites. After checking in, I had my bags sent up to my room and took a seat in a red velvet booth in the circular bar near the lobby.

When you're the CEO, people tend to wait for you, not the other way around. But I didn't mind waiting for James and Innerva. I'd emailed Innerva when the plane landed, but I knew they'd show up whenever they felt like it. They always did. And I had a big night planned so I figured I'd ingest some caffeine and do a little people-watching while I waited.

I ordered a double espresso and scanned the TVs mounted over the bar. Half of them were on sports channels, the rest on news. One of the news channels was local, and was covering something about a shooting in Las Vegas. But I didn't pay any attention to it because I was taking in the scene.

Until a few years ago, I hated Vegas. But that was because I didn't know what it was really like. I had an outdated view borrowed from books, movies, and probably some anti-gambling after-school-special I'd seen as a kid. If you haven't been to Vegas in a while, close your eyes and picture it. What do you see first? The Rat Pack, Bugsy Siegel, fat Elvis? Or maybe showgirls, cheap buffets, and cheesy slot machines? Don't get me wrong, you can still see some of those things. But now there's much more.

In 1957, Vegas made 70% of its revenue from gambling. In 1987, it was 65%. Today, it's only 30%. But Vegas is booming, so where does all the money come from? Shows, clubs, shopping, food, booze, and rooms. And now that gambling is just one of Vegas's many attractions, you'll find a more diverse class of tourists in high-end resorts like The Wynn. To my left, a table of Asian men in nice suits talked loudly on cellphones. In front of me, a beautiful young couple watched soccer on an iPad while trying to corral a sticky toddler. To my right, three men with matching biceps ate burgers and talked MMA. Behind me, a table of gorgeous young women glanced at each new man as he walked in, looking for someone to buy them drinks. A bro in flip flops was doing shots at the bar, about to become that someone.

And then there was me. Another forty-something guy whose business-casual attire got nicer over the years as his belly got softer, eyes dancing from TV to TV, praying that the magic of Vegas would make him cool again. At least for a night.

I was pulling out my phone when Innerva slid into the chair across from me. She wore a black turtleneck and blue jeans as always—her Steve Jobs look—but she didn't make eye contact as I expected.

I looked around the bar. "Where's James?"

"Dead."

Innerva never lied. I'm not even sure she knew how. But at first I didn't believe her. "Seriously, where is he?"

"James was killed. This morning."

I didn't say anything. Just stared at her. Her hair was wet, her eyes were puffy and dark, and her voice was barely audible. I kept hearing his name in my head, repeated over and over like when I was a kid and I'd repeat a word to myself until it lost all meaning.

"Alex, this is real. He was killed."

"James was...Are you sure? I mean...are you okay?"

"I don't know how I am. I'm in shock."

So was I, and I didn't know what to say. The phrase *was killed* flashed in my head like a neon sign. He hadn't been hit by a car or died of a heart attack on the treadmill. He *was killed*.

James had always been vague with details, but over the years he'd led me to believe that he and Innerva were behind some huge stories. There was the oil spill IMG Oil didn't want you to know about, for example. James and Innerva managed to get their hands on all the records, including IMG's efforts to cover it up. Or the time the Prime Minister of India tried to sell seats in Parliament and Innerva leaked recordings of his phone calls. They'd even leaked the emails of a Major General who'd had six women dishonorably discharged after they accused him of sexual assault. The bottom line: any number of people would have wanted James dead.

I leaned to the side to try to meet her eyes, but they were fixed on one of the TVs. She pointed at the screen without looking at me. "James was there. *The Gazette*."

I'd ignored the shooting earlier. Like a lot of people, I went numb after Sandy Hook. But now I read the segment bar at the bottom of the screen: *Six Dead in Mass Shooting*. The TV showed a talking head on the left and video footage from a helicopter on the right. The scene was a one-block strip mall with parking in the front, an alley in the back, and one of those large, back-lit plastic displays by the street that lists the six or eight businesses in the strip. I'm embarrassed to admit it, but my first instinct was to open my phone, to distract myself with a little Angry Birds or Plants vs. Zombies. Maybe scroll through my social media feeds. I turned my phone face down on the table.

According to the scroll on the bottom of the screen, police were confirming that there had been only one shooter. He'd killed all five people who were at *The Gazette* at the time, then taken his own life. So far, no survivors or witnesses had been identified. That was when I started to form my mental picture of the shooting.

"How can you be sure he was there?" I asked. "It says the names of the victims and the shooter haven't been released."

"He *was* there."

Innerva never spoke without knowing she was right, but her news didn't feel real. Five minutes ago, I'd expected James to slide into the booth, hug me awkwardly, then drink six Cokes or six Diet Cokes—depending on whether he was dieting or not—while telling me the CliffsNotes version of their latest info grab. Two minutes ago, I was imagining which of his stories had gotten him killed. Now Innerva was telling me he'd been killed in a random mass shooting. Like I said, it didn't feel real.

Then I remembered something. "When you emailed me this morning, why'd you say that James had a story for me? Why didn't you tell me he was dead?"

Innerva said nothing, but I could tell she was concealing

something by the way she was biting her bottom lip.

"It's because you don't think he was killed by a random gunman. And you didn't want to say that in an email." Innerva's emails bounced between ten countries and six levels of anonymization before landing on my laptop, but she was still cautious about what she put in writing.

She reached across the table, took my hand, and met my eyes for the first time. "Look, Alex. I probably shouldn't even be here. I don't know for sure what happened. I really don't. I'd tell you if I did."

"Were you and James involved in anything especially dark lately?"

She was quiet for a full minute as I glanced back and forth between her and the screen, feeling like she both wanted and *didn't* want to tell me something. Finally, she pulled a cheap red backpack from under the table, unzipped it, and swung it onto my lap. She said, "This was our most recent side project."

Inside the backpack was a plastic case that reminded me of the food dehydrator Greta used to make salmon jerky and chia crisps.

Innerva said, "It's a hard drive. We got it about a week ago. James was at *The Gazette* to meet with Benjamin Huang."

"He's the editor there, right?"

"*Was* the editor. He's dead, too." She paused a beat, then said, "James took it to see if Ben could get the data off it. I'm good with code and security, but I don't know old hardware like he did. He knew computer collectors and was tied into the local maker community."

I took out the drive, which was heavier than it looked. Ten pounds, maybe. "If he took it to *The Gazette*, how am I holding it?"

"We had two. Sent James with one just to see if Huang could get the data off."

"Do I want to know any more?"

"No, but here we are."

"Have you spoken to the police?"

"If the police knew who I was, I'd be one of the most wanted women on earth."

"So, no."

"Right. No."

"And you think this drive had something to do with the shooting?" I pointed up at the TV. The segment bar at the bottom now read: *Domestic Terrorism or Deranged Loner?*

"Probably not. I don't know for sure. But I know I'm leaving town and I'm leaving the drive with you."

"And you don't know what's on it?"

"No. Very few people have the parts to get readable data off a hard drive that old. We were hoping Ben would."

"Where'd you get it?"

"From a guy."

"Where'd he get it? I mean, where's it from originally?"

"We're not sure."

"But you have a hunch?"

"James and I had some educated guesses."

I like to get to the point as quickly as possible, and Innerva usually did as well. But her vague answers were starting to piss me off. I returned the drive to the backpack. "I don't want it. If you thought it was important enough to send James with a decoy, then—"

"Alex, I'm not going to tell you what to do. I know James is dead. I know it probably has nothing to do with this drive, but it might. Either way, there may be something interesting on it. In a minute I'll be gone and it will be sitting on your lap. Throw it away if you want, or leave it here. Whatever. But you may be able to get a story out of it. This could be your chance to be a journalist again."

She said it without judgment. As if it were a simple matter of fact that I was not a journalist. I'm sure James had been pushing the "Alex is a sellout" narrative for years, and I couldn't exactly argue the point.

When James and I split up, I kept News Scoop going and James kept me honest by feeding me serious stories from time to time. But do you know what happened when we ran pieces revealing the media's worst shenanigans? Unless they involved sex, racial slurs, or public drunkenness, no one clicked. After a while, James started giving the best stuff to the big, international papers and throwing me the leftovers, the stories he was too embarrassed to give anyone else. They were still big news, but not the nation-shakers he gave to the people he actually respected. Six years ago, News Scoop had become *The Barker*. And as James grew more radical and I grew more shallow, we lost touch. He stopped calling me to Vegas, and his old email addresses stopped working. I'd taken our baby and turned it into one of the most successful websites in the world, but journalistically just one rung above *The National Enquirer*. I *was* a sellout. A dealer in listicles. A clickbait whore. I'd become the guy we'd started News Scoop to investigate in the first place.

So, what do I do all day?

Remember the story about the granite-jawed NFL quarterback cheating on his wife with the babysitter? Or the video of the A-list actor running over a prostitute in the parking lot of a bodega in east L.A.? I was behind those stories. I run the stuff real news outlets refuse to cover until it goes viral and they can swoop in with their condescending meta story: "Internet Goes Crazy for Celebrity Scandal, Journalism in Peril."

Our biggest winner last year was a video of Dusty Price—the actor who does the voices on that Laughing Dinosaur show—calling some poor valet parker a "faggot" outside the Windswept Club in San Diego. You probably watched it at work before deleting your browsing history. To create the video, I'd purchased the silent footage from a security camera and an audio-only recording from some random guy's cellphone. Then Bird had spliced them together. We even hired a lip reader for the day to help out. Maybe Price is homophobic, maybe he's not. I don't especially care. When I bought the video, I cared about only one thing.

Clicks.

In my business, clicks equal ad sales and ad sales equal

money. Within twelve hours, every entertainment show in the country picked up the Dusty Price story. Eight million people shared the link on social media. Eighty-million watched the video. *The Barker* made more money. Plus, a bunch of parents got to learn that the hilarious dinosaur their kids adore is played by an asshole. The point is, the story took over the world for a few hours, and I made it happen.

Sure I feel crappy about some of the stories we run, but it's not like we're the only ones. Take *Vanity Fair*, for example. They've run some of the best investigative pieces over the last decade: AIDS in Africa, The Secret Life of Kim Jong-Il, Inside Guantanamo. But can you guess their best-selling issue ever? It was "Call Me Caitlin," which might as well have been titled "C-List Celebrity Sex-Change Shocker!" Eighteen extra printings. Four billion impressions on social media. So before you join the truth-crusaders like Innerva and James on their high horse, check your browser history. You like gossip as much as I do. Well-written, deeply-investigated news is great, but I'm not a snob about it. I'm as happy watching *Friends* as I am watching Fellini. To Greta's dismay, I'd stop for Chicken Nuggets on the way home from a $200 sushi dinner. If people don't click on Fellini, I give them *Friends*. They're scrolling past sushi? I sell them a damn Happy Meal.

I didn't say any of this to Innerva, of course. What I said was, "If you don't know what's on the drive, and if you don't know if it had anything to do with the shooting, why are you saying it's my chance to *be a journalist* again?"

Innerva stood up. "Two reasons. First, I have a feeling there's something good on this thing. James thought so, too."

"And the second?"

"Because *I* can't do it. I'm disappearing. Today."

"Where are you going?"

She just stared at me.

"Will you contact me again?"

"Possibly."

"Can you at least tell me *why* you're disappearing?"

"I don't usually need a reason."

"But you have one this time."

I studied her face until I was sure she wasn't going to tell me anything else, then said, "Okay, I'll look into it." I didn't know if I actually would, but it seemed like the thing to say. I zipped the backpack closed and slid it to the floor near my feet.

Innerva stood, tossing an index card across the table. "You can find a hardware expert back in Seattle, but if you want someone local, tell The Overclocker I sent you. She's who we would have asked if Huang couldn't help. She's a little odd, but you can trust her."

I looked down at the card. An address on some Las Vegas street I'd never heard of. "What's an Overclocker?" I asked.

When I looked up, Innerva was walking towards a row of slot machines.

***

My mind darted between panic, despair, and blankness. James was dead. I understood this intellectually, but it hadn't actually hit me yet. I didn't want it to, so I picked up my phone.

The shooting was already trending on Facebook and Twitter. By this point, Captain Shonda Payton had issued a generic statement to the press and the old man who'd called in the shooting was doing the rounds on TV, enjoying his five minutes of fame. But the names of the victims and the shooter still hadn't been released, and a motive was not yet being discussed. The posts I read followed the pattern of most other mass shootings: thoughts and prayers, rants about thoughts and prayers not being enough, memes blaming guns and the NRA, memes defending guns and the NRA, infographics of gun deaths in the U.S. compared to Europe, and dozens of comments expressing sadness, horror, and confusion.

One Facebook post from an anarchist news site showed a screen-capture of *The Gazette* offices surrounded by police tape with the caption: "Newspapers are *Finally* Dead." Even on a page that supported the overthrow of all forms of government, the commenters mostly agreed, "Too soon."

I shot back my double espresso, now cold, then waved down the waitress and ordered a vodka and soda. The TV was on a commercial for dog food so I let my eyes roam around the bar and the casino floor. Under normal circumstances, I would have loved to watch the evening crowd pour into The Wynn. But the conversation with Innerva was floating through me like a dream, and the scene looked surreal. Lights flashed, beautiful people walked around with purpose, a slot machine rang with the sound of a jackpot. Everything looked and sounded far away. It all *felt* far away. I stared down at the table and traced the wood grain with my pinky finger. *James is dead. James is dead.* I tried to make it sink in, but I was coming unglued.

My chest was heavy, my head spinning, my arms and legs tingling with a new, horrible sensation. Each cell in my body felt like a fingernail scraping a chalkboard. It was one of those times Greta had told me about: I could choose to be present in the moment, to meet my feelings head on, or I could slink out the back door without looking them in the eye.

I was counting the lines in the wood grain, trying to decide what to do, when the vodka arrived. I squeezed the lime wedge until I'd extracted every drop of juice, then mashed it into my drink with the little red straw. I drank it in two long sips, then I did what I usually do when I'm feeling things I don't want to feel.

I made plans to eat.

CHAPTER 4

Cafe Gil isn't actually a cafe. It's a secret restaurant hidden behind an unmarked door in a low-traffic corner of The Wynn. Named for celebrity chef Alvaro Gil, it serves a farm-to-table Spanish tasting menu of twenty-one courses over three hours. Gil doesn't do any of the cooking, of course. He's too busy overseeing his food empire and winning Iron Chef, but they serve the style he's known for. Avant garde tapas halfway between fine dining and experimental carnival food. You can only get a reservation if you know about it, and most people don't.

The dining room was no more than 200 square feet and adorned with Cubist art and strange knick-knacks, like wine bottles filled with marbles and shoes wrapped in red lace. I took one of the nine seats at the brass bar that framed a single workstation of gray marble, behind which a red velvet curtain hung from brass hooks.

I'd eaten at most of the top restaurants in the country, and I'd been meaning to try Cafe Gil for a year. Under normal circumstances, I would have been excited. But I immediately felt out of place surrounded by the happy diners drinking cocktails and sangria. I was thinking of bailing when three young chefs appeared from behind the curtain. The tallest of the three had short cropped hair and heavily-tattooed forearms. He stepped in front, gave a brief introduction, then reached into a hidden fridge under the marble counter and began spooning caviar onto white crackers. A minute later he slid a plate in front of me. The "cracker" turned out to be dehydrated Asiago cheese and the "caviar" was something he called "beef tartare molecules." A single leaf of micro-arugula sat on top. A diner to my left asked him a question about the molecules, but I wasn't listening. I'd already popped the bite into my mouth, chewed, and swallowed it without pleasure.

I know what you're thinking. James was dead and my response was to shell out $300 for a fall-of-Rome level culinary extravagance. I'm not proud of it, but we all have our ways of coping with pain. Some turn to drink or weed, some zone out in front of the TV, some call their friends and gossip, some exercise obsessively. When something terrible happened when I was poorer, I inhaled an extra-large pizza and a six-pack of Miller Lite, then played Words with Friends until I passed out. Now I eat gourmet meals. The purpose is the same. It's the price tag that's different.

The problem was, it wasn't working.

After six courses, including pureed chickpeas with white truffle and crispy chicken skin *en escabeche*, I was feeling even worse. And there were fifteen courses to come. As much as I tried, I couldn't shake the video of Payoff Plaza and *The Gazette* I'd seen earlier. When I blinked, my mind would zoom in through the roof of the building and see James, arms and chest bulging out of his jacket, lying dead on the floor. And that reminded me of the hard drive, which was tucked under the stool, nestled between my feet.

A waiter set down a single spoon of frozen sangria, spherified with sodium alginate. A palate cleanser. I ignored it and pulled out my phone, thinking I'd do a little research about the hard drive between courses. Then I saw that I'd missed a series of texts from Mia and I got that little hit of Oxytocin-positivity that accompanies social media notifications or new texts.

Dexter Park confirmed!

I let out a quiet "Yes!" under my breath and shot back the sangria. I read the second text.

10 am Sunday, yoga mats and lunch will be delivered to his room at The Bryant. Paid in full out of your personal account.

Maybe it was selfish, but all I could think about after that was my plan to convince Greta to give me another chance.

We'd separated the day after Thanksgiving and I'd spent most of the winter in shock. All spring I'd been waiting to get a letter from a fancy-sounding law firm, informing me that she'd filed for divorce. But the letter never came, and early in the summer I'd hatched a plan that started with a Google search for "Romantic Gesture to Win Her Back."

As it turned out, the first hit was a listicle from *Love Hound*, a men's site *The Barker* acquired a couple years ago. According to the piece, there are five types of romantic gesture that "All Women Want to Experience." Each type of romantic gesture illustrates one of five specific messages. And the message is the key, because it's not about the object or even the experience. Focus on the message you want to send, the piece assured me, then craft the gesture, gift, or experience around the message. And the five messages were: 1) *I'm Sorry*, 2) *This Day is All About You*, 3) *I've Been Planning This for Weeks*, 4) *I'm Ready to Be Open and Honest*, 5) *I Must Win You Back*.

Before you start rolling your eyes, I *know* these lists are nonsense. *All women* don't want the same things, just like *Four Daily Habits* won't double your productivity, and *Three Amazing Superfoods* won't melt away thirty pounds in six weeks. But I love Internet lists anyway. They give me a starting place on how to think about something and, in this case, I was desperate.

My biggest issue with *this* list, though, was that it encouraged the reader to pick just *one* gesture. When I'd read the article, I'd tried to reflect on our relationship. What had Greta told me? What had she tried to tell me that I wasn't ready to hear? What intel had trickled back to me through friends? I wanted to figure out the ways I'd disappointed her so I could know which type of gesture to choose. For example, if I'd made one major mistake in an otherwise solid relationship, I'd choose #1, the *I'm Sorry* gesture. If I'd been consistently selfish, ignoring her needs, not taking her life seriously, I'd choose #2, the *This Day is All About You* gesture.

After reflecting on our marriage, I'd picked all five. My plan was to incorporate all of them in a single, monumental anniversary surprise. Greta's schedule and the fact that we weren't communicating were the only problems.

Greta had once been a massage therapist, but she'd slowly transitioned into a life coach for the rich and famous, so her schedule fluctuated. Some days she'd have five or six clients, some days she'd have no clients. On occasion she'd even accompany a CEO or movie star on a trip for a couple days. So, to make sure she'd be free, I'd had a friend of a friend book a day of her time, telling her it was to accompany him to an all-day board meeting on Sunday. Four and a half days from now.

Was it a good idea to start off my grand, reconciliatory gesture with deception? Probably not. But I didn't have any better ideas.

So the friend of a friend had set it up to meet Greta at Mee Sum at 10 am on Sunday because it was near her office and near where his board meeting would take place. But the real reason was that, when she got there, I'd be there holding a plate of *Cha Siu Bao*, those little buns stuffed with pork. You see, Mee Sum is a little Chinese pastry shop near Pike Place Market in Seattle. On our first night in Seattle twelve years ago, we'd watched an old man stuff pork buns for half an hour and eaten three buns each while breathing in the salty, fishy air from the Puget Sound. It wasn't a memory Greta and I talked about much, but it meant something to me, and I hoped it would to her.

When I met her at Mee Sum instead of her client, I'd be saying *This Day is All About You* and *I've Been Planning This for Weeks*, all in the first minute. This was phase one.

Phase two was Dexter Park, her first yoga teacher back in New York City and, to this day, her closest mentor. I was flying him in for a day of yoga and couples counseling. Phase two would reiterate the *I've Been Planning This for Weeks* message and transition to what, for Greta, would be the most important message of all: *I'm Ready to Be Open and Honest.*

The honesty part I could handle. The openness, not so much. Before we'd moved to Seattle, Greta was pregnant and I was over the moon. But Rebecca had been stillborn, and, despite talks and plans and dreams, we'd never had another child. I'd never been able to talk about it.

The waiter set down another course, something about Spanish olives six ways, but I was about to bail on the dinner. That's when I read the final text from Mia.

You got a letter from Shapiro, Hawley, and Jackson, LLC. Certified mail. Should I open it?

CHAPTER 5

Wednesday, June 14, 2017

Mornings in Vegas are underrated, and I'd planned a nice one. Sleep in, eggs Benedict and a couple mimosas, maybe an hour or two of people-watching in a cabana by the pool before my flight to Seattle. But they're not as pleasant when you'd received a certified letter from the top divorce lawyers in Seattle the night before.

After texting Mia back and learning that she'd already left for the night, I'd abandoned dinner between courses sixteen and seventeen, tossed and turned until two a.m., nodded off for a couple nightmare-ravaged bursts, then given up at five and called to get an earlier flight. In the last two hours, I'd consumed five cups of coffee while huddled over my laptop, worrying about the letter and reading every article, blog post, and tweet about the shooting. At seven, I dragged my suitcase past the koi pond and hopped in a taxi for the airport.

In the daytime, all the glittery Vegas dreams of the night

before come crashing down. The sky is washed out, the sidewalks cracked and veiny. And you notice all the homeless people, pawnshops, and billboards for divorce lawyers you'd missed the night before. I was bleary-eyed and jittery, hollow except for a violent twist in my guts.

I'd never wanted out of Vegas so badly.

At 7:30, I rolled my suitcase into the airport, laptop bag over one shoulder, the drive over the other. It was still in the thin red backpack Innerva had given me, but the zipper was starting to separate, so I decided to find a luggage store to replace it. I'm not a computer historian myself, but I know people who are. The drive was a work of craftsmanship that had survived for decades, and I wasn't going to let it shatter on the floor of an airport. Plus, there was a miniscule chance it had something to do with James's death.

A source "close to the case" had leaked the name of the shooter to the Associated Press an hour earlier and every network in the country was running with it, so Baxter Callahan's creepy face was plastered across every TV in the airport. A mugshot from his most recent arrest. His face was pale white and wore a blank expression, like he was drugged or incredibly bored. He had short, dirty-blond hair, and a scruffy beard that matched. What stood out was his nose. It was crooked and very large, like it had been broken multiple times and healed out of shape.

The names of the victims, some crime scene photos, and the basic chronology of the shooting had also been leaked, so my version of the shooting was starting to crystallize. And the news networks were doing what they always did. After mentioning the victims for a minute or two, they pivoted to the issue on everyone's mind, the issue that would occupy the police and the pundits for the rest of the day. Motive. Once we know the *who* and the *how* of a mass shooting, and once we know that the shooter is dead so there will be no trial, *motive* is all that's left. But so far there was no manifesto from Baxter, no threat against *The Gazette*, no social media trail of hate. Just a couple of interviews with neighbors from his apartment complex who characterized him as "quiet" and "reclusive, but friendly." One woman even mentioned how they'd bonded over a shared love of *Star Trek* when Baxter revealed that his dog's name was Worf, and wept over the fact that the dog had now been taken by the police.

My guess was that it would turn out *The Gazette* had run some inane story that conflicted with a belief Baxter clung to like a life preserver in the typhoon raging inside his head. Maybe they'd reported on the efforts to bring an NFL team to Las Vegas without mentioning the $750 million price tag for the stadium that would be passed along to taxpayers. Maybe they'd refused to run his op-ed about the UFOs the government uses to steal our life force. Hell, it's possible the receptionist had cut him off in traffic that morning and he'd followed her to the office. Who knows? In mass shootings, the motive is never as important as the shooter thinks it is.

I was contemplating all this as I walked into the luggage shop.

"Are you Alex Vane?"

A man's voice, behind me.

"I am," I said, turning around.

He looked generic, like the dad of ambiguous national origin in the photo that comes with a cheap picture frame. The only difference was that he was wearing a cream-colored linen suit that must've cost two grand. He smiled at me and held out his hand. "I'm Kenny Atkinson. This is Holly."

Holly stood to his right and wore a light blue pantsuit cut with sleek, fashionable lines. She was about ten years younger than him and had curly red hair and bright red freckles on both cheeks. "Do you have a second?" she asked.

She looked like she should have a friendly Irish accent, but she didn't. Her voice matched his appearance. Steady and professional. Generic.

I get approached in airports from time to time. Sometimes by fans of the site. Sometimes by haters. I didn't really care which these two were, but I didn't feel like chatting. "I've gotta catch a flight," I said, shaking their hands quickly and shuffling toward a wall of luggage at the rear of the store.

"Sorry if this is strange," Kenny said, hurrying after me. "We're recruiters for the GNL App."

"And we're big fans of *The Barker*," Holly added. "It's so funny we're running into you. We were actually in Vegas for the Tech Roundup Conference. We're headed back to San Francisco now."

I reached the racks of luggage and began inspecting a large black backpack. It had wheels and a retractable handle so it could work as both a backpack and a rolling suitcase. Space for the drive, plus three or four side pockets of varying sizes. I tried to look busy, but they couldn't take a hint.

"In Vegas for business or pleasure?" Kenny asked.

"Little of both."

"Were you at the Tech Roundup Conference, as well?"

He was fishing for something, but I didn't know what. "Who were you with again?" I asked.

"We're corporate headhunters," Holly said. "Have you heard that GNL is focusing on their app? It's going to change the media landscape. Honestly, you're on our list to contact about it anyway."

The more I heard her voice, the more it creeped me out. I mean, she looked like Nicole Kidman from *Far and Away*, but her voice sounded like it was being run through a computer that smoothed out the highs and lows, filtering out the humanity.

"We're putting together a team," Kenny added. "The best and the brightest, so to speak. Melissa Monroe from Yahoo News, Greg Chang from BuzzFeed."

GNL stood for Global News Link, a site that creates customized digital "newspapers" based on your social media use. You give them access to all your accounts—Facebook, Twitter, Google, and so on—and their program tracks every link you click, how long you stay on the page after clicking, and so on. I'd heard someplace they were focusing on their mobile app because their web traffic was anemic.

"Lemme guess," I said, "you want to know if I'm interested in leaving *The Barker*?"

They both smiled.

"I'm not." I unzipped the new backpack and set it on top of a rotating stand that displayed nuts and inflatable airplane pillows.

"Too bad," Holly said, plucking a mini toothbrush off the rack. "Where'd you stay in Vegas?"

"The Wynn."

I leaned down and struggled with the zipper on Innerva's backpack. It stuck, so I just ripped it open, ruining the bag. But it didn't matter. It would be in the trash in five minutes. I pulled the drive out and set it into the new backpack, just to make sure it would fit. It did, and with space left over.

Holly and Kenny were hovering. They'd each stepped a little closer.

"What's that?" Holly asked.

Her tone had changed a bit, like a spark of personality was squeaking through her mask of professionalism.

"I don't know," I said, zipping up the new backpack with the drive still in it.

"Odd to have such an old hard drive," Kenny said.

I gave Kenny a long look. "If you knew what it was, why'd you ask?"

He stared back at me for a moment, then smiled. "Well, Holly asked. I just meant, where'd you get it? I know a guy back in San Francisco who collects—"

"I've really gotta go," I said, grabbing the bags. This was getting weird.

"Well, it was great to meet you," Holly said. Her generic voice was back, but I barely noticed because I was striding toward the counter.

They didn't follow me, but I watched them over my shoulder while paying $200 for a bag that would have cost $80 online. Kenny was in the far corner, talking on his cellphone. Holly stood next to him, inspecting a purse. After paying, I stepped out of the store and spent a few minutes padding the drive with t-shirts and socks, then shoved my laptop bag into the empty space I'd created in my rolling suitcase.

Kenny and Holly must have lost interest because, by the time I'd finished repacking, I didn't see them around. For corporate headhunters, landing a guy like me meant a finder's fee of 20% of my first-year salary, which would be low seven figures if I ever left *The Barker*. That meant that Kenny and Holly would see around a hundred grand each if they convinced me to join GNL. As odd as it was to approach me in the airport, I decided they'd just been excited to meet me.

Five minutes later I was at Alaska's first-class desk handing my driver's license to a pimply kid who looked no more than twenty. He began typing and spoke without looking up from his screen. "And what's your final destination today, sir?"

"Seattle. I'm on the 8:55. I was wondering if there are any first class upgrades available."

"I'll be happy to check on that for you, Mr. Vane."

He tapped at his keyboard for a few seconds, then looked up, frowning. "I'm sorry, sir, I can't let you on a plane today."

"What?"

"If you would step aside, I can get someone to answer any questions you might have."

I smirked, then chuckled. "You're kidding, right? I mean, look at me. I know I don't look like a terrorist."

"We don't profile based on appearances, sir. You'll need to step aside."

"Wait, what? Can you check again?"

The kid checked the line, which was growing behind me, and sighed. "Please step aside and I'll find an agent."

I walked to the edge of the check-in counter and, a couple minutes later, an older man appeared out of a green door next to the luggage belt. He gestured to the corner of the check-in area and I followed him. "What's the problem, sir?"

"The kid said I can't fly."

"And?"

"Look, I know you're just doing your job. But I'm

obviously not a terrorist."

"Have you traveled to the Middle East recently, or participated in any anti-government protests?"

"No, but why would that—"

"Do you have any outstanding warrants? Sometimes that can do it." He seemed like he'd had this conversation before. "If you haven't yet, you should receive your letter from DHS TRIP in the next two to four weeks."

"DHS TRIP?"

"The Department of Homeland Security Traveler Redress Inquiry Program."

"Am I being punked?"

"Sir, we're very busy here."

"Are there ever mistakes?"

"Sure."

"But you can't let me onto the plane?"

"No."

"Really? This is *really* how it works? I can't get home and you can't give me any more information? And I'll get some letter? I. Flew. In. *Last. Night.*"

The man looked past me like he wanted to move on, then let out a deep sigh. "When you are added to the No Fly List, DHS TRIP sends you a letter informing you of your status and providing you the option of submitting a form to receive additional information. If you choose that option, DHS TRIP will provide a second letter identifying the general criterion under which you have been placed on the No Fly List. Sometimes they include an unclassified summary of the specific reasons for your inclusion on the list."

I just stared at him, blinking. He gave me a long look, like he was making sure he'd shut me up, then turned and walked back through the green door.

I'm usually a pretty confident guy, but I was genuinely rattled. I knew it was a mistake, but a dozen people were staring at me like I might be carrying a bomb, and now I was stuck in the airport with no way to get back to Seattle. Plus, I was reminded of a fight I'd had with Greta about a year ago.

I'd just gotten back from a two-day trip to Silicon Valley, where I was in talks to purchase a tech gossip blog, and, within minutes of getting home, I'd made the mistake of telling her I had to go again later in the week. Long story short, we'd argued about how much I was working, I'd assured her that the only thing she'd catch me with in a hotel bedroom was an empty pizza box, and she'd threatened to report me to Homeland Security. To get me added to the No Fly List.

It was one of those things people say when they're mad. Like when someone leaves their clothes on the floor over and over and you let it build inside you until it explodes outward and you tell them they're the messiest person on earth. The kind of thing you regret immediately. I'd said stuff like that to Greta before, but she rarely got that mad. Later, she apologized and pleaded temporary insanity, but I'd found it kind of funny. Of course, I'd assumed she'd never actually do it, and the thought of Greta on the phone with a buzz-cutted guy at the Pentagon made me smile. It probably wasn't her, but at this point it didn't matter.

I walked to an off-brand coffee shop at the other end of the airport and opened my laptop. Then I did what I always did when I was confused. A Google search.

Another thing Greta likes to say is, "As bad as you are at feelings, you're that good at Google searches." Of course, that was her passive-aggressive way to get me to do research for her, but it flattered me, and I have to say that it worked. Any time she wondered something out loud, I'd slide up next to her while tapping away at my phone. Seconds later I'd present her a double-sourced answer, like a cat leaving a mouse on its owner's porch.

After a double espresso and a few minutes of Googling, I'd confirmed what the man told me about the letter I'd get from DHS TRIP. I'd learned some other things about the No Fly List, too. Before 9/11, there were a dozen names on the list. After the Bush administration passed the Patriot Act, it grew rapidly for six years before ballooning to over 50,000 names under President Obama. Turns out, people get added to the list for all sorts of reasons. Many are legitimate terrorist threats, sure. Others are journalists traveling home from foreign countries, protesters who rubbed someone the wrong way, or family members of suspected terrorists who refused to cooperate with law enforcement. There are even reports of simple name mix-ups. Senator Ted Kennedy was once refused a boarding pass by mistake because there's a T. Kennedy on the list. Of course, Kennedy was able to board his flight when his secret service detail cleared things up with the TSA agent.

But I'm not a senator.

According to the ACLU's website, getting a name removed from the list takes a month or more, and that's with a good lawyer. *The Barker* retains a great lawyer back in Seattle, so I Skyped her. But she didn't know much more than me about the No Fly List and, after a few minutes, she advised me just to get home, promising to look into it immediately. I slammed my laptop closed, drained my remaining espresso, and scanned the cafe. I'm not the paranoid type, but I couldn't shake the interaction with Holly and Kenny. They certainly weren't following me now, but something in them had changed when they saw the drive. Or maybe I was imagining it. Maybe it was just Innerva's fear rubbing off on me. Either way, I needed to figure out what it was, so I pulled the drive out of the new backpack and onto my lap.

Despite running a website and living in one of techiest tech hubs on earth, I know next to nothing about computers and I'd never seen a hard drive. To me, data storage is the platinum-plated, 100 gig zip drive on my keychain. I knew the drive was old, and that communities existed online to discuss and trade old computers and parts.

So I searched again, quickly finding photos of similar drives on a couple blogs and on the website of a computer museum in the Netherlands. Within a couple minutes, I knew what I had. It was an IBM 2314, built between 1967 and

1969. Originally, it would have lived in a drawer with a bunch of matching drives, all accessed by a central control unit. It held eleven double-sided magnetic disks separated by spacers, totaling 29 megabytes of storage. How much is 29 megs? Not much. Ten years ago your first iPhone had 140 times that. The drive was a relic, and my guess was that the tech guys back at the office would geek out when they saw it, if I ever made it home.

I rotated the drive within the bag, checking for any defining marks that would help me pinpoint the year. That's when I noticed the small white sticker on the bottom. It was peeling off and one of the corners was ripped, but the black ink was still legible.

Destroy Per Directive 6/35.

I ran a few searches for the phrase, including all sorts of variations, inclusions, and exclusions, but couldn't figure out what it meant. But I knew someone who might know, and I couldn't think of anything else to do, so I checked the index card Innerva had given me. I figured I could meet the computer expert, then catch a bus or a train back to Seattle and be home by midnight. According to my phone, her house was located in *Biltmore Estates*, a neighborhood I'd never heard of just south of the Fremont Street Experience in Downtown Las Vegas.

The Overclocker was a twenty-minute Uber ride away.

CHAPTER 6

As I stood in the street, I began to wonder whether Innerva had been messing with me.

I'd always imagined computer experts living in sleek lofts with floor-to-ceiling windows that looked out over Puget Sound. They'd sit in minimalist chairs, surrounded by silver laptops and neatly-bundled cables, sipping cold-brew coffee as clean racks of servers blinked reassuring patterns of blue and green light into the darkness. In my mind, their homes were as modern and efficient as the technologies they'd mastered.

The Overclocker's house was a dumpster fire.

It was a tiny bungalow covered in light brown stucco that had been washed out and cracked by decades of Vegas sunshine. The right side of the roof was held together with duct tape and plastic garbage bags. On the left side of the house, a ragged blue tarp fluttered in the hot wind, partially covering a patch of exposed metal lattice.

I checked the address on the index card again, just to be

sure, then walked over a patch of dead grass to the front door. Before I could knock, I heard a series of muffled sounds. A quiet clang, metal on metal. A dull thud, like something hitting the floor. Then a floor creaking. Footsteps.

I tapped on the door, but no one answered.

I noticed a flash of movement through the half-open blinds in the window to the right of the door. I peered in but saw no one.

"Helloooooo," I called.

Nothing.

"I'm looking for The Overclocker."

Still nothing.

I knocked again, harder this time, then angled my head between the rusty window bars and looked through the crack in the blinds. The house was still. All I could make out was a patch of blonde wood flooring, dotted with stains.

Innerva told me once that only ten people knew her real name, so I figured that if Innerva was comfortable enough with The Overclocker to send me to her, that meant they were either close friends or trusted professional allies. A name-drop would be my best shot at a response. I leaned in toward the window, mouth between the bars, and yelled the name this time. "Do you know *Innerva Shah*?"

More noises, more footsteps, but no answer. The Overclocker was in there but she clearly didn't want to come out and chat, so I scanned the neighborhood, trying to figure out what to do.

The house was surrounded by similar bungalows, all painted a shade of brown or gray and all baking in the sun. A few old cars and motorhomes were parked along the street, but the only signs of life were the malnourished palm trees that rose from the sidewalk every forty feet or so. Then I noticed something. A few blocks to the south, the red and white sign of Binion's Casino peeked out above an overpass, which reminded me that I was just a couple blocks north of downtown Las Vegas, old school Las Vegas. Binion's was one of the casinos that put Vegas on the map. It was the first to add carpets, the first to offer comps to all gamblers, and the first to offer high-limit tables. The World Series of Poker had even started there. Tourists loved it because you could take your picture with the million in cash they kept stacked in the lobby. I could hop in a taxi there and be on a bus to Seattle within the hour.

As I stepped toward the curb, I heard a sound behind me. A quick, piercing screech like a subway train grinding to a halt. The door opening. Before I could react, a hand gripped my arm, twisting the flesh and jerking me into the house. A moment later I was in the living room.

The dead bolt clicked and a woman stepped to within two feet of my face. "Who the hell are you?"

The first thing I noticed was her smell. Sweet at first, then a hit of citrus and burnt metal. Like gummy bears mixed with soldering fumes. She wore jeans splotched with black and brown stains, a white V-neck tee, and a black vest covered in pockets and zippers. The kind photographers and fishermen wear. Her frizzy black hair was tied back in a messy ponytail and her forehead, nose, and upper cheeks were dotted with reddish-tan freckles. Her body reminded me of Greta's—lean, athletic, and not super curvy. But she was a half-foot taller than Greta. Probably almost six feet, so I barely had to tilt my head to meet her shifty eyes.

"I'm Alex Vane."

"How'd you know Innerva's name? Where is she?"

I was about to answer when the smell of the room hit me all at once. It was a sour, chemical stench that reminded me of old magic markers. Halfway between sickening and alluring. I inhaled deeply and my knees buckled slightly. "What's that smell?"

"Solvent. Adhesives. Where's Innerva?"

"I...I don't know. She told me to come talk to you."

She took a step back and I looked around the room. To my right, a threadbare recliner sat next to a wooden chair with three legs. In front of me, a few milk crates full of books blocked an arched doorway that appeared to lead to a kitchen. To my left, a giant table was buried under computer monitors and external drives, and littered with soda bottles, food cartons, wires, small cans and bottles with labels I couldn't read, and various tools I didn't recognize.

"I know you from somewhere," she said.

"I run *The Barker*. The website. Maybe you've seen me—"

"Innerva hates that piece-of-shit site." She paused a beat. "Who told you about her?"

I'd known Innerva for years, longer than almost anyone. Longer than this woman for sure. I knew I wasn't at the top of her "journalists-I-respect" list, but it stung to find out that she'd been badmouthing my site to a woman I didn't know. I was trying to figure out what to say when she grabbed my arm like she'd decided not to wait for an answer. Her grip was strong and I felt my bicep bruising as she yanked me toward the door. I probably could have stood my ground if I'd tried—I had at least fifty pounds on her—but between the chemicals and her tone, I was pretty dazed.

I figured she was going to throw me out, but instead she put both hands around my ribcage and slammed me up against the door. She got right in my face. "Who told you about Innerva?"

"I've known her for *years*. Our friend James was *killed* yesterday." I was trying to sound tough but there was no way I was going to fight her, if it came to that. The last time I got in a fight, I was twenty. And I lost.

"James who?"

"Stacy."

"He was your friend?"

"Yes. And so is Innerva." I switched to my reasonable, calm-the-bear voice. "James was shot yesterday at *The Las Vegas Gazette*. Innerva gave me a hard drive. Said you might be able to help me."

She loosened her grip a little. "Hard drive? That thing got blasted yesterday. It no longer exists."

Now I was confused. I said, "The drive is *literally* in my bag right now."

She stepped back. Said, "*You* have the drive? Let me see it."

I rubbed my arm where she'd been holding it, glared at her, then unzipped the backpack. She lunged forward when she saw what was in it.

"No," I said, turning my shoulder to block her. I held up the bag to let her look inside. "Innerva said you might be able to get the data off this thing."

She grunted in a way I couldn't understand. "She tell you where she got that drive?"

"No."

"Do you have *any idea* what it would take to get the data off that? It's fifty years old, you yuppie dipshit."

"Why'd you say the drive was destroyed yesterday?" I asked.

Another grunt.

"Why?"

She ignored me and walked a little square around the living room. One pace in each direction with slow, 90-degree turns after each. Then she did it again. It was as though she'd forgotten I was in the room.

"They must've had two," she said to herself at last. "A decoy. Damn, Innerva is smart." She paused a beat, then met my eyes. "Maybe they turned you?"

"They who? I'm a *friend of Innerva*."

"Turned you, Mr. Innocent. The Company In Action. Conspiracies In America. Covert Infiltration and Assassination. Charlie fucking Indigo fucking Alpha, you Jack Ryan motherfucker."

It was *possible* that this woman was a computer expert. Too early to tell. But the words she spoke out loud seemed to be squeaking out at random from an ongoing internal conversation. She was clearly paranoid, and possibly something worse. I looked at the floor, trying to decide whether to make a run for it or continue what was quickly becoming the strangest conversation of my life.

Then it hit me. Jack Ryan. "Are you talking about the

CIA?"

"I'm talking about the owners of that drive you brought into my house."

"You think the CIA *turned* me? Are you crazy?"

"I'm a little bit crazy, but that doesn't mean I'm wrong."

I smiled because it was a good line, one I assumed she'd used before. And I had to admit that she was right. I know there's no such thing as normal, but when I said I'm good at reading people, I meant people whose chemistry and personal history have landed them somewhere near consensus reality. The Overclocker didn't qualify. Her demeanor had become a little less aggressive than before, but she still wouldn't meet my eyes. I had no idea what she was thinking, what she was feeling, or what she'd do next. All I knew for sure was that the drive had gotten her attention. She wanted it. Or maybe needed it.

And I wanted to find out what she knew—or thought she knew—about the drive, and about James. Much of journalism is simple manipulation. Sometimes it's just a matter of saying the thing that gets a source to tell you what you already know they know. And part of that is pretending you don't need them. That you have ten or eleven other sources who'd be happy to tell you what you want to know. I knew she wanted the drive, and it didn't seem likely that she was going to kill me for it, so I decided to try the oldest trick in the book.

I said, "Look, I have no idea what you're talking about. I have not been turned by the CIA. I came to Las Vegas, Innerva gave me this hard drive, and told me to come see you. Said she had to disappear. I'm sorry to bother you. I'll just head out."

I closed the backpack, turned abruptly, and reached for the doorknob.

"Wait." Her tone had softened and I knew I had her.

I turned back. "What?"

"When did you say you met Innerva?"

"About thirteen years ago."

"When did she and James meet?"

She was quizzing me, but I decided to play along. "At the same time."

"You were working with James then?"

"Yes, we co-founded News Scoop."

"That was a good site, until you ruined it."

"Thanks."

"What did Innerva love best about James?"

"She talked to you about that?"

"She did, and if you really knew them, you'd know as well."

This was an easy one. Computer hackers could be white hats, gray hats, or black hats, depending on how they used their skills. The media tends to focus on the black hats, the ones who use their powers for illegal or destructive hacks. But there are plenty of white hats out there, hackers who test systems, recover data legally, and so on. I said, "Innerva loved James's moral certitude. She sometimes described herself as amoral, and James kept her hat from getting too gray."

She nodded and walked another little square around the living room, then said, "If you're not CIA—*which I will choose to believe for now*—I need to tell you something. I'm leaving this house. Soon and forever. And that drive is coming with me, with or without you attached to it."

She spun around, stepped over the crates of books, and walked into the kitchen. A minute later she was back, carrying a gray canvas duffle bag that was probably white twenty years ago, a can of steak and potato soup, and a sparkler. The kind kids get at the Fourth of July.

"Why are you leaving?" I asked. "And what were you saying about the drive being the real target? And by the way, what's an overclocker and what's your *actual* name?"

She ignored me and walked to the large table. She was mumbling something, but I couldn't tell what. *Batter?* Or maybe *Axes?*

She set the duffle bag on the floor and slowly peeled a piece of tinfoil off the soup can. She peered inside, then replaced the tinfoil and set the can on the stack of servers in the center of the table. She jammed the handle of the sparkler through the tinfoil so it stood straight up in the can, then rummaged through the mess on the table. Cables, trash, and bits of metal fell to the floor. She dropped to one knee and began rifling through the debris. She was still mumbling, and I was beginning to understand what she was saying. It was just one word, repeated over and over.

Baxter. The name of the shooter.

"Are you saying 'Baxter'?" I asked. She didn't respond. "Are you hearing *any* of my questions?"

Still on the floor, she pulled a red lighter out of a balled-up napkin that had been stuffed in a coffee mug. "Ha!" She held it up like a trophy.

She stood and lit the sparkler, which was still sticking straight up out of the soup can, then turned to face me as the blue and gold sparks erupted behind her. She didn't smile, but her face looked relaxed, like the paranoia was gone. "An overclocker is a particular kind of hardware specialist. I make computers run faster than they're designed to run, do things they're not supposed to do. I'm leaving because James was murdered yesterday, but not by Baxter Callahan. Someone else killed them both, and killed four others to cover up the crime. For now, I'm choosing to believe it wasn't you, but whoever it was will be coming for me next. And because you're holding that hard drive, they'll be coming for you, too."

She looked at the sparkler, which had burned down about an inch. The sparks were bouncing off the foil on the soup can, tumbling over the servers and fading out on the table below. She looked straight at me, and for the first time I got a clear look at her eyes. Her small black pupils were surrounded by streaks of white and pale blue that grew darker toward her outer eye. Like a white star exploding in a blue sky. They were wild and wide open, like a madman, and staring straight at me.

"My name is Quinn Rivers," she concluded. "And we have sixty seconds."

CHAPTER 7

Journalists get lied to all the time, so if you don't learn to read people, you don't make it far.

Years ago, I took a weekend class from a former FBI agent and learned the basics. First, you study visual clues like age, body type, the presence or absence of a wedding ring, and so on. Then you establish a behavioral baseline using the subject's normal facial expressions and gestures. Do they cross their arms or close their eyes at certain times? Do they discharge nervous energy with foot tapping, fidgeting, or excessive blinking? That sort of thing. From there, you ask questions and study reactions. You watch for deviations in the baseline. It's actually easy. But the basics only take you so far. Greta taught me that you can only truly observe someone if you're deeply grounded within yourself. If you're distracted or stuck in your own head, you're going to miss something. And the *deeper* your own peace, the more you'll notice about the world, and the person standing across from you. That's the idea, anyway.

But with Quinn, I didn't know what to think.

On the one hand, she was finally looking at me, and her eyes had me frozen. In a different time and place I might have called them beautiful, but in that moment, they were simply transfixing. She seemed clearer than before, though not calmer, like all the nervous energy in her had coalesced into a plan of action. And part of me felt like I could trust her. On the other hand, I didn't know what was in that can.

I assumed it had something to do with destroying her computers and everything else on her desk. Seems like what a paranoid person might do. But I didn't feel like waiting around to find out. I was ready to get as far away from Quinn Rivers as I could, and I was taking the drive with me.

I decided to bolt out the front door, find a taxi, and head to the bus station. I held her gaze for a moment longer, then scanned her up and down, trying to figure out whether she'd chase me, or fight me, when I tried to leave without her. And that's when I realized that she was dressed like Han Solo. It was a passing thought, a ridiculous thought given the situation. Back at *The Barker*, we have a life-size cardboard Han Solo stand-up and, intentionally or not, she was dressed just like him, right down to the black leather boots.

I turned for the door just as I heard a car passing out front, so I peeked through the blinds. A silver Chevy Suburban was easing to a stop in front of Quinn's house, a patch of bright red hair visible through the passenger window. Holly, from the airport. She wasn't looking at me. She didn't see me. But I was pretty sure it was her.

"Weird," I said.

Quinn must have been in sync with me, because she bounded toward the window with four long strides and peered out, standing shoulder to shoulder with me.

Something silver flashed in the window of the SUV. "Was that a gun?" I asked. "I'm pretty sure that's the woman I saw at the airport and—"

"Shut up."

Quinn jumped behind the door and pulled me away from

the window. "You saw her at the airport? Do they know you have the drive?"

"Yeah, they saw it."

"They're here to kill me. And probably you. I'm leaving, and I'm taking the drive with me. Give it to me."

All I could manage was a weak, "No."

"Alex, Mr. Listicle, we have about thirty seconds until that sparkler ignites the 300 grams of blue thermite in that soup can. At that point, the plastic, metal, and silicon will literally begin to melt and the paper and wood will catch on fire. If you want to wait here, that's fine. Have a chat with the folks in the SUV, go buy them a Frappuccino or whatever people like you drink these days. And by the time they're wiring your balls up to a truck battery, I'll be two states away." She glanced at the sparkler. "Twenty seconds."

As stupid as it sounds, my first instinct was to walk out the front door and shake hands with Holly, or whoever that was. I was sure there'd be a reasonable explanation for all this, and Quinn already seemed like the bigger threat to my health and safety. But there was a chance she knew something I didn't, and the sparkler was already more than three-quarters burned.

I looked back at Quinn, whose eyes were fixed on mine. "Prove it," I said. "Prove you know something I don't."

"Have you looked at the drive?" she asked.

"I have."

"There's a sticker on it, right?"

I nodded.

"It says 'Destroy Per Directive 6/35'?"

"How'd you know that?"

"Because I'm telling you the truth. C'mon."

"What does it mean?"

"I'll tell you when we're out of here. Five seconds."

At this she grabbed my hand and pulled me toward the table. The sparkler had burned down to just above the tinfoil. I didn't know how much space there was between the tinfoil and the blue thermite underneath, but I was convinced that I'd be safer with Quinn than in a thermite fire. On our way past the table, she scooped up the duffel bag, then shoved me through the kitchen and into a small bedroom.

A loud *click-whoosh* came from the living room. Like a huge match being lit. Then there was a heavy knock at the door. *Thack-thack-thack.*

Quinn slid into an open closet door on her knees and I glanced around the bedroom. Slivers of light streamed through cracked blinds, illuminating a twin mattress on the floor in the corner. The mattress was surrounded by stacks of books, bits of wire, and a few hand tools. Two egg crates, one of jeans and one of t-shirts, sat by the foot of the mattress.

Quinn was pulling up a loose section of floor inside the small closet. The floor opened into a dark hole and the top few rungs of a cheap aluminum ladder started about a foot below floor level.

Quinn said, "You first."

I dropped my suitcase to the bottom and climbed down, holding the backpack over my head so I could fit. About eight feet down, the ladder stopped at the mouth of a low tunnel with dirt walls and cheap plywood planks along the ground.

I heard the closet door close above me. Quinn's duffle bag struck my shoulder and fell to the ground. I heard her feet hit the ladder. "Go," she shouted.

Suddenly the tunnel went black. Quinn had replaced the closet floor above us. I took my phone out and turned on the flashlight, then swung the backpack over my shoulder and scurried down the tunnel in a half-hunched slump, pulling my suitcase awkwardly behind me.

"Where are we going?" I called.

"To my other house."

I'd only gone about twenty feet down the corridor when I saw a glint of silver rising out of the dirt floor. The bottom rungs of the second ladder. It matched the first and led up a slightly wider space that ended abruptly about twelve feet above me. I gripped my phone in my mouth—flashlight aimed up the ladder—and held my suitcase over my head. I climbed, pressing my chest into the rungs and sucking in my stomach so the drive on my back wouldn't get crushed against the back wall. My shoulders were burning by the time my suitcase ran into a piece of plywood.

Quinn was right behind me, at the bottom of the ladder. "Push hard," she said. "There's a layer of dirt."

Using my suitcase as a wedge, I popped up the plywood. Dirt rained down on my head and onto Quinn. She cursed as I reached the top of the ladder and rolled onto the floor of a tiny shed. "*This* is your other house?"

Quinn made her way up the ladder and stood next to me, breathing hard. "It's the shed behind the house. I have a truck nearby." She slid a deadbolt on the thin metal door and peeked out. I heard pounding coming from the other house. They were still knocking.

"What do we do now?" I asked.

"They're at my front door, so we've got a clear run through the vacant space behind those houses, then we've got shade from that fence. We get to the other side of the fence and it's a straight shot to the truck."

She held out her hand. "How about I take the drive?"

I offered up a blank stare.

"Fine," she said. "Follow me close and move at the speed I move and remember I'm being generous right now." When I nodded, she pushed the door open and ran out of the shed. She wasn't limber, but she *could* run. Like someone who never worked out but was constantly moving, constantly walking, and stayed in pretty good shape despite a lack of regular exercise. I watched her for a moment, debating whether I should follow, then ran after her.

We covered the thirty yards of open ground at a pace that made me realize just how out of shape I'd gotten, then stopped in the shadow of an old wooden fence. I glanced back at the shed. Nothing. I couldn't see the front door of Quinn's house, but through the holes in the blue tarp on the side window, I saw flames. She hadn't mentioned that after the blue thermite lit the table on fire it would spread down the table legs to the floor and curtains and walls, but I figured it had been her plan all along. Quinn was burning down her house.

She slid through a broken section in the fence and I followed her.

She took a few confident steps, then froze.

"Where's your truck?" I asked.

"I can't remember where I parked it."

She closed her eyes, mumbled something to herself, then paced in a little square. I was beginning to recognize this as her contemplative stroll. She took off suddenly, heading north.

A block later, we came to an unmonitored parking lot next to a boarded-up grocery store. Quinn pulled out her keychain as we came alongside the truck, an extra-large Ford F-series from the eighties. Dual-tone brown on light brown. Ugly thirty years ago, now it was just sad. She fumbled to find the key, but she made it into the cab, stowed her bag in the footwell, then tugged on the passenger door lock until it popped up.

I looked back. No sign of pursuit. I hopped in.

"Check the drive," she said. "Did it get cracked in the tunnel?"

I didn't need to check it. "I was careful," I said. "It's fine."

Quinn leaned back, jammed the key into the ignition and, for the first time, smiled. "We'll be on the freeway in ten minutes."

"Then you'll tell me what 'Destroy Per Directive 6/35' means?"

"Yes. And I'll tell you about Baxter. About all of this. The parts I know, anyway."

"Good," I said.

"Good," she said, turning the key.

Damn thing didn't even click.

CHAPTER 8

I should've known her truck wouldn't start.

"Any other ideas?" I asked, brushing some dirt from my hair onto the floor.

Quinn's face was sweaty and dusty, and frozen in a blank expression. But I could tell her mind was racing. She tried the key again. Nothing. "Motherless son of a—"

"Did *you* see a gun in the window of the SUV?"

"No, but I didn't need to," she said, staring down at the key. "They *always* have guns."

I wasn't *sure* I'd seen a gun. Just a flash of silver that could have been a cellphone. And I wasn't even positive that the person I'd seen in the SUV had been Holly from the airport. I hadn't gotten a good look at her face, and hadn't seen the driver at all.

Being around Quinn was messing with my head, and I was doing another thing Greta liked to accuse me of: trying to convince myself that everything was okay, that the status quo wasn't being disturbed. Greta would tell you that this particular failing was why I'd never dealt with Rebecca's death. And I was probably doing it again now.

I grabbed my phone from the backpack. "If they're still following us, we should call the cops."

Quinn slapped my phone to the truck floor. "These guys *are* the cops, you *asshole*. Or at least on the same payroll. They're here to kill us, like they killed Baxter."

"Baxter shot my friend through the chest with a shotgun," I said.

Quinn grunted. "Because your TV told you that?"

I was starting to recognize two distinct grunts from Quinn. One was a dismissive, *hell-no* grunt. She'd grit her teeth and release a deep bass note out of the side of her mouth. The other was her slightly-less-dismissive, *ambivalent-yes* grunt. An open-mouthed, higher-pitched sound that felt like a shower of rainbows compared to the first kind.

Her latest grunt had been the first kind.

"Tell me about Baxter?" I said.

Another grunt, the second kind.

She looked out all the windows, like she was expecting us to be surrounded by a SWAT team. "Well, if you want proof he didn't kill himself, here's some. He loved dogs as much as I do. Worf was his best friend. Even if he'd let his demons get the best of him, even if he *had* planned to kill himself, he never would have left that dog alone in the apartment for the police to find."

"But you didn't have a dog at your house."

"Only because I knew I might have to disappear one day. But anyway, there's another thing about Baxter. He *gave* James the drive."

"No way." As usual, she'd buried the lede, but I didn't buy it. I knew that the press screwed up rapidly-developing stories all the time, but they wouldn't have plastered Baxter's face across every TV in the country if they weren't sure he was the shooter. And they wouldn't be sure he was the shooter if the police hadn't leaked it to them.

I also knew that, if Kenny and Holly *had* followed me to

Quinn's house, something weird was going on. So, as sure as I was that Quinn was wrong about Baxter, I agreed with her that *something* was up.

But she seemed to have no idea what to do next.

I looked through a smudge in the dust collector that was the back window of Quinn's truck, but didn't see anyone. A few blocks to the south, peeking out above an overpass, I saw the red and white sign for Binion's, then I caught something out of the corner of my eye. A flash of red emerging over a slight hill about two blocks away. It was partially covered by a hat or scarf or something, but the hair was unmistakable. Holly.

"C'mon," I said, opening the door. And because I had the drive on my back, Quinn followed me.

We walked north for a block, away from her house, then turned left twice to land on Fremont Street. A few blocks away, a thin line of smoke was rising from the area of Quinn's house. I pointed at it. "You're burning down your house, huh?"

I think her mind was on the truck because she'd been passing the key from hand to hand, glancing at it every few seconds like it had let her down. As though the truck not starting was the key's fault and not the fault of the owner who'd let it rust, unmaintained, for years.

"Data destruction," she said at last. "Bastards aren't going to get a single byte out of me. And where are we going?"

"Fremont Street," I said, ignoring the sigh Quinn let out when I was halfway through the first word. "If that *was* a gun, and if those *were* the two people from the airport, I figure we can disappear there."

A block later, we passed under the overpass and entered the Fremont Street Experience. The crowd wasn't huge, but it seemed to be growing, and I wanted to be around people. To our left, a graying singer with a mic and a cheap amp was doing a terrible cover of Prince's "Purple Rain." To our right, a gang of buff guys in Red Wings jerseys laughed loudly, sipping colorful drinks from two-foot tall plastic cups from

Fat Tuesdays. A hundred feet above us, a couple flew by on a zip line attached to a curved, translucent roof. If Kenny and Holly were following us, they seemed to be hanging back, because I hadn't seen them since we left the truck. We walked toward the bright blinking face of the Golden Nugget, the largest of the old-time, downtown casinos.

That's when I spotted them.

About a hundred yards behind us, Kenny and Holly were jogging slowly and in something close to rhythm, like the Secret Service alongside a presidential motorcade. Kenny in the amazing linen suit and Holly in the light blue pantsuit. She now wore a matching hat, the brim tilted down, shadowing her face, but patches of red peeked out from the side when she turned her head.

I turned to Quinn and shouted, "Let's run."

She'd fallen a few yards behind and was gazing up at the twinkling lights wrapping around the facade of the Golden Nugget Casino. I took off before she answered, my rolling suitcase in one hand and the drive on my back. I raced across a little intersection and past a crowd that was watching a guy spray paint onto t-shirts. Quinn was on my tail and, as we ran, I swung the backpack off my left shoulder and pulled my phone out of the side pocket.

Quinn seemed to be keeping up with me, because I could hear her yelling something, but the light show was starting to the thunderous applause of the crowd, so I couldn't tell what she was saying. I entered my password without looking—0618, which stood for June 18, the date Greta and I got married.

Suddenly a pop song from the nineties filled the air and, above us, a surreal underwater scene appeared on the arched screen as the crowd stopped and stared at the lights. In another block, we'd be out of the covered area of the Fremont Street Experience and into more deserted territory, so I needed to hurry. With a swipe and a tap, I was in the ZipCar iPhone app. After two more taps, a map popped up showing three cars near us. All my info was already on file, so it only took three more clicks to reserve a red Toyota Corolla four blocks away. Problem was, it was south, well away from the crowds.

I slowed my run a little to allow Quinn to catch up with me. Kenny and Holly were still jogging about a hundred yards behind us. For a terrifying instant, I thought Kenny was holding a gun, but then I realized that he was talking on a cellphone. Both he and Holly had seemed fit—more fit than Quinn or me, at least—and I was getting the sense that they weren't trying all that hard to catch up with us.

When she'd pulled abreast of me, Quinn said, "You...you didn't call...?"

"Call the police? No. I got us a ZipCar."

"Is that the...the thing where...where you get a car that already has a tracking device in it?"

"You're welcome." I slowed until Quinn was a half-step ahead of me and gave her a slight nudge from behind. "We're gonna need to run faster."

The light show above had switched to a psychedelic scene of butterflies and flying horses with sweeping, Enya-like music. Some *oohs* and *ahhs* came from the crowd and someone screamed with excitement on the zip line overhead. I glanced behind us. Holly's eyes were locked on mine, like she'd been waiting for me to turn around. Kenny still appeared to be on the phone.

"Follow me," I said, cutting sharply to the right down a side street that led into an industrial area.

For two blocks we ran north, dodging occasional groups of tourists streaming toward Fremont Street. Every few seconds, I checked my phone to make sure we were on track. I was hoping we'd lost them with the quick cut down the side street, but I soon realized that we hadn't. About a block from the little green ZipCar icon on my phone, I shot a glance over my shoulder. Quinn was slowing down and Kenny and Holly were maintaining their pace behind us, no more than a block away. Kenny was no longer on the phone.

"Quinn," I yelled. "You have to sprint. We're almost

there."

Her sweat had washed most of the dirt off her forehead and down her face, leaving a line of sweaty mud where her neck met her t-shirt. Looking like an eighteen-wheeler trying to accelerate up a steep hill, she picked up the pace.

I spotted the Corolla half a block ahead. I sped up and turned back at the same time. Quinn looked like she might pass out.

Meanwhile, Kenny and Holly looked fresh, like they were in a commercial for businesswear, *so comfortable you can jog in it*. I was pretty sure they could catch up with us if they wanted, but I wasn't going to wait around to find out.

I got to the Corolla and waved my phone across the sensor on the windshield, unlocking the doors. I threw my bags in the back and slid into the driver seat, slammed it all the way back to make room for my long legs, and leaned across the passenger seat to open the door for Quinn. When she was about ten yards away, I pulled the keys out from their spot under the gear shift and started the car. Quinn collapsed into the car, panting and cursing under her breath. Something about the CIA. Unintelligible.

I checked my rearview mirror as I peeled out and ran a stop sign at the corner. Holly was still running after us but Kenny had stopped. He seemed to be on his phone again. As relieved as I was to get away from them, I had to wonder what the hell they were doing. They hadn't seemed all that determined to catch us, and if Kenny was on his cellphone now, maybe it *had* been a cellphone before. But they had definitely followed me from the airport, and even the most aggressive corporate headhunter wouldn't do that.

I lost sight of them as I turned west toward the highway. We were both out of breath, but as I merged onto Highway 95, Quinn managed to say, "The first thing we do is get rid of this Lojack mobile."

As crazy as she was, I had to agree.

I was driving one of the world's most trackable cars.

CHAPTER 9

After five minutes, Quinn told me to exit the freeway. Part of me still wanted to get as far away from Las Vegas as possible, but this was her city and I decided to let her take the lead.

I turned onto a little street called Pico Drive, Quinn pointing at a cellphone tower disguised as a palm tree. "Good," she said, "pull up there."

I stopped the car abruptly, but left it running. "What?"

She held her hands on her head, pushing back her hair from her forehead, "You are holding a drive that formerly belonged to the CIA. You do know that, right?"

"I don't know *what's* on this thing."

"Okay, no, yes, I'm sorry. What I mean is that we have a long drive ahead of us and we can't do that in a car that's literally designed to be tracked by any idiot with a cellphone."

Her tone was somewhere between exasperation and condescension, but I decided not to let it get to me. I said, "Hang on. I know *you* say it is. But, no offense, I don't want to just take your word for that."

"Oh, no offense. Well, okay then. I'm glad you said that. I

mean, the worst thing that could happen here is I might get offended, and that simply *wouldn't* do. But all right. You are holding. A drive. That someone wants very badly. Maybe it's not even the CIA. Could be *annnnnnyone* in the world. And that someone has sent at least two agents after us. Unless you think we *weren't* being chased just now?"

"Well, yes, we were being chased, but that doesn't mean —"

"Please, please do not tell me you don't think it's connected to that drive. Just… please."

It did seem like the obvious explanation, and I nodded reluctantly.

"Okay then. So, given that people are after us and given that it's about that drive, and given that they are serious murderers, and given that we need to drive but can't drive another mile in a car any five-year-old could track, *mayyyyyyyyyybe* we should get into a different goddamn car before we get waterboarded!"

Ignoring most of what she'd said, I asked, "We need to drive where?"

"To where that damn CIA drive came from. Well, not originally, but where Baxter got it from. Who he got it from, I should say."

"You know where he got it?" I asked.

"From someone we both know. I don't know her real name. Weird collector, trades old tech. She's based out of—"

"Where?"

"I'd rather not say right now," Quinn said, gesturing meaningfully around us.

I stared blankly at her for a second, then I realized what she meant. "Are you saying you think this car is *bugged?*"

"Safe to assume it is, yeah. I probably shouldn't say another word in this damn car, but we're not exactly *teeming* with options right now."

"You think the CIA knew in advance I was going to pull up the ZipCar app and arranged to have *this exact car* pre-bugged and waiting for us?"

"No, I don't."

"So, what, every ZipCar is bugged? That's your theory?"

"I don't know for sure, but it's safe to assume. We *know* they're tracking them, why not get a little more info while they're installing things?"

I stared at her for a long moment, mouth hanging open a little. I was about to go off on her. Call her paranoid, crazy, and so on. But she started her rant first.

"Think about your comfortable world of dotcom douchebags back at *The Barker,*" she began. "Has there ever been a time when you passed up a chance to collect and store information about your customers? No, there hasn't. You try to collect every speck of info you can on your customers— age, gender, location, education level, shopping habits."

She was right, of course. Most sites do that so they can serve ads based on the particular customer. It's really not all that nefarious. The average American consumes fewer commercials and ads now than ever before because of DVRs, streaming video services like Netflix, and pop-up blockers. The *least* a customer can do is let us customize the ads, seeing as how we give them millions of words of free content every month.

I was about to say this when Quinn said, "And you're a little shitty site. Now think about your friends at Google and Apple and Facebook, because I'm *sure* you have friends there. Have they been fully up-front about how much information they're filing away on their customers? Or what they're using it for? They're vampires. We're a damn food source for the bosses and their goal is to make us into herd animals. And— yes!—that means that their convenient little car-shares are bugged because somewhere in the terms and conditions that you didn't read, there's a little clause about how *Conversations and vocal expressions conducted within a ZipCar vehicle become the property of ZipCar Incorporated.* They like to have legal cover, some way to hide behind their own system, because the law is *their* system. It exists just to keep them safe from people like me. To them, I'm the dangerous one. And if *you* aren't willing to become dangerous, *we're* going to die."

I was beginning to get a sense of Quinn. She was smart, that much was clear. But, by her own admission, she was a little bit crazy. The trick with her was going to be finding the line where the smart turned into crazy, and backing away slowly before crossing it. In this case, it was somewhere mid-rant. She'd taken facts known to most people—that all tech and web companies gather all sorts of data about us—and turned it into a crazy conspiracy that led to our Zip Car being bugged. Finally, I said, "Would you feel more comfortable if we got out of the car?"

We walked to a bus stop about twenty feet down the block, in front of a crummy apartment complex. Her eyes were darting from the street to the apartment complex, but, after a minute or two, she calmed down.

"What's the plan?" I asked.

She was staring at the plants alongside the walkway. They were some sort of shrub, but half dead, and the dirt they were in was half sand. Quinn shook her head. "I've never seen a city so hated by its natural environment. I swear, if you turned off the sprinklers, Las Vegas would be a desert again in forty-five minutes."

"Quinn, what—"

"I know where the drive came from."

"You said Baxter gave it to James."

I still didn't buy it, but, like any decent journalist, I knew it was smart to get your source's version of the story, no matter how crazy it was. Quinn was quiet for a moment, like she was deciding whether she wanted to tell me. I said, "You already decided I'm not with the CIA, remember?"

"The Duck Valley Indian Reservation. That's where Baxter got it."

"Never heard of it."

"Well, of course you haven't," she snapped. "The whole point of Indian reservations is to move the genocide survivors someplace folks like you don't have to see them or think about them!" I started to object, but she held up a hand.

"I'm sorry," she said. "Sorry. That's not the problem we're trying to deal with right now. I get distracted sometimes. Sorry."

I shrugged.

"Anyway, there's a…a specialist there. She runs a server farm, goes by the handle Tudayapi. Paiute, someone told me. She collects old tech, trades it sometimes, you know how it goes."

I didn't, but I said, "Sure."

"Baxter got the drive from her. I don't know where she got it. But she walks with God-as-she-perceives-him, and I know she's not CIA, so I want to talk to her. I think…I think we should both talk to her."

"How far away is it?"

"Not far."

I was racking my brain for a different solution, a better solution. In that moment, I came up blank and couldn't bring myself to argue with her. "Got it. Okay then, you're right. We can't keep the ZipCar. What do you suggest?"

She sat on the wooden bench and set her duffle bag on her lap.

"We can just use my phone," I said.

She looked at me like *I* was the crazy one. "You haven't powered down your phone?"

"Why would I—"

"You know it has GPS on it, right? That it's even more trackable than that stupid car?"

I decided to humor her. I pulled my phone out of my pocket and powered it down, holding it right up to her face so she could watch the screen go black. "But how will your laptop be any better?"

"My laptop runs a proprietary OS, designed to keep out snoopers."

I watched over her shoulder as she opened her laptop, a small black one encased in a dented plastic shell. She talked as she connected a little black box and various wires. "It's a little clunky, but it's as secure as anything's reasonably going to get.

The black box I put together functions as a wireless modem, piggybacking on cellphone signals and running multiple layers of encryption in and out. It's not as fast or convenient as the Wi-Fi you take as your birthright when you're in a Starbucks, but it *does* let me transmit and receive information without immediately sending the NSA a transcript of the whole thing. I mention this so you'll understand that when I hop onto Craigslist, it's not without precaution."

By the time she'd finished talking, she was on the site, searching for used cars under $500. "We're *not* getting a five-hundred-dollar car," I said.

"I've got eleven-hundred and four dollars in this bag," she said. "That's it."

"Well, I've got at around four hundred in my wallet."

"The hell are you carrying four hundred bucks around for?"

"Tips," I said. "Also, I think we can safely get some more."

"Oh, you think so? You're an expert on living underground now? Hey, enlighten me."

I'd already thought this through. "Listen. Assuming that people with serious information access are tracking us, they know I'm in Las Vegas someplace. Like, we can agree on that, right?" She nodded. "So, I can hit an ATM and get cash out and advances on a couple of my cards, and all that tells them is I was in Las Vegas today, which they already knew. Right?"

She gave me the second grunt. "As long as you don't hit any ATMs *after* this time and place."

"So that's another nine hundred, giving us a total of twenty-four hundred bucks, give or take. I think we'll get further in a thousand-dollar car than a five-hundred-dollar one. That's all I'm saying."

She nodded slowly and changed the search parameters.

We'd passed a little bodega on the corner when we'd turned onto Pico Drive, and I could see a red and white ATM sign between the beer and cigarette posters in the window. I pointed at it and Quinn nodded before turning back to her computer.

I jogged down and pulled out the max of $200 from my checking account, along with $200 from each of three credit cards.

When I returned, Quinn was talking into her computer. "We'll need to see it first," she was saying.

A man's voice came through the computer speakers, tinny and a little distorted. "How soon can you be here?"

"Ten minutes," Quinn said, rotating the computer so I could see the Craigslist ad. It was a 1997 Ford Thunderbird, its faded blue paint cracked and speckled like it had a rare and deadly skin disease. Once blue, now it was blue-and-scabies. It had 194,000 miles and was listed at $1,000. The ad said that the guy was moving out of state and needed to sell ASAP. And, like all Craigslist ads for cheap cars, it said, "Runs Great!"

"It really is a steal at this price," the guy was saying.

"We can talk price when we get there," Quinn said. I held up the money. "And we're bringing cash."

***

The car was about five minutes away, in a part of Vegas you'd prefer not to visit. It's called D Street and it's on every list of America's worst neighborhoods. Not that I knew that at the time. I was one of those guys who flew first class, stayed in a posh room, then flew home. For me, slumming it in Vegas meant hitting the buffet at the MGM Grand after a concert. Before this trip, I'd never even considered what the rest of Vegas was like.

I'd gotten a hint of it when I arrived at Quinn's house, but her place looked like a suite in the Bellagio compared to the Sunset Vista Apartments on D Street. As I pulled up across the street and turned off the engine, I could see that the building was six or eight stories of beige stucco, with a couple internal stairwells that opened onto a concrete patio. The patio had a couple of vending machines in metal cages and led to a large patch of dry grass. On the grass, a group of men and women sat on milk crates and an old sofa. They were passing a couple joints around and laughing raucously.

Quinn reached for the door.

"Wait," I said. "I want to scope it out before we just walk up."

"Then you're a fool. We sit across the street from the apartment with our lights off, you know what they'll think?"

"That we're here to shoot them?"

"You're catching on, Internet Boy." She opened the passenger door and stepped onto the curb, then walked around and opened my door. I have to admit, I was scared, but Quinn wasn't going to let me sit in the car. I held onto her arm once I got out, giving myself a minute to scan the area.

So, as I held Quinn's arm and pretended to be fumbling with the keys, I did a quick scan. Eleven people total, seven men, four women. Facial expressions all looked friendly, no one seemed to be excluded from the group, no one seemed to be dominating. The sun was on its way down and the temperature had cooled to the low eighties, so they seemed like a group of friends just hanging out on the grass. A casual get-together on a Wednesday evening.

Quinn tugged me forward and called out when we were still a hundred feet away from the group. "Any of you guys Hector?"

"You seem awfully friendly for a paranoid recluse," I said to Quinn.

"I'm paranoid about guys like you, not folks like this."

As we approached, a girl called out from an old blue recliner. "Who's asking for Hector?"

"I'm Moira. I just spoke with him about an old Thunderbird he's selling."

The girl stood and stepped to within a few feet of Quinn and pointed at me. "What the hell kind of name is Moira? And who's the white dude?"

"Moira is a Dutch-African-German name, and this is Abraham."

The girl stared at me, then at Quinn, then glanced back at her friends and broke out laughing. "Hector went up to get the keys and title."

A minute later, a short guy with bushy black hair and a black goatee came out from the stairwell in between the apartments and walked right up to me. "You here for Baby Blue?"

"Yes, I mean, I guess. Is that what you call the Thunderbird?"

"More like Baby Trash," Quinn said. I nudged her in a *let-me-do-the-talking* way, but she ignored me. "We'll pay $500 for it."

"Five?" Hector wasn't having it. "The parts alone are worth two grand. Things got eighteen-inch G6 rims, and a NT-5 Wing Lid Trunk Spoiler."

"It looked like a fine car in the ad," I lied. "Can we see it?"

"It's a piece of crap," Quinn said.

Hector looked at me as if to say, "Can you shut her up?"

Quinn had probably watched enough cop movies to feel right at home in the "bad cop" role—or maybe it just came naturally to her—but I wasn't going to try to stop her. I shrugged at Hector and he led us around the perimeter of the apartments to the car. It looked just like the picture, except that now it was covered by a thin layer of dust, like it hadn't been driven in a few months.

"Looks like the picture," I said.

"Looks worse," Quinn said. "Four hundred cash right now if it starts."

Hector chuckled. "No way you're taking Baby Blue for four hundred, and it doesn't just start. Baby purrs."

He slid into the driver seat and turned the key. I breathed a sigh of relief when it started right up. And he was right. The thing sounded pretty good.

"The papers are clean?" Quinn asked.

"Yeah, grandma gave it to me a few years ago. I pimped it out myself."

"And you're moving out of state?" Quinn asked.

Hector shot her a confused look. "Why?"

Quinn walked around the car, running an index finger

along the edge like a snobby maid checking for dust. And, of course, her finger came up covered with grime. "You said in the ad you're moving out of state."

"Man, my cousin wrote the ad."

"So you're *not* moving out of state."

"Look, you want the car or not? I got shit to do."

Quinn frowned at me. "Let's go." I was stunned. I knew she didn't want to get back in the ZipCar, but she didn't seem to be bluffing. "He's a liar," she said, loudly enough for Hector to hear.

I looked at Hector apologetically and moved toward Quinn like a dad in a grocery store, shuffling away from the jar of jelly his kid just knocked onto the floor. Hector raised his shoulders as if to say, "So?"

Quinn was walking her little square. "We're not gonna do better than this," I whispered to her.

"I can't. He lied."

I looked over at Hector, who was staring at us with an amused smile, then led Quinn a couple yards away as Hector pulled a cellphone out of his back pocket. "Quinn, what the hell are you doing?"

"He lied about leaving town. That was one of the reasons I chose this car."

"Why does that matter?"

"If they come looking for us, and *they will* come looking for us, I wanted the owner of the car to be gone, unreachable. Or at least a little more unreachable."

If we were going to swap cars, this was the one. There was no way I was going to go through this process again, but I needed to get Quinn on board. I decided not to address her paranoia right there, standing on the street with Hector glaring at us.

Instead, I tried a practical approach. "Quinn, if we don't get this car, we have to go back, sit in the ZipCar, open up your laptop, and find someone else on Craigslist who happens to want to make a deal on a Wednesday evening. It could take hours. We might have to get a hotel, sleep in the car or the street, wait till tomorrow, steal a car. Something." I paused for effect. "*This* is the car. If it's alright with you, I will go chat with Hector, get the best price I can, and in ten minutes we'll be driving out of Vegas."

Finally, Quinn folded her arms, gave me her *ambivalent-yes* grunt, then walked back toward the ZipCar.

With Quinn out of the picture, it didn't take much to talk Hector down. I started at $400, where Quinn had left off, figuring we'd end up at $800 or $900. To me, speed was more important than a couple hundred bucks. But Hector was a terrible negotiator. Every time he tried to highlight a feature of the car—the rims, the strangely incongruous beaded seat cover in the back, or the spoiler, which it turned out used to light up—I just said, "I get it, but those features don't add value for us."

After five minutes, we settled on $650. I paid him in cash, and twenty minutes after we'd arrived at the Sunset Vista Apartments, I was back at the ZipCar, holding a registration slip, a set of worn keys, and a sales slip handwritten on notebook paper.

Quinn was sitting on the hood of the ZipCar and she didn't look up even when I gave the top of the car a double-tap, the sort you give a taxi after you've gotten your luggage out of the trunk. "Let's go," I said. "We'll leave this thing here. How far is Duck Valley?"

"Five or six hundred miles," she said, sliding off the hood.

Earlier, when she'd said it was "not far," I'd assumed that meant twenty minutes, an hour, tops. "What?" I managed.

"Nevada-Idaho border," she said casually, pulling the hard drive and her duffle bag out of the ZipCar.

I was trying to convince myself I wasn't making a big mistake.

CHAPTER 10

The ZipCar abandoned, we were rolling north on 93 in the godforsaken Thunderbird. Our bags were in the back seat, stacked protectively around the backpack holding the drive. I was driving and Quinn was staring at the splits in the velour upholstery, closing the glove compartment every time it fell open, which was every time we hit a pothole or one of those rumble strips on the shoulder of the highway.

Since meeting her, I'd been too busy to be annoyed with Quinn. But as I watched the power lines thin out, giving way to strange and beautiful rock formations along the highway, I was no longer wondering if I'd made a mistake. I was wondering how big a mistake I'd made.

Within five minutes of meeting her, I'd known that Quinn was eccentric and probably paranoid. But in the sixty minutes that followed, she'd burned down her house, refused to call the police, and claimed that the CIA was behind the mass shooting that killed James and five others.

And that was before she'd convinced me to drive through

Nevada in an antique Thunderbird.

The ZipCar had the new-car smell of freedom. The open road, possibility, and some sort of chemicals that are terrible and lovely at the same time. I'd never been in a Thunderbird, but I'd always pictured something sleek but solid. American-made speed and toughness. This thing looked like a fat guy sat on a beat-up Toyota Camry, flattening and widening it but leaving the uninteresting lines and uninspired styling. It smelled of stale cigarettes with a hint of curry. Like someone had spilled a couple orders of chicken tikka masala in the trunk eight years back and it had slowly become part of the car. The only nice things I could say about it was that the air conditioning worked, and it suited Quinn well.

About an hour outside of Vegas, we passed a road sign that seemed to rise up out of the dust: TWIN FALLS: 400 MILES.

Twin Falls is the first real city you hit after leaving Nevada from the north, and it was just an hour or two east of the Duck Valley Reservation. At an average speed of seventy miles an hour, we had at least seven hours of driving ahead. The traffic had thinned, and we were cruising down a dark stretch of highway, jagged mountains on both sides. It was just past dusk, and the sky had faded from blue to gray to brown.

I turned to Quinn, knowing that she'd probably be wrong, but wanting to hear her story, just in case she wasn't. "So, what do you think happened?"

She said nothing, so I tried again. "I mean Baxter, the shooting, the sticker on the drive. All the stuff you were talking about before. Start from the beginning."

"This whole thing must be kinda screwed up for you, huh?"

Not what I expected. "What do you mean?"

"Just, you know. I've been planning for something like this for years. Decades, possibly. Why do you think I had my bug-out bag ready, full of cash, couple passports, clean t-shirt, underwear, and pistol."

"You have a gun in there?"

"Sure, and I'm guessing your life doesn't usually involve driving a car like this. With someone like me. Or having people trying to kill you."

"How do you know they were trying to kill us?"

"Are you...they killed six people yesterday, then followed you, showed up at my house with a gun, and chased us through that tourist hellscape. What do you think they were trying to do, sell us Amway?"

"Okay, first off, I have no reason to believe they killed those people. No, let me finish!" Quinn was trying to interrupt. "And they didn't exactly seem like they were trying to shoot at us on Fremont Street. That guy had a cellphone in his hand, not a gun."

"These days you can kill a lot more people with a cellphone," she muttered.

"They were running after us like...like a jog, almost. Like they weren't even trying to overtake us. It was weird."

"So your theory—being as you're the sane one here—is that two armed people followed you from the airport and then decided to run after us for a mile because, what, we were like a pace car for their morning jog? I guess the guns were for extra weight, build some muscle tone. Yessir, okay, that makes perfect goddamn sense, I sure am sorry I tried to make that sound crazy."

"Look, if I thought that, I wouldn't be in this car with my cellphone turned off," I said, and it sounded a little too much like I was implying that having my phone off was the worst part of the whole ordeal. Quinn shot me a withering look, which I only caught out of the corner of my eye. I said, "I just don't understand it yet."

"Me, I don't plan on dying of overthinking. The CIA's been after me for years, and today they finally made their move. I don't need to pin down every little detail to know that."

"Okay, you keep bringing up the CIA, so let's start there. Why did you say the drive used to belong to the CIA, and why do you assume Kenny and Holly are——"

"Who?"

"When I met them at the airport, they said their names were Kenny and Holly. Claimed to be with Global News Link. I don't believe that, obviously, but they *did* seem corporate."

"Ah yes, your highly-trained instincts in spotting intelligence operatives."

"Hey, if there's one thing I've met a lot of in my life, it's corporate types. They had that feeling, like at any minute they might break into a PowerPoint presentation."

She laughed slightly, which made me feel good, like the ice was starting to melt. "Whereas, I've been tracked by the CIA for years," she said wearily, "so I'm just going to assume that without further information, these are the same bastards who've been ruining my life all along."

"See, that's what I don't get." I paused, trying to put it as delicately as I could. "I'm just not sure the CIA devotes that many resources to tracking and stalking...you know, people like you."

"Well, they do."

"How do you *know*, though?"

"Pattern recognition, dammit! When you get a rash every time you eat fish, you figure out you're allergic to fish by recognizing the pattern. And when you get rejected for car loans or credit cards all the time, you figure out that the secret number three unelected agencies have assigned you is low, right?"

"It's called a credit score."

"I know what it's called! So, when your credit score drops lower and lower the more you dig into the CIA, when weird coincidences rob you of your job and your friends, when the more you figure out what they're *really* up to, the worse your life just *coincidentally* gets, that's what you'd call a recognizable pattern! They don't like people finding out their secrets, and they make sure that anyone who does is miserable and poor. An 'outsider' nobody will listen to."

She paused for a moment, and I was about to try to bring her back to the subject, but she was just getting started.

"Think. Just...think. This is an organization that is designed to find out secrets and to keep secrets, right? *That's what they do.* It's what they're *for.* So, think about what they let you know, what they don't keep secret. They will tell you—Cheerfully! Happily! With a big smile!—that they killed a guy in the whorehouse they were running to test mind-control drugs. They'll tell you that they were founded on information straight from Adolf Hitler! They don't think it's important to keep secret that they funded terrorist training camps with the money they got from selling heroin to veterans. That's all public record. So how—I seriously mean *how*—do you think that's *all* there is to know? Do you think that tracking people who try to expose their secrets is somehow beyond them? Like, oh sure, we'll assassinate people left and right, overthrow elected governments, yeah, but monitoring our critics? Goodness me, no! We'd *never* do that!"

I knew a couple of the references she made, but not most of them. "Adolf Hitler?"

"Reinhard Gehlen," she said tiredly. "You can look it up."

"Okay, so if I can grant, *for now*, that you're right about the CIA, will you answer some direct questions with short, on-topic responses?"

"I'll try."

I still wasn't buying that the CIA was after her, but I needed some straight answers. "Baxter. Who was he?"

"Kinda like me. Bit of a loner. Traded old computer hardware with him from time to time."

"Why do you think he didn't do the shooting at *The Gazette* despite what every news agency on earth is reporting?"

"Isn't the fact that 'every news agency on earth' is reporting it enough to know it's not true?"

"No, it's not. And you promised me straight answers."

She sighed. "Okay, look. I'm not going to pretend Baxter was a saint. He had some anger issues, but he wouldn't have done anything like that shooting. The people he was mad at are the same people I'm mad at. Baxter cared about the little guy. The guys getting screwed by your Apples and Googles and CIAs."

"Enough with the editorializing," I said.

"Fine, but he was *not* out to get some poor receptionist at a struggling newspaper. *Not* a crooked old editor who couldn't ever get his life right. And *certainly* not James Stacy, who he respected the hell out of."

"And he knew James and Innerva?"

"Sure, he *gave them* the drive."

"How do you *know* Baxter gave James the drive?"

"Same way I know about the sticker. He told me."

She had my attention now. "Baxter did?"

"About a week ago, Baxter emailed me a photo of a box of goodies he'd gotten in trade. The drive was in the box. He asked me what I thought the sticker meant because he'd gotten two drives. One with the sticker and one without. He was confused because they seemed identical in design, and in age. You know, most likely from the same place. But one had the sticker, one didn't."

I was pissed at her for burying the lede, for making me listen to a ten-minute rant about credit scores before getting to the important stuff. "And I assume you researched it?"

"Directive 6/35 was issued by CIA director George Tenet in 2003. It was pretty routine. It called for the destruction of *certain computers, hard drives, and related materials deemed of no historical value.*"

I decided to believe this part of her story for now, though what remained of my journalistic instincts wanted to confirm her story with a second source. "You said that last part like you were quoting something."

"I *was* quoting. CIA Directive 6/35. And no, you can't just Google that. I got it off the Dark Web."

"Assuming that's true, why did Baxter give the drive to James and Innerva?"

"Once I told him what the sticker meant, the first thing he wanted to do was to find out what was on it. But he also knew that he wanted no part of a CIA drive. James and Innerva specialize in hacked and stolen information. They're truth crusaders. Plus, they have some technical skills. Not with hardware so much, but enough to get by. Anyway, he figured if he gave it to them, he'd still get to find out what was on it, but so would a lot more people. If it was something interesting, he'd pass the risk along to James."

"Did he own guns?"

She looked at me skeptically. "Yeah, why?"

"News reported that the shooting took place with two guns, both of which were purchased *by* and licensed *to* Baxter. And that he was found dead by his own hand at the scene."

"Framed."

I didn't know what to say. Of course, it was *possible* she was right. But it didn't seem likely. "By the way," I said, "since we may have to do a lot of communicating over the next few days, here's a tip. If you want to bring me on board with one of your arguments more quickly, start with facts, like the CIA sticker and destruction directives, rather than credit scores and Hitler conspiracy theories."

I glanced at her and thought she cracked a smile, but all she said was, "I'm telling you, Google the Hitler thing. Public record."

She said it with a sigh, like she was talked out. And I was happy to have some time to think about what she was saying.

The sun was long gone and the road was straight and black ahead. I could still see the faintest glow of orangish-black behind the mountains, but the area had a feeling of desolation. My mind flashed on what we would do if the car broke down, but it worked for now, and we were only another four or five hours from the Duck Valley Reservation.

Quinn had said the word 'framed' as though she was sure of it, as though she already knew the details. Of course, she couldn't *know* the details, but she thought she did, and I was curious.

As a journalist, your job is to know things, *then* to write them. Problem is, in order to know things you have to rely on sources, and sources can be deceiving. Some are trying to play you—to get you to print something that serves their interest rather than the interest of truth. Many think they know more than they actually do. They're sure they have the complete story even though they're only looking at a tiny corner of it. Like the blind men and the elephant. One touching the rough skin, one the hard tusk, one the rope-like tail, all certain they have the complete version because their experience seems real.

For example, when I was still in high school, I interned at a tiny paper on Bainbridge Island, Washington, where I grew up. I wasn't there to write anything, though. I was there to get coffee, research things for the real journalists, and so on. But one night a reporter called in sick before a big Town Hall meeting and the editor sent me out to take notes, get quotes from at least five residents, and bring it back so she could punch it into a story.

The first guy I interviewed for the piece was a local contractor and he was happy to give me a quote for the story, but it's what he told me afterwards that I remember. He said, "You know what you should *really* be covering? The use of school funds. You know they paid twelve thousand for the new sprinkler system at the soccer fields, eighty-thousand for new bleachers. Could have done both for half the price by hiring local contractors, but the superintendent wanted some big, out-of-state firm to get the work. Those guys are criminals."

Now, in my little seventeen-year-old brain, this sounded like a big scoop. Corruption within the school board. Wasted funds. Great headline material. And the guy seemed sure of himself, too. He had the figures off the top of his head, after all. I dutifully recorded what he said and told him I'd look into it.

But he was the blind man, just holding the tail. And, like the blind man, he wasn't wrong, exactly. He was *partially right*, which is how most of us are, most of the time. He was correct about how much everything had cost, but it turned out the money had come from a state infrastructure bill designed to help make Washington State greener, and green materials cost more. The new sprinkler system would use half the water of the old one. The new bleachers were made of some special kind of alloy that would last sixty years, as opposed to the twenty-year lifespan of aluminum.

Not to mention, the guy had an axe to grind. I found out that his contracting company had bid on the sprinkler and bleacher installation project, only to find out it had been pre-awarded. It wasn't even the superintendent's call. The state had negotiated a deal with a supplier in Oregon, then awarded the money. My 'source' had just read the budget report showing the costs of twelve grand for the sprinkler and eighty for the bleachers, and jumped to a few wrong conclusions.

Just like Quinn, he'd started with a fact, then editorialized his way to a fiction.

All that is to say that, as I turned to Quinn, I was nervous to ask the question, but even if she was only holding the tail, it was worth a try. "So, if Baxter didn't do the shooting, who did? Given your creative imagination, I'm sure you've thought about how it might have gone down."

Quinn grunted, a new kind of grunt, which I immediately labeled "Type 3." Slightly softer, almost like she was saying "yeah" under her breath, but swallowing the word as it came out.

I stared out into the darkness, watching the white lines in the center of the road and scanning what I could see of the shoulder, illuminated by the uneven headlights. Then she started to speak.

"I know you're not gonna believe me," she said, "but here's what happened."

CHAPTER 11

"James was already on a lot of lists because of his naughty habit of leaking the truth to people. The kind of lists you *don't* want to be on. When he entered the offices—if you can call them that—of *The Las Vegas Gazette*, he was met by Benjamin Huang, whose record as a faker of stories is a matter of public record.

"James was carrying the drive. Well, one of the drives. Until you showed up, I figured he'd taken the one with the sticker, the important one. He was there to tell Huang about what was on the drive, spill the CIA secrets it contains, maybe even ask for Huang's help to leak it."

"That's not what Innerva said." As little as Quinn respected my opinion, I knew I had facts from Innerva's mouth that would get her attention. "Innerva said they didn't know what was on the drive, that they were there to ask Huang to help them extract the data. Plus, they never would have leaked to a paper like *The Gazette*."

She grunted, the second kind. Reluctant agreement. "Fine,

but if they still needed to get the data off, why didn't they come to me? I know ten times as much as Huang."

I could think of a few reasons, but I didn't say anything.

"Anyway," Quinn said, "even if you're right about that, it doesn't change the point. So James was there to get help with the data. You can bet that if it took me a couple hours to figure out what that sticker meant, it took Innerva half that time. Anyway, Huang called in Deirdre Bancroft, a Godly woman who did tech support. It makes more sense that she was in the office, if what you just said is true. They could have called her in to look at it."

"That's what I assumed as well."

"Here's where I'm guessing our stories will diverge. As the three of them sat or stood in Huang's office, a black SUV stopped in the alley. It had tinted windows and only four numbers on its license plate. Its doors flew open with choreographed precision and four masked commandos in urban tactical gear climbed out. Maybe your pals Kenny and Holly were two of them, maybe not. They had the standard H&K MP5s that all their kind seem to carry, but those were slung. In their hands, two of them had identical cheap pistols and two had identical cheap shotguns. One of them was also dragging a stumbling, semi-conscious man: Baxter Callahan. My buddy."

She spoke steadily, matter-of-factly, like she was reciting the story from memory. And as we passed mile after mile of darkness on all sides, two things became clear to me. First, Quinn became more talkative when she was spinning a conspiracy theory. And second, she'd been thinking this through from the moment she'd heard about the shooting.

"Baxter was a smart man," she continued, "a computer engineer, a database specialist. He fixed databases that had gotten corrupted or fragmented or just stuffed full of garbage. He literally ferreted out information for a living. He'd done a lot of work on a lot of very important jobs, many of them under the table. Some of those jobs involved access to classified information, so highly-placed people were aware of him, and aware of his bad habit of asking questions, and his even worse habit of questioning the answers. He wasn't willing to swallow what they fed him, not when he had the brains and the know-how to find out the truth for himself. I always told him that he was going to get himself killed if he didn't watch out, and he always told me that he was careful. I guess he hadn't been careful enough. Hell of a way to learn that."

I grunted as if to say, *not likely.* Quinn's communication style was rubbing off on me.

"He'd already been drugged when they dragged him out of the SUV," she continued. "Not that you'll ever see a toxicology report admitting that. It made him easier to handle as the commando stood him up next to the conveniently unlocked back door of *The Gazette,* and put a 9mm pistol in Baxter's mouth.

"And the three of them—James, Deirdre and Huang— were just sitting there, yapping away about that ridiculous old drive, when they heard the first shot from the back door. That was Baxter.

"James and the other poor bastards didn't even have time to react. This team had drilled for days in a perfect mockup of *The Gazette* offices, ever since they found out James would be there with the drive. They came through the hallway like a breeze of death, guns blazing, incidentally killing the paper's sole remaining salesman and the young woman they kept at the front desk to look pretty and keep out riffraff."

"Gil Kazinsky and Esperanza Martinez."

"Yes, them. Within seconds, the team burst into Huang's office. First, they shot the drive on the desk with a 12-gauge, destroying it completely. Just like that, a whole load of the CIA's dirty laundry disappeared, and you have to ask yourself why. They've already *admitted* to a lot of nefarious stuff, so what's bad enough that they'd kill to keep it secret?"

To Quinn, it was perfectly reasonable that they'd killed six people just to destroy the drive, but I was growing more skeptical by the second.

"The primary target being disposed of, the commandos pumped several more rounds into the three human beings in the room, a Godly woman, an honest man, and a failed liar.

"Their job done, they scattered a few more 'random' shots around so it would look nice and plausible that a crazed loner had done this, because everyone vaguely assumes that crazed loners have lousy aim. Except when they have mysteriously perfect aim and magic bullets, but it's considered rude to bring that up. Then they marched out the back door in single-file formation, placed the appropriate weapons in the hands of Baxter's dead body, leapt back into their SUV, and vanished before any of the neighbors could even get to the alley to see what the noise was. The entire operation took less than a minute and left no traces they didn't mean to leave.

"Of course, your made-for-TV version doesn't even mention the drive, which was the point of the whole operation."

I let her story hang there for a minute, then asked, "Other than the sticker on the drive, do you have *any* evidence of any of that? I mean, the team of commandos, the use of the back alley, Baxter being shot first. Come to think of it, ballistics have already been released matching the bullets to his guns. How do you explain that?"

"Maybe they took his guns from his house when they kidnapped him. Maybe they used his guns to kill everyone."

***

We switched positions at a rest area after a couple hours, and now Quinn was driving. I told her I needed to get a little rest and think through her version of the shooting, so we'd moved the luggage to the trunk and I'd taken the back seat. I'd been worried about her driving, but she seemed to know what she was doing. Plus, it kept her distracted and gave me time to consider her version of events.

In theory, I could see it going down the way Quinn had described. In *theory*.

But there were some holes in her story. First, her assumption that James had been there to leak the contents of the drive to Huang had already been contradicted by Innerva. Second, I didn't think that James would have set up the meeting with Huang more than a day in advance, so her theory that a team had trained for the mission didn't add up. Finally, I wasn't buying her explanation of how Baxter's guns had ended up on the scene.

But the biggest issue was that I still believed my version of the shooting, the official version. Reporters were digging all around this story, talking to Baxter's neighbors and trying to piece together a timeline. If it had happened the way Quinn thought, someone would have found out. Or, at least, they'd have disproved some aspect of the official version.

The truth was, I didn't want to think about the shooting any more. Every once in a while, I'd be hit by a wave of disbelief that James was gone, but I didn't even want to think about James.

The only person I could think of was Greta.

Crisis after crisis had kept me from thinking about her, about the letter. And now that I had a moment of downtime, I couldn't use my phone. I was stuck with Quinn for at least another day, so I figured I'd try to get to know her.

I sat up in the back seat and leaned forward. "You married?" I asked.

She grunted something inaudible, her eyes moving in a steady rhythm from the road to the rearview mirror. Four seconds on the road, one second on the mirror. Repeated endlessly.

I wasn't going to give up that easily. "Married. I asked if you are married."

"Do I *seem* married?"

"No. I can't say that you do."

We rode in silence as an eighteen-wheeler passed us on the two-lane highway.

"Are *you* married?" she asked at last. She spoke robotically, like a computer inside her had just booted up the "small talk" program. But at least she was trying.

"I guess you could say that. Greta and I got married in

2005, but we separated eight months ago." I watched her eyes to try to figure out if she was listening. Four seconds on the road, then one second on the rearview mirror. She'd added a new wrinkle to the routine, where every couple minutes she'd glance at the side mirrors. First her side, then the passenger side.

"You've been married eight months?" she asked.

"Twelve years. *Separated* for eight months."

"Oh, sorry."

She clearly wasn't, but I appreciated the effort. "We're working it out, though, sort of. We only live about ten minutes apart and I've been trying, I really have, to change."

"Change? Why?"

She seemed to genuinely not understand what I was talking about. As though the daily compromises and accommodations of marriage—or, really, any relationship—were entirely foreign to her. "Have you *ever* been married?" I asked.

She grunted. The second, more-dismissive one.

"Boyfriend? Girlfriend? "

"No."

"Not ever?"

"I had a boyfriend once. And I've had men in my life, plus a couple women here and there. But I don't have anyone I'm itching to contact, like you do. *Obviously*, that's a good thing." She went quiet as a train of three cars passed us. She seemed determined not to go over the speed limit, which I assumed was to avoid a possible interaction with the police. "Most of the last fifteen years, I would have said it was a good thing, anyway. I knew one day I'd have to bug out, disappear. And if that's gonna happen, it's not good to be tied to someone."

She paused again, this time for longer and I thought she might be talked out. I felt my phone pressing against my thigh. "But it's not a hypothetical anymore," she continued. "I'm living in the worst-case scenario here. It's a good thing I didn't have someone to leave behind, someone I need to call, someone who might be targeted with propaganda. I can see the headline now: 'Crazed Loner Tries To Kill CIA Agents With Arson, Boyfriend Being Investigated For Terrorism Connections,' or whatever. They'd staple his balls to his legs until he gave me up. So, like I said, it's a good thing I don't have someone."

Her small-talk robot had turned off and she was speaking more quickly, growing irritated.

"Who was he?" I asked. "The boyfriend you had *once.*"

She glanced at me in the mirror for a second, breaking her routine. "Jack."

"When were you with him?"

The lights of the car behind us hit our rearview mirror and I caught a glimpse of her eyes, which were quieter and sadder than usual. "Before 9/11," she said.

I could tell I'd hit a sore spot.

Quinn's eyes were now fixed on the rearview mirror and I felt the car drifting a little. We also seemed to be slowing down. I tapped her shoulder as the car behind us changed lanes to pass, but we were drifting into the center lane. I leaned over Quinn, trying to reach the steering wheel. "Quinn, the road!"

Now that the other car was in the other lane, our car was dark. But she seemed to be blinking away tears. "Quinn!"

I got a finger on the wheel, but couldn't control it from the back seat. We were about halfway across the center line and now the car behind us was honking its horn. I wedged myself between the seats and grabbed the wheel as the car passed, half in the left lane and half on the left shoulder. After I steered back into our lane, Quinn pushed me back and took the wheel again.

"I'm sorry," she said.

"Me, too," I said. "I mean about Jack. I don't know what happened, but...well...if you ever want to talk about it."

After a few seconds that seemed like a few minutes, she grunted in ascension and I got the sense that she was back.

A minute later, she turned on the radio and scanned until the static turned into coherent sound. It was light Christian rock. When the first song ended, she began her routine again. Four seconds on the road, one on the mirror. Something about 9/11 had set her off, maybe something about Jack, but my guess was that it was 9/11.

I added "Jack" and "9/11" to my list of topics to avoid with Quinn. Already on the list: CIA, fire, and social media.

And speaking of social media, I couldn't take the blackout any more. I said, "I'm gonna try to sleep for a bit. Just lemme know if you need me to drive." But instead, I pulled my phone out of my back pocket and powered it on, careful to press the screen into my sleeve so it wouldn't light up the back seat.

Next, I opened up the Facebook app, figuring I'd just pop in for a sec to make sure the world was still turning. I get hundreds of Facebook notifications every day, and most days I scroll through them all, just to get a sense of what people are saying about me and *The Barker*. But this time, something was different. I had a few thousand notifications. Person after person was tagging me in posts. Even more were tagging *The Barker*, and it only took me a few seconds to figure out what was going on. I checked the news list and there I was, at #2.

I was trending on Facebook.

CHAPTER 12

I angled my body so my head was right behind Quinn's seat, then stared at the headline for a few seconds:

Alex Vane: Wife of The Barker CEO Files for Divorce.

I tapped on the link and a little summary of the story popped up:

> *Greta Mori, life coach and wife of Barker CEO Alex Vane filed for divorce in Seattle Court today, claiming that the marriage was "irretrievably broken." The two married in 2005.*

I hadn't seen this coming, but I wasn't shocked. And I'm not gonna lie. My first instinct wasn't to call Greta or grieve the impending dissolution of my marriage. I just wanted to know what people were saying about me. How the narrative was playing out online.

I clicked through a few of the links. TMZ, BuzzFeed, HuffPo. Most of the sites were treating the story respectfully. Greta had filed for divorce, a couple grafs of backstory, but no real detail and no narrative-shaping quotes. It was news because much of what I did was news. I was the public face of one of the most valuable independent sites left on the web, and I'd put myself front and center in many of the controversies that had hit *The Barker* over the last few years, rebuffing takeover attempts, winning some lawsuits and losing others. In short, I wasn't famous, but I was known to everyone in the media and a lot of people out of it. It didn't hurt that I looked like an intellectual Backstreet Boy. At least I had until the last few years when I started packing on the pounds. Apparently, enough people cared about the end of my marriage to get it trending. But there was nothing incendiary in the first few articles.

Then I saw it.

A site called Media News Online had a slightly different angle on the story, and it was the quotation marks that made me stop scrolling long enough to read the headline.

Alex Vane's Wife Files for Divorce, Cites "Scumbaggery."

It gave much of the same information as the other articles, but also contained a few grafs detailing the reasons Greta had filed. I knew right away that Greta was the "source close to the story." Not only was "scumbag" her favorite way to insult me, but the piece had details only she knew. For an educated man, who tries to convince himself that he's a decent person, "scumbag" is one of the worst insults. It implies classlessness, possibly chauvinism, and a kind of immorality that brings to mind used car salesmen, strip club owners, or ambulance-chasing lawyers in cheap suits.

The particular scumbaggery she was referring to was my tendency to publish articles that, to me, were on the margins and, to her, were "immoral, invasive, sexist, and offensive." She didn't mention a specific story in the article, but I knew the one that had pissed her off the most. You probably do, too. Remember the upskirt shots of Kelsye Sparks, the child star turned singer, turned actor? I bought those. I published them. And I'd do it again, too. It's not like I snuck into her bedroom or anything. In a reckless phase in her mid-twenties, Kelsye hit the L.A. club scene wearing a miniskirt and no panties. It just so happened that a paparazzo I know snapped a couple pictures as she got out of the limo.

Before she'd swallowed her last shot of tequila, I'd paid him $15,000 for three digital images and run the story. By the time her head hit the pillow, it had been shared nine million times on social media. For me, it was just another payday, but Greta treated it like a final straw. I'd stayed late to run the story, then stayed later to deal with the backlash, and had stumbled into our apartment overlooking Lake Union at around 8 a.m., just as she was rolling up her antibacterial yoga mat. It was one of those mornings when I knew the fight was coming before I'd even put my keys and phone on the counter.

She glared at me as I stepped in. "Red Bull?" she asked. I looked at the can in my hand, which was empty. For a moment, I wondered why I hadn't thrown it out in the lobby as I usually did when I wanted to hide my food or drink consumption, but then I realized I'd been begging for the confrontation.

"I needed to stay awake," I said, hurling the can into the recycling bin loudly and stepping into the living room. The TV was playing the closing credits of the yoga video, along with some spiritual-sounding music. Long, slow strings punctuated with bells that sounded like drops of water falling into a serene pool.

"Do you *know* what that stuff does to your system?" she asked.

"You've mentioned it, yes."

I'd promised to eat better and I think she genuinely cared for my physical health and couldn't understand why I'd drink Red Bull instead of the organic, probiotic, cold-brew coffee she'd started making.

But we both knew we weren't fighting about Red Bull. This was about the Kelsye Sparks photos. I'd known we'd have this fight since the moment I'd clicked "upload" on the story. But it was also about me neglecting our relationship and failing to effectively process what happened with our daughter, at least if you asked Greta. If you'd asked me in the moment, I would have said that it was about Greta being a controlling, judgmental shrew who believed that the only way to deal with difficulty was through hours of psychosomatic processing, of which she was one of the world's experts. If you asked me now, I'd probably admit that she was right.

She took a seat on the couch and stared at the TV. "Alex, we need to talk."

I sat next to her. "I'm sorry I had to work all night," I said, putting my hand on her knee. I could feel her warmth through the blue yoga pants. She didn't say anything and I tried to come up with an excuse that didn't contain the words "Kelsye" or "Sparks."

"I'm never going to forgive you for running that story," she said, not looking at me.

"Never? Really? Never?"

"She's twenty-three. It was practically kiddie-porn."

"If we hadn't done it, someone else would have."

"Scumbags have been using that excuse for thousands of years."

Was it a terrible story? Sure. But, for some reason, people care more about a teenaged starlet not wearing panties than they do about anything else. And if I hadn't bought those photos, someone else would have snatched them up five minutes later. Plus, the profits from that story would pay our mortgage for a year. Not to mention the fact that it would keep the lights on at *The Barker* and allow us to do *better* stories while keeping seventy people employed.

I nudged her hand playfully. "Why aren't you looking at me?"

As much as we'd drifted apart, the truth was, I was still in love with her. If I'd fallen out of love with anyone, it was myself. And I guess I felt that if I kept loving her, that was enough. I would have bet that we'd never, *never* break up. But, as she turned toward me, eyes glued to her lap, I knew that's exactly what was about to happen.

"Alex, this hasn't worked in a few years. We both know that." She looked up and took my hand as she said it, but let it go a second later. "I don't know what's going on with you, but we both know this isn't working."

"Not working," I repeated. I meant to say it as an indignant question. *Not working? How dare you describe our love that way.* But it came out flat, like a comment. "Not working."

That yoga music was driving me crazy and I grabbed the remote from the armrest, smashing at the "off" button. I thought of throwing it across the room, but, instead, I just dropped it on the floor.

"Remember when we first got together," she said, "and we talked about how you're the perfect blend of selfless and selfish?" I remembered. A billionaire's widow had said that about me just before James and I founded News Scoop. Greta and I had gotten together soon after and, at the time, I'd found the sentiment to be a useful way to understand myself. I'd bought into it and even tried to live up to it. Really, though, I was just another privileged guy who occasionally did altruistic things to block out the guilt of being a jerk much of the time. "Well," she continued, "it feels like the selfish side won out." She paused and met my eyes. "Alex, I want you to find an apartment."

Here's the thing about moments like that. Years later, when we write the books and screenplays of our lives, we have to make the key emotional insights of our characters line up with key actions or moments. As in, "When she smiled at me at the top of the Space Needle, that's when I knew she *truly* loved me."

But real life doesn't work like that. Not for me, at least.

In that moment, I should have been struck with some revelation about our marriage, or myself. Some insight that would bring reconciliation, or change, or peace. But when she said she wanted me to find an apartment, all I could think about was a sign I'd seen on my walk home from *The Barker* that morning. It was an advertisement for high-tech condos starting at $2,400 a month. Standing in the dawn light, sipping my Red Bull, I'd wondered what "high-tech" meant, and I wondered it when Greta told me to find an apartment. A T1 line, probably. Maybe a built-in Bose sound system, managed by iPad. I wasn't sure. But right then I saw myself plugging my phone into a built-in USB charger in the wall, snuggling into bed, and turning off the lights with my voice.

"You know I've never cheated on you," I said.

"I know. And, as you're fond of pointing out, you could have. Many times." It was her way of calling me callow. "But it's not about that, Alex. You know I still love you. I do. Probably always will. But you're the kind of guy who lives his life on either side of a narrative he creates. Like there's a story of Alex in your head that is never actually aligned with your life. When you're behind it and trying to catch up, you get depressed. When you're out in front of it, it's like you can't see yourself, you don't know where you are, and you fill up with anxiety. The actual moments don't exist to you. Without the story, you're nothing. And I don't mean 'nothing' in bad or judgmental way. Just, *not anything*. An absence of a person. It's like all events and actions and people have to eventually find their way into your narrative or they don't exist." She paused to let that sink in, then said, "Remember when you told me you'd never lie?"

"I said I'd never lie to *you*."

"And you haven't. You don't lie. What I've figured out is that people or events that don't have a place in your narrative just get omitted. You just won't see or remember the things that don't go with your story."

"Aren't we all like that?"

"We are, but my life is dedicated to becoming less like that. To living a life of meat and sweat and spirit. To letting the stories we tell ourselves *fall away*." She stood, turned toward the bathroom, and took off her sports bra. She wasn't being sexual. She undressed wherever and whenever she wanted, and that was just a sign that she was about to take a shower.

"This is about us not having children, right, and about Rebecca?"

We'd named her at a hot dog stand in Central Park a few weeks before Greta's due date and, a few days later, she'd been stillborn. The death certificate read, "Stillbirth caused by fetal infection." To this day, I don't like to talk about it.

She threw her sports bra on the arm of the couch, took a few steps toward the bathroom, then returned and sat back down. I'd said the right thing. Enough to keep her from walking away, at least.

"It's not just about her," she said. "But, of all the people you omit from the story you tell yourself, Rebecca is number one."

She was right, and I knew it. I felt genuinely incapable of talking about it, but I needed to try. "I will...I mean I'll...Greta, I...Ever since Rebecca, I've—"

That's when my cellphone rang.

I've trained myself to ignore my normal ring in Greta's presence, but this was the special ringtone that sounded like ducks quacking. It was Bird, my number two at *The Barker*. Before I knew what I was doing, I'd taken two steps toward the kitchen, where my phone was still sitting on the counter. I turned back when I heard Greta sigh. In one deft motion, I spun around, took a long stride, and flopped back down on the couch. "Rebecca," I said. "Um, where was I?"

"You got up before even considering the fact that you were in the middle of a sentence."

"I—"

There was nothing I could say that didn't taste like bullshit coming out of my mouth. I stretched out my legs and scooched down the couch a bit so I could rest my head on the cushion. The ceiling was bright white and the fancy LED kitchen lights danced in a patch of sunlight. I thought about that sign. $2,400 a month was doable. I'd get a six-month lease and Greta and I would work it out in that time. Things would be fine.

Greta stood up and stepped gracefully out of her yoga

pants. She was naked and no longer sweaty, but sex was the last thing on my mind. For some reason, that was the moment I realized it: I loved her and hated myself.

I opened my mouth, but nothing came out.

As she walked to the bathroom, Greta said something. I'm not sure if she was speaking to herself or to me. She'd said it the day we'd decided to get married, and she said it the day she kicked me out. I still didn't know what it meant, but on that day, it felt like a kick to the stomach. "We were supposed to be walking each other home."

***

I stowed my phone in my pocket and thought about Quinn, who had calmed down and was driving carefully, though still a little slowly for my taste. I could tell she had the potential to be violent, though I wasn't worried she'd be violent toward me. What I was wondering was whether, if I tried, I could get her to turn the car around.

I was sure there were private flights back to Seattle all the time, and I'd find one. In three hours, I could be back at McCarran Airport. A few hours after that, I could be at the door to our old apartment, begging Greta to call off the divorce. Hell, I'd charter my own plane if need be. I could afford it.

I sat up and leaned into the space between the two front seats. "Hey, Quinn, can I fly on a private jet if I'm on the No Fly List?" It seemed like the kind of thing she might know, but she was focused on her road and mirrors routine. She didn't respond.

I felt stupid for asking. Chartering a plane and racing back to Greta was exactly the kind of thing I'd do. I'd swear we could work it out and I'd work my ass off to do it. But it would all be an elaborate plan to avoid feeling what I was feeling in the moment, which was that my heart had fallen through the floor of the car and was now five miles behind us on the highway.

"Quinn! Private flights. No Fly List."

Quinn glanced back at me. "No," she said. "They cross

check the No Fly List on all flights within the U.S."

"What about busses?"

"Yeah, you can travel by bus."

By dawn I could be at the bus station and by midnight tomorrow I could be home. But that was twenty-four hours from now, and that was if I could convince Quinn to turn around.

I had to talk to Greta, and I resigned myself to the fact that it wasn't going to be in person, at least not today. I was already feeling stupid and guilty that I'd turned on my phone, even though it had only been for a few minutes. "I'm not necessarily granting it's the CIA," I said, "but I get that you know more about info security than I do. Is there a way I can make a phone call without sending up a flag to...whoever it is?"

"No."

"What about on *your* laptop?"

She thought for a minute, checked the mirrors a few times, then looked at me in the rearview mirror. "There are three problems with that. First, there's no way you'd be familiar with my operating system, so I'd have to do everything for you. Second, the crypto I use tends to throttle bandwidth, and if you want to make a voice call, that might be tricky. Third, and most importantly, there's no way I'm letting you use my computer. No offense, but...just...no. Do you have TorFone on your computer?"

"No, but I've heard of it and I can get it. I *do* have a VPN account for encrypted communication, if that helps."

"With who?"

"TorGuard. I...well, to be honest, I mostly use it for torrenting movies and stuff."

"Well, at least they're not CIA. And this wouldn't be a long connection, right? We can't hang around while you read every Ten-Reasons-To-Wear-Capris listicle out there."

"In and out," I said. "I just need to call my wife."

"Well, better to do it through an encrypted laptop, rather than waiting until you get nervous enough to turn your phone on."

I felt guilty, but was glad she hadn't noticed. "So, will you help me set it up on my computer?"

"How about we make a deal? After we talk with Tudayapi, I'll set it up."

"I'd really rather—"

"That's the deal, okay? You get what you want when I get what I want."

I slid awkwardly over the divider and into the front passenger seat. Quinn flashed something close to a smile and nodded out the passenger side window, where, in the faint glow of our Thunderbird's crooked headlights, I could see the sign: TWIN FALLS, 300 MILES

PART TWO

CHAPTER 13

Thursday, June 15, 2017

I took the wheel the last 100 miles, exhausted but still wired enough to keep my eyes on the road. The dim, crooked headlights of the Thunderbird didn't illuminate much, but in the last hour we'd passed miles of odd rock formations, some road signs dotted with bullet holes, and one that read: SPEED ENFORCED BY SNIPER.

Finally, we passed a small painted sign: WELCOME TO THE DUCK VALLEY INDIAN RESERVATION.

The town was dark except for a few streetlamps and a sign that blinked the message *Welcome to Owyhee,* and the time: *1:09 a.m.* Luckily, the main road through town led straight to the motel, a six-room mess that looked like a double-wide trailer and abutted a small hill. Thin windows and AC units faced out to the street. I pulled the car up in front of room six.

We'd stopped at a truck stop a couple hours earlier and Quinn had called the motel from her laptop, still not wanting to let me near the thing. She'd told the guy we'd be arriving between midnight and one in the morning, and offered him an extra $50 to wait for us. He'd said he'd just leave it unlocked and throw the keys on the bed.

I'd driven the last hour with a forced concentration interrupted by occasional waking dreams, or possibly hallucinations. I'd reached the point of fatigue that I imagine torture-victims experience. Too tired to keep their secrets. Willing to betray the ones they love for sleep.

Once in the room, I stowed my bags in the closet, fell on the bed, and scanned the furnishings, which might have passed for decent twenty years ago, but were now just shabby. Carpet so thin you could see the padding showing through, two twin beds too close together, a boxy TV of the sort I'd forgotten ever existed. The walls were covered with typical motel art, desert themed. But it was clean and the bed was soft, and I was thankful to be there.

Quinn came in just after me and seemed to be doing a thorough inspection. First, she checked the closet and the bathroom, then she bolted the front door, turned on the AC unit, and drew the curtains. I was getting used to her paranoia by now, so I didn't need to ask what she was doing.

I changed into a clean pair of boxers and a t-shirt. The bathroom was outdated, but clean, and I watched myself in the mirror as I changed. I looked like hell. My eyes were dark, my hair greasy, and the 36-hour beard made me look strange to myself.

Sliding under the sheets, which were stiff but felt heavenly, I noticed Quinn lying on top of the blankets, fully clothed and staring at the door. From my angle, she looked like she was spooning her filthy duffle bag.

I grabbed my phone from the bedside table. "What time should I set the alarm for?"

Quinn didn't say anything, so I tried again.

"Do you think your friend rises early?"

Nothing.

"You said she has a data center here?"

Quinn grunted, her slightly-less-dismissive, *ambivalent-yes* response.

"Do you know anything else about her?"

"She trades old machines. Baxter got the drive from her, like I said, but I don't think she knew what she had."

"I'll set the alarm for seven. How's that?"

Quinn's head was moving slightly, and I imagined her eyes shifting from the door to the window and back. I closed my eyes for the first time and immediately felt the fatigue I'd been pushing away. Time was, the run through the Fremont Street Experience wouldn't have had a noticeable impact on me, but now my whole body felt sick. I knew the feeling from when I used to run a lot. After a hard run of ten or more miles, my body got that feeling and I knew it meant that I'd wake up with stiff, achy legs. Plus, I was seeing visions.

The mosaics and butterfly carpets of The Wynn, the glittering lights of The Golden Nugget. Long expanses of shadowy road.

Greta liked to say that trauma is just unprocessed experiences and emotions that get frozen inside us. Her work was about locating, re-experiencing, and releasing those traumas. She used techniques from talk-therapy, body work, and art-therapy to help people process the experiences in a safe environment. I'd spent a lot of our relationship thinking that her work was pseudo-science, but now I wished she was here, because it was as though all my experiences over the last thirty-six hours were recurring, now that my body had temporarily relaxed. They were coming at me in fast-forward, and I was feeling things I didn't want to feel. Confusion. Sadness. Anger. But mostly fear. Terrible fear.

I was watching Quinn's version of the shooting, playing in slow motion in my mind.

"I wasn't always this crazy."

When I heard Quinn's voice, I thought I was awake and thinking but, jolted by her voice, I realized I'd been half asleep and dreaming. I sat up with a start. "What?"

Quinn turned to me, body still wrapped around the duffle

bag, back now to the door. "I wasn't always this crazy."

"What do you mean?"

I said it without thinking and I knew right away it was the wrong question. *I wasn't always this crazy* was the first piece of self-reflective personal information Quinn had volunteered since we'd met, and I didn't want to blow it. For better or worse, I was tied to her, and I wanted to know as much as I could. I wanted to know how she'd ended up this way, sure, but mostly I wanted to learn how to determine where her paranoia ended and her rational mind began. When she didn't respond, I tried to squeeze the dreamy images from my head as I booted up my inner-journalist: ask open-ended questions, not too pushy. If the subject gets defensive or clams up, pretend you didn't care about that particular question and shift to something else.

"Are you thinking of a particular time?" I asked.

"Nine-eleven."

Now we were getting somewhere. But sometimes a subject will regret a major admission right away, so the next step is to pretend like the revelation wasn't a big deal, like you'd already heard it from three other sources. I chose a classic approach: share your own story as a misdirection, then come back to the main point. "Nine-eleven? I was in New York City back then. Court reporter. Job was mostly boring as hell but from time to time I got into some interesting stuff."

"Did you cover it?"

Perfect. Quinn was thinking that I didn't notice or care that she'd admitted that 9/11 was at least part of the origin of her crazy.

"I didn't cover the Towers, no. It's something I'm pretty embarrassed about. Want to know where I was that day?"

Of course she did, but she'd never admit it. She gave me grunt number one.

"At the time, I lived in a little studio uptown, five miles north of the Towers. I covered cases in the downtown courthouses most days, so I was around the Financial District a lot, but not that day. I'd been out partying the night before and woke up late. Turned on CNN as I drank my coffee. Within minutes my phone was ringing. Friends, mostly, but also my boss from the paper. I worked at *The Standard.*"

"That thing is an unconscionable waste of trees."

I shouldn't have mentioned *The Standard*. When trying to draw someone out, it's better to avoid details that could cause a reaction. But I hadn't lost her. "Want to know what I did when my editor called? You'll like this because it makes me seem like a shallow coward." I swung my legs around and sat on the edge of the bed, facing Quinn, but she wouldn't look at me. I shifted to a casual, confessional tone, like I was sharing an embarrassing story reluctantly. It *was* an embarrassing story, but I'd come to terms with it years ago. "I ignored the calls. I knew that he'd ask me to go to Ground Zero, to cover the story. I mean, we all knew right away that this would be the defining story of the year, the decade. So he wanted everyone down there. I ignored his calls and watched CNN all day. Emailed him halfway through the day and told him I had the flu."

I'd learned that admitting my own imperfections was often enough to get a source to open up. But Quinn had closed her eyes halfway through and I didn't know if she'd fallen asleep, so I raised my voice. "At the time I still had two journalistic ideals in my mind. One was of the crusader journalist, the one who shines the light on the dark places, exposes corruption, all that stuff. The kind of journalist you'd like. The other was the breaking news hero-journalist. Reporting the hurricane from a hundred yards away, the fire as it burns, or the war from within the battle. That day I proved I was neither. I was scared."

She turned onto her back, resting the bag on her belly. She drew a deep breath and I knew I had her. Everyone likes transparency, everyone responds to vulnerability. And, in the end, everyone wants to talk.

"Austin," she said. "I was in Austin at the time, piecing together a living by overclocking computers for smart people and teaching dumb people what the Internet was."

When you know you're about to go deep with a source, sometimes it's good to interject a seemingly meaningless question. It shows that you're not *too* hell-bent on getting at the good stuff, and it actually increases the chance that they won't clam up before they get to it. "What landed you in Austin?"

"I moved out to work for a tech company. That was when Austin was supposed to be the Silicon Valley of Texas. Didn't work out. They were assholes—and so was I—so I split off to go it alone."

"So what happened? On 9/11, I mean."

"It wasn't one thing. First, it was the immediate reaction. Flags and flag decals on trucks. The wars. The message boards full of theories. The Internet got *really* ugly. A lot of things got really ugly. You probably think I'm gonna go conspiracy-theorist on you, right?"

She'd read my mind. I'd been expecting an expletive-filled rant about the CIA or NSA or FBI. Or possibly a detailed theory about Building 7 or the melting temperature of steel beams. But I lied. "Not at all. I just…what else happened around then?"

"I don't know about the conspiracy theories, okay? Could the CIA have been involved? Maybe. Could the Pentagon have planned it? Maybe? Or could thirty-seven hijackers have planned it and carried it out simply because they hate America? Possibly. I don't know. But it was the aftereffects. It was all gradual—and I didn't notice any of it until Jack told me—but I started isolating myself. I just felt down. I already knew that the CIA was after me—possibly for the off-the-books overclocking I was doing, possibly something else. But I'd come to accept that. Then the buzzing started. Up until then I'd been able to quiet it. Even to silence it for days on end. But each new theory I heard, each new horror story I read, the buzzing just got louder. Sometimes when it got too loud out in public I read people's thoughts just to have something else to do."

"Jack was your boyfriend?"

"In Austin, yeah."

Now we were getting to it. I knew 9/11 had impacted people deeply, and differently. In addition to all the people who were personally affected, 9/11 cast people in all sorts of different directions. Military enlistment rose, but only modestly. Some folks rushed to learn Arabic. Some journalist friends of mine fought to get embedded in Afghanistan and Iraq. Nine months after 9/11, birth rates rose by twenty percent in New York City. Make of that what you will.

But it went the other way, too. After the 2016 nightclub shooting in Orlando, a bunch of classmates of the shooter said that he'd first started acting crazy after 9/11. He'd started joking about the attacks, making airplane noises all the time, things like that. In the years after 9/11, a lot of people went down a lot of different rabbit holes. My sense was that Quinn was one of the people who never came out.

"What happened?" I asked.

"He left."

I waited to see if she'd continue, but she didn't. The first question I thought of was "Why," but that was the wrong question, too direct. So I said, "Where'd he'd move to?"

"He didn't move. Just left me. Told me he loved me but that I needed help. Said I needed to get on meds—*fucking* meds. I saw him once a few years later and started shouting at him in the street. Told him I wanted the truth, why'd he leave me, all that stuff people say. Said he was fine with me hearing voices, but 9/11 was when I started believing them."

"A man. It's always about a man, am I right?" I knew it was a mistake as I heard it come out of my mouth. Not only was it a cliché, it was pseudo-chummy bro talk, like we were about to do a shot at a club in Vegas. Quinn rolled so she was facing the door again, clutching the bag tight. "I meant, what was that like for you?"

Nothing.

"How long had you been with him?"

I'd lost her and, after, a few minutes of racking my foggy brain for a way to undo it, I was asleep.

***

I silenced my alarm before it woke Quinn, who was snoring loudly, slipped on some jeans and shoes without socks, and snuck out of the room. In the motel office, a kid of no more than twenty was sitting on the floor behind a desk, playing with a toddler. He stood when he heard the bell on the door.

"Are you one of the couple who came in last night. Moira something?" He was as tall as me, and thin, with thick black hair and even-thicker eyebrows.

I slid $40 across the desk and extended my hand. "Thanks again for taking our reservation. Everything was great."

The toddler squawked and he picked her up.

"Your daughter?" I asked.

"Niece."

He didn't seem like he wanted to chat, but he wasn't rude. He just seemed to be waiting for me to say something. I wanted to ask about the mysterious computer woman, but didn't want to ask directly. I spotted an iPad on the floor, open to something that looked like a toddler-friendly version of Tetris. Big, colorful blocks dropping slowly into place. "Is that the new iPad? The thirteen inch?"

"No."

"I hear the next one's gonna have a sixteen-megapixel camera."

He shrugged and put the girl down. She sat next to the iPad and pawed at the screen.

"Hey, I heard something about a data center around here? I work in the tech industry back in Seattle, where I'm headed, and—"

"Brenda."

"Huh?"

"You mean Brenda's place. She lives out at the edge, just before the Idaho sign, down Shale Road."

"I thought her name was Tudayapi?"

"She goes by that, too."

"What does she do?"

"I don't know, but something with computers. Data

storage or something."

"What's she like? I mean, I'm always curious about tech stuff. Might want to drop in and check out her setup."

He just shrugged.

"I mean, do you think she'd mind a drop-in?"

"Don't know. She's a two-spirit. Doesn't come out too much anymore."

The Seattle area is surrounded by reservations—the Puyallup, the Quinault, the Swinomish, the S'Klallam, and the Suquamish, the tribe of Chief Sealth who had given an Americanized version of his name to the city of Seattle. I grew up with many Native Americans, some of them good friends, like my buddy Bearon, who was still back in New York. I'd tried to learn as much as I could about the tribes around me, but I was far from an expert, and I'd never heard of the Duck Valley Indian Reservation or the Shoshone or Paiute Tribes who lived here. And I'd never heard the term "two-spirit."

"What's that mean?" I asked, as he scratched the address on a sticky note.

"You'll see."

CHAPTER 14

Thursday, June 15, 2017

I woke Quinn and waited while she got ready to go, which didn't take long. Her personal grooming habits were pretty much what you'd expect: tie back her hair, put on her shoes, and go. Yes, she slept in her clothes. But I didn't care, because the sooner she was ready to go, the sooner we'd be at Tudayapi's, and the sooner we'd know what was on the drive, or whether we'd ever find out.

Tudayapi lived at the end of a mile-long dirt road on the edge of the town of Owyhee. From about a quarter mile away, the house appeared from behind a stand of trees. It was brown and white and small and my first thought was: How can she run a data center out of that thing?

I was about to say this when Quinn pointed. "There. That's the server farm."

A structure that looked like a large aluminum shed was

appearing from behind the house as we made our way down the driveway. The morning sun glinted off the metal roof.

"I know this is going to sound stupid," I said, "but what exactly *is* a server farm?"

Quinn sighed, like she didn't have the time to explain it to me. Then she cracked a smile. "You run a major website and you don't know what a server farm is? Do you know what a *server* is?"

"Not exactly."

"A server is a computer, the box, ya know. Not the monitor, or 'screen' as you probably call it. A server farm is just a large collection of them, used to store data, to host websites, and so on."

"Okay," I said, parking the car behind an old red pickup truck. "But why would a tiny town like Owyhee have such a big server farm?"

"This is actually a *tiny* one, relatively speaking, and I'm not entirely sure of her business model. But my guess is that she stores data for some people who may not be entirely above board. In some circles, data stored on an Indian Reservation is considered more secure, all else being equal."

"Because the government recognizes reservations as sovereign?"

We got out of the car and began walking slowly toward the house, the hard drive locked safely in the trunk. "Exactly. Don't get me wrong, if the CIA or FBI wanted those servers, they would just come take them. But, between lower levels of law enforcement—local police, state police, and so on—jurisdictional issues can sometimes make it tricky."

"You're saying she probably stores data for criminals?"

"Or grey hats."

"Like you."

Quinn knocked on the door, and Tudayapi answered right away. She wore a 1970s-style knit pantsuit in light aquamarine, with big gold earrings and a matching necklace. Her hair was short and had been styled into a kind of 1980s power-helmet. She looked like she was around forty, but she dressed like she was seventy.

"Come in," she said in a low, husky voice. She barely looked at me and I was surprised at her response. It was like she'd been expecting us. I didn't feel in danger, but, at the same time, it didn't feel quite right.

Tudayapi's living room looked like a set from *The Golden Girls*. In the center, she had a wicker furniture set, including a glass-topped table with four coasters and a neat pile of magazines, two chairs and a sofa with cheap cushions covered in floral patterns. The carpet was somewhere between beige and gray. A color so boring it doesn't even have a name. The prints on the walls matched the flowers on the cushions. Big, flowing orchids. And they didn't just kind of match. They were identical, like she'd purchased them from the same company. The room would have been a great fit in a low-budget condo in Clearwater, Florida, but it seemed wildly out of place at the end of a dirt road on an Indian reservation on the Nevada-Idaho border.

Quinn sat in one of the chairs and I sat in the center of the couch, facing the door. Tudayapi disappeared into another room and came back a minute later with a pitcher of what looked like iced tea.

"It's warm out," she said. "Would you like a drink?"

"Don't you want to know who we are?" I asked.

Quinn slid her coaster over to Tudayapi, who had taken the chair next to her. "Don't be rude, Alex." It was odd to get etiquette advice from Quinn, but she seemed to be in her element.

Tudayapi set glasses down and poured tea in each, then carefully slid the coasters and glasses in front of me and Quinn. "Jamie, from the motel, called me. I was expecting you."

I sipped the iced tea, intent on letting Quinn do the talking. It was like drinking a bag of sugar, and I almost spat it out, but managed to get it down.

Quinn gulped hers like it was perfectly normal, then said, "Do you know why we're here?"

"Not really, but I assume it has something to do with Baxter. I've seen the news."

"I'm Quinn Rivers. We've traded parts before. I got the Apple 2e from you last year, sent you the Commodore 64."

"Quinn, yes, I remember you. And this is Alex?"

Quinn nodded toward me. "That's Alex. And you seem to remember Baxter."

"Did he really kill all those people?"

Quinn shook her head slowly. "No, he didn't. But he *is* dead."

"*Please* don't tell me it had anything to do with me."

"It may have," Quinn said. "Do you remember a pair of drives you sold him?"

"Sure, IBM 2314. Two weeks ago."

Quinn looked around the room. I got the sense that she was nervous. "Tudayapi, is it safe to talk in here? Is there any chance it's bugged?"

Tudayapi reached across the armrest and took Quinn's hand. "It's safe. I rarely leave the house anymore."

"Do you know what was on those drives?" Quinn asked.

"No."

"Where did you get them?"

Tudayapi pulled her hand back and took a long, slow sip of her tea. She smacked her lips in a kind of faux-satisfaction, like she was the star of a Sunny-D commercial. "I don't think I want to say anything more."

"Why not?" I asked.

Tudayapi ignored me and spoke to Quinn. "They were supposed to have been destroyed."

"We know that," Quinn said.

"How?"

"The sticker. Why did only one of them have a sticker on it? Were they both from the same place?"

"How'd you know about the sticker?"

"Because we have one of them."

Tudayapi was quiet. She crossed her right leg over her left, then sipped her tea and crossed her left leg over her right.

"Would you like a tour of my home?"

I started to object, wanting desperately to get to the point, but Quinn said, "Sure," and Tudayapi was already standing.

The living room led to a formal dining room, which matched the living room and was so clean I wondered if it had ever been used. The dining room led to a kitchen with a bright linoleum floor and beige counter tops and—you guessed it—a small wicker table. I half-expected to see Betty White and Bea Arthur eating cheesecake and talking about their day. Tudayapi didn't show us the bedroom, but I imagined a wicker, four-post bed, floral printed curtains, and a polyester robe that looked like silk.

But when we passed through an immaculate laundry room into the garage, things changed.

It looked more like Quinn's house. Disorganized, dirty, and full of tools, wires, scrap metal, and old computer parts. The only light came from five metal contractor lights, dangling from bent nails in the ceiling above work tables, giving the place a sense of dark corners and brightly-lit work areas.

I glanced at Quinn, who was smiling as if to say, *This is more like it.*

Tudayapi took three steps down into the garage and threw on a pair of brown coveralls that had been hanging on a greasy hook. Next, she stowed her earrings and necklace on a little shelf and put on a white trucker hat stitched with a LINUX logo. She now looked like an auto mechanic. "Better if we talk in here," she said.

Tudayapi walked to the center of the garage and leaned an elbow on a table made from two sawhorses and a sheet of plywood. Quinn followed as though this was all perfectly normal, and sat on a swiveling black stool next to the table. I followed and stood awkwardly behind Quinn.

I tried to catch Tudayapi's eye, but she was staring at Quinn. "I should probably ask you to leave," Tudayapi said.

"But you won't," Quinn said. "Because you're curious."

"I don't want anything to do with those drives. If what you

said is true, I don't want anything to do with them."

"Please," Quinn said. "If you won't help us get the information off this *antique data depository*, at least tell us where you got them."

Tudayapi thought for a moment, then said. "I'll tell you where I got them, but that's it."

It was a start, I thought.

"Before I made the transition, I was a private contractor, one of the best in the region. I got my start setting up computer networks for the tribe in the nineties. Word spread to other tribes in the area and as far as Washington State, so I started getting jobs all over. I never intended to go to school—I was already making a good living—but the tribe offered me a scholarship to get a degree. I specialized in data management, the storage of data. And, of course, the *destruction* of data. After college, I started getting more jobs, and I set up a real business. Ended up getting gigs switching out computer systems. In the early 2000s, before everyone was doing it, I was a hot commodity. Basically, if a big company wanted to overhaul their entire computer system, they called me. I'd handle everything. Backing up data, purchasing the new machines, installing software, everything. I even had partnerships with some trainers who would come in and teach the staff how to use all the new systems."

"So how did you end up working for the gestapo?" Quinn asked.

Tudayapi frowned.

"Quinn means the CIA," I said. "The government."

"I never *worked for them*. I once *did work* for them. Anyway, it was ten years ago or so. I'd done a job for McGregor Ham, a major regional distributor of—"

"Ham?" I asked.

Tudayapi looked up at me, stared into my eyes, and gave me a strange smile, the kind you'd give a child who is doing and saying ridiculous things but you love them anyway. "Yes," she said. "Ham. Anyway, they were down in Boise and I came in with a bid that was half of the local bigwigs. I did the job—nothing big, just installing a new system to track orders and shipping—but the CEO asked me to train him personally, so he could review the sales and shipping data himself. I did, and a couple weeks later, I got a call from a guy who said McGregor had personally referred me. Guy said he had a job for me."

"Who was the guy?"

"Yeah...don't remember his name, but he was with Allied Regional Data Security. ARDS. They were looking for contractors and, long story short, they hired me. And these guys had a ton of money. Too much money. They really didn't know what they were doing *at all*."

"What kind of stuff did you do for them?" I asked.

"Mostly swapping out systems, but over the second and third year, more sensitive stuff. Data destruction, encrypted backups, and so on."

Quinn was walking her little square, listening intently. "So how did you end up with the drives?"

"I was getting to that, honey." She nodded at me. "I thought *he* was supposed to be the impatient one." She closed her eyes. "It was my third year with ARDS. I got called in and told I had a job down in Bakersfield, California."

Quinn stopped abruptly. "CIA western district headquarters."

"That's right," Tudayapi said. "My boss said I'd earned bigger jobs. Said there'd be security clearance and a $10,000 bonus. I went down and it turned out I was there to destroy data for the CIA."

"Why wouldn't the CIA have their own people to do that?" I asked. "I mean, you wouldn't think they'd be looking in the yellow pages for that."

"Well, we weren't exactly in the yellow pages. ARDS was the biggest in the region and half of their contracts were government or intelligence. ARDS isn't one of them—they had a private sector business established beforehand. But after 9/11, *billions* of dollars started flowing in for all sorts of security projects. The stuff people know about—the war on terror, the Iraq and Afghanistan wars—were just the tip of the iceberg. Most of the money actually went to expand the size of the security systems in the country. There was money to spend. You can bet that if I was going to get a $10,000 bonus, ARDS was charging them half a million for the job."

Quinn asked, "Did they hook electrodes up to your balls when you got there?"

"They were actually super nice. Just regular working folks. I flew down and met the guy. Brown or Butcher or something. He said he'd heard great things about me from McGregor, which I took to mean, 'We've studied your background extensively and we know what you ate for breakfast at the airport.' But I didn't care. As screwed up as America has treated us natives, it was after 9/11, so I was proud to serve my country."

Quinn scoffed at this. "Did you ever do another job for the CIA?"

"No, I told my boss I wanted to stay more local after that one. He was disappointed, but what was he going to do? I was the best they had and they'd rather have me local than nothing at all. The sense I got was that, if I'd wanted to, I could have worked there full time, some sort of partnership between ARDS and the CIA."

"But you didn't want to work for them again?"

"I didn't know if I wanted to leave the Rez, and, as flattered as I was, I didn't know if I wanted to work for the CIA. I had no problem backing up or destroying data, but part of me wondered whether I'd end up giving that speech that Matt Damon gives in *Good Will Hunting*, you know, the one about using his skills for evil."

"So the drives were part of the data destruction, and you lifted them?" Quinn asked.

"Basically, yeah. The job had four parts. Back up the old systems, install new, modern systems, then destroy the old systems. The fourth part was to render old data invisible and destroy what they told me to destroy. I destroyed over five hundred IBM 2314s that month. And all sorts of other hardware."

"They didn't want to wipe them clean and sell them or anything?"

Tudayapi chuckled. "They were paranoid, and they were right to be. Everyone knows that even after data has been erased, there are sometimes ways to recover it, or at least parts of it, like file headers and whatnot. So they wanted me to physically destroy the machines."

"And you just couldn't bring yourself to do it?"

Tudayapi smiled. "Those drives were works of art. And I *did* destroy all but two of them."

I was growing impatient. As interesting as it was to hear how she'd stolen them, I couldn't forget that her theft a decade ago had landed me here, on the Duck Valley Indian Reservation, with less than three days until my wedding anniversary.

I tried to catch Tudayapi's eyes, but she was talking Quinn through the specs of the drives and occasionally going off on tangents about other drives. It was clear that, while Quinn *did* speak her language, Tudayapi knew much more about old computer hardware. But they still weren't getting to the point. "Excuse me, sorry. Tudayapi, please. Bottom line, do you have the equipment to get the data off this drive?"

"I was just saying, it'll take—"

"I know, it'll take a connecter systems interface module drive joystick, or whatever. *I don't care.* Do you have the stuff or not?" It sounds rude now, but it didn't come out that way. As meandering as Tudayapi's speaking style was, I could tell there was part of her that appreciated directness.

She looked up and smiled, then whispered something under her breath.

"What?" I asked.

"Nothing. Just a digital storage joke. You wouldn't get it."

Quinn smiled, "She said 'Five years, or whichever comes first.'"

She was right. I didn't get it.

"It's a saying in the data world," Tudayapi said. "'Digital

information lasts forever, or five years. *Whichever comes first.*" I had no idea what they were talking about, and Tudayapi knew it. "It's a riff on what everyone used to say. That digital data won't deteriorate. It's not like paper, that can burn, or stone tablets, that can break. In theory, data lasts forever."

Quinn butted in, "But the technology changes so fast that storage devices are obsolete within five years."

"And if you can't *actually get* the data off a device, the data is, effectively, destroyed."

"There are floppy disks all over the country that you'd have to go to a museum to read," Quinn said. "The information is there, but it's locked. Data never dies."

"Okay," I said. "But *this* data isn't locked, and you *can* access it, right?"

"I can," Tudayapi said. "But there's no way I'm helping you."

"Why the hell not?" I asked. This time it sounded rude, and I meant it to. We were surrounded by wires, connectors, soldering irons, tins of tiny screws, panels of black and beige and silver metal and plastic, and maybe twenty old monitors and fifty old hard drives. She'd just spent fifteen minutes describing how she acquired the damn things, knowing the whole time that we'd want to know what was on them.

"While I was telling you that story, I was thinking. About you two showing up here, about Baxter, about the drives, and about the day I took them, why I took them, and why I never cared to open them. I didn't really know Baxter, but I looked into him a little bit more when I saw that he was being named as the shooter. He was paranoid. He was—"

"He was *not* paranoid," Quinn said. "He was a truth seeker."

"Call it what you want, but it's not what I was. Those drives sat in here for ten years and I never once thought of figuring out what was on them. Honestly, I had too much respect for the CIA to do that. I think that's what allowed me to steal them in the first place. I had *no intention* of stealing secrets or *seeking the truth*. In my heart, I'm a preservationist. I want everything to remain exactly as it was made."

I smiled, but it turned out she didn't mean this as a joke. She saw me smiling and rolled her eyes. "Well, *almost* everything. But, in any case, I won't help you because it wouldn't be morally right, and because it's too dangerous. I seriously doubt that this thing has anything interesting on it. I mean, do you know how little data these things have on them? And even if it does, it likely has nothing to do with the shooting." She paused and passed a little black screw between her hands a few times. "I'm sorry about your friend. I really am. But I'm a practical person. There's just nothing to gain from me helping you, and a lot to lose. I think you should leave."

CHAPTER 15

I was hungry and eager to have Quinn set up the call to Greta, as she'd promised. The place to go in Owyhee was the *Tammen Temeeh Kahni*, a grocery store attached to an ACE hardware, a deli, and a gas station. According to Tudayapi, it was the *only* place to go in Owyhee, both for food and for free Wi-Fi.

I hadn't given up on getting Tudayapi's help, but, after a few minutes of listening to Quinn try to convince her, I'd gently suggested that we get a late breakfast and think about our next move. We needed a new approach, but first we needed to eat. And I needed Quinn to hold up her end of the bargain.

I parked the car along the side of the bright blue building and hopped out. Quinn followed reluctantly, still sulking.

"I know what you're thinking," she said, not looking at me as we walked in. "You want to make your damn call."

"That was the deal, Quinn. How about you set it up on my laptop while I get us some food?"

The *Tammen Temeeh Kahni* was a basic, medium-sized

grocery store with four checkout counters and a special rack of dreamcatchers and carvings made by local artists. We walked to a little sandwich stand in the corner of the store and Quinn waved toward the food shelves as she slid into a booth. I handed her my laptop and turned to get the food, then I realized that we hadn't eaten since we left Vegas, and I had no idea what she ate. She could have been a meat eater, a vegetarian, or a paleo lady. She might have eaten only Hamburger Helper for the last six hundred meals. Nothing would have surprised me.

"What do you want to eat?" I asked.

"I'm a Freegan. Get me some snacks while I fix your machine." It was such a Quinn thing to say. She'd said "Freegan" like it was a common word. A word everyone should know. It isn't a common word, but it just so happened that we had a Freegan named Fern back at the office. Basically, he ate a vegan diet if he was paying for the food, but he'd also eat roadkill or pick meat out of the trash. He'd eat anything that was going to waste, or free. To him, this was the most environmentally friendly thing to do and the best way to stick it to the "industrial farming system."

Anyway, it was lucky for Quinn that I knew what it meant because, if she'd had to explain it to me right there in the *Tammen Temeeh Kahni,* I think we both would have lost it.

I was about to tell her this, but she was already opening my laptop, frowning, and leaning away from it like it might explode. I was running a Virtual Private Network, or VPN, which added a layer of security to my emails and Internet usage, but Quinn was not impressed. I knew she was constantly judging me in her head, and doing her best to keep it to herself, but the lack of security features on my laptop was too much for her to contain. Within a few clicks, her frown turned into violent head shaking, then into cursing. But at least she was doing it under her breath. I headed for the wall of fridges along the back wall, and, by the time I'd filled my hands with Red Bulls, iced coffees, and water, her face was red. Somewhere between rage and sorrow.

I grabbed nuts, turkey jerky, granola bars, and some fruit, then paid, used the restroom, and slid cautiously into the booth across from Quinn.

She ignored me for a couple minutes, then looked up. "I didn't have much time," she said. "So I did the basics. First, I installed Tor." Even I'd heard of Tor. It's a piece of free software that anonymizes everything you do online by directing traffic through a worldwide network of more than seven-thousand relays. James had told me about it years ago, but it seemed like something only criminals or the paranoid would ever need. But if Quinn was happy, then fine.

"Next, I installed TorFone," she continued. "I'm still not happy about you making calls, but, if you must, this is the *only* way to do it." I'd never heard of it, but Quinn explained that it was like Skype for "non-idiots."

I asked her a few questions about it as she connected her headset to my computer. I didn't understand much of what she said, and I had to interrupt her rants about the technical specs and the Dark Web, but she seemed to know what she was talking about. Basically, TorFone was a way to make totally anonymous, Internet-based calls.

She explained things directly and clearly, then stood and took my chin in her hands, turning me toward her. "Alex, as confidential as the call is from our end, it won't be from her end. Do *not* say where we are or anything about anything."

I sat where she'd been sitting and put on the headset. "Enter the number here, then hit enter," she said, pointing at a little box on the screen. "And don't say *anything*."

I started entering the number from memory, but Quinn interrupted me. Her face was in the bag of snacks. "You didn't get any dark chocolate?" She said it like I'd disobeyed a direct order.

"No," I said casually. She sighed and walked away as I finished entering the number.

The ring seemed slow, drawn out. I knew it was just my anticipation, but it didn't matter. After four rings, she answered. "Alex?"

"How'd you know it was me?"

"I'm actually surprised you didn't call sooner."

"But how'd you know it was me?"

She just let my question hang there. She did that sometimes. She liked me to think she could read my thoughts. And she often could. Not because she's psychic, but because she knows me better than anyone and because I'm pretty predictable. As the silence hung there, I figured she had been waiting for my call since the divorce story broke. I hadn't asked Quinn how the TorFone call would appear on her caller-ID, but I'm sure it was either "blocked" or gibberish. So when she saw a number she didn't recognize on her personal cellphone, she assumed it was me.

"Did you hear that I was in Las Vegas?" I asked.

"Yeah. Why aren't you calling me from your cell?"

"Long story. How'd you hear I was in Vegas?"

"I talked to Wesley yesterday." She was close with Bird, but Greta wasn't a nickname kind of person. "He said you were there to meet James."

"You haven't heard?"

"Heard what?"

"James was killed."

I think that, for a moment, she was wondering whether it was an attempt to get attention or sympathy, because it took her a while to say, "What? No! How?"

"The shooting in Las Vegas."

"I saw that go by on...something. Some screen or another. Tuesday morning? I haven't seen the news today."

The combination of talking about James and speaking to Greta was getting to me, and I fought back tears. "James was there. He's dead, Greta."

She didn't say anything, and I didn't know if I should say more. I looked around the store. A man in dirty jeans was paying for beer at the counter. A couple of matching blonds talked loudly about different brands of water in the back. The whole scene was surreal, like it had been back at Wynn.

"Greta, did you hear me?"

"I just looked it up on my phone. You're right. He's listed. I just can't believe it. Did you see Innerva?"

It was the exact kind of question Quinn did not want me to answer. "No," I lied.

"How are you?"

"I don't know," I said.

"I wouldn't have filed if...if I'd known that—"

"You couldn't have known. Plus, you must have filed days ago. A couple weeks ago."

I pictured her crinkling her nose and moving her cheeks from side to side with subtle twitches of her facial muscles. I'd asked her about it once and she'd said something condescending like, "It's yoga for my face. *You* might want to try it sometime."

I pressed the headset closer to my mouth. Whispered, "Why didn't you tell me you were going to file? Why'd you have to do it like *that*?"

She didn't say anything and, in the silence, a phrase popped into my head: *Don't Be Pushy*. It was from another listicle I'd read on one of our blogs, *The Guy Zone*. And before you accuse me of sexism, we own *The Lady Zone* as well. Anyway, I rarely click on any of the crap on *The Guy Zone*, but the headline had called to me: *Five Ways You're a Jerk in Your Relationship*.

Item number one, which I was trying to take to heart, was *Don't Be Pushy*. The idea was that, in most relationships, guys are overly controlling. They're used to having a privileged place in society, used to reality conforming to their style of discussion, their style of conflict resolution, and so on. If you want a woman to truly love you, she needs to feel free. She needs to choose you from a position of power, and from within her feelings. Your tendency to press for answers, the article concluded, will just drive her away.

I didn't think of myself as a control-freak, but I could tell I wanted to push for an answer that would satisfy me, even though, on a deeper level, one of the things I loved most about Greta was the fact that she *didn't* satisfy me. She *never* answered questions in the way I expected. She *didn't* conform to the expectations I had. And I loved it.

I took a deep breath. "Greta, I know I don't know what you're thinking or feeling. Just tell me why you needed to go public with the article. With the 'scumbag' stuff?"

"I wanted to take you down a notch. I'm sorry. I was going to file anyway, and the guy from Media News Online called. He said he already had the details of the divorce. Someone at the court must've leaked it."

"But you gave him quotes."

"I gave him a few quotes. I...I'm sorry about that." We were both quiet until she said, "I know now's not the time, and I'm so sorry about James, but there's something else, Alex."

My heart was still somewhere back on the highway, but right then it felt like it was getting run over by a tractor, because I knew it was about a guy.

But it wasn't about a guy.

"I may have called DHS on you."

"May have?"

"I did. I did call them and, before you say anything, let me just say that I'd had some wine, I was angry and stewing on our marriage, and—

"What did you tell them?"

"That you'd been acting funny lately, that I'd seen Al Qaeda sites in your search history, that you were planning a trip to Kuwait."

It's ridiculous, I know, but all I felt was relief. "Kuwait is a U.S. ally," I said. "You should have said Iran."

"I was thinking on my feet, or trying to. It was a moment of temporary insanity. It was stupid, and I regret it."

"What else did you tell them, Greta?"

"That *The Barker* was a front and that you used the money to support secret terrorist cells in Oregon and Washington State."

I was almost laughing with joy. Both because the "something else" hadn't been a serious relationship and because the words coming out of her mouth were so un-Greta like. She barely followed current events and almost never "acted out" her anger. I was about to say something clever when she said, "Alex, there's something else."

And that's when I knew. If the first something else was reporting me to the Department of Homeland Security, the second something else had to be a guy. When breaking bad news to people, we tend to save the worst for last. Not for their benefit, but for our own.

"Are you serious with someone?" I asked. "It's okay if you are."

She said, "Not serious, but *yes*, I've been seeing people. Just coffee, mostly."

I'd stopped listening. "Okay" was the last thing it was, but of course I'd known this day might come since the day she'd kicked me out eight months ago, and I'd expected it for the last two. "Okay" was a bald-faced lie, and it damn near killed me to say it.

I hadn't rented that high-tech apartment after all. Instead, I'd rented a loft in the Northgate neighborhood and, for the first few months of our separation, we'd met for coffee every Sunday afternoon. We'd decided on a soft-separation, where we'd keep in regular contact as we wound down our marriage. Of course, that was what *she* wanted, not what I wanted. But I'd agreed to it because it was my only option. My plan all along had been to get her back.

But after a few months of regular meetings, in which I tried to enact the various lists I'd been reading online, she started canceling every once in a while, coming up with excuses not to meet me. Every time she canceled, I tried to find out why as casually as possible. *Don't Be Pushy.*

"Oh, something come up at work?" I'd ask. I knew how pathetic it was, and I knew that she knew, as well. I may as well have said, "Are you canceling so you can hit the town with someone else who's better than me in every way?"

That's when I started checking her social media. She'd never been an active user but, all of a sudden, the frequency of her posts starting picking up. "Wow!" a recent post had exclaimed, "I think I'm learning to appreciate classic cars. Can you see me in a 1965 Mustang powered by lithium ion batteries?" Greta hated cars, so if she was at the Seattle Electric Muscle Car Show, someone had convinced her to go, and I'd imagined the worst.

The next week, she posted a picture of Lake Washington on Facebook. It was the view from our apartment, which looked east across the lake into Bellevue. On clear days, Mount Rainier appeared to be rising up out of the floor of our living room. Greta posted a photo of the view at least once a month, usually with an inspirational quote, but sometimes with a little note about what she was eating or thinking. As in, "Mango-chia smoothie and this," with a photo of the morning sky and Mount Rainier in the distance. As corny as it sounds, I used to love those posts. Anyway, she'd posted a photo with the caption, "Leftover linguini for breakfast? Don't mind if I do." In the foreground of the picture, which I knew she'd taken from the little loveseat in our breakfast nook, was a recycled cardboard container. The kind you get for leftovers at a fancy restaurant that would *never* use Styrofoam. I assumed it was the pasta. But on the corner of the box, on the far right of the picture, I could see a tiny gold sticker with the word "Altura" printed in a cursive font.

Altura was probably the best Italian restaurant in Seattle, one I'd been asking her to try for two years. When we were still together, she'd been "trying to cut down on gluten," so we'd never gone, despite my assurances that they could do an entire tasting menu without a bite of pasta. As soon as I'd seen that sticker, that photo, I started picturing the guy lying in my bed who had convinced her to go there the night before.

"Alex, did you hear me?" I'd closed my eyes and Greta's voice brought me back to myself, back to the grocery store. Even though she'd said it wasn't serious, the thought of her dating wrecked me. I couldn't say anything, and it turned out

I wouldn't have the chance because Greta said, "Alex, I'm sorry I gave those quotes, I really am. And I'm sorry about James. And we can talk about this again. There's just…too much happening right now. And I know you're going through a lot. But I have to go."

I sat there for a few seconds after she hung up, just wishing I'd thought of something better to say.

I thought of finding Quinn, but instead I did what *of course* I would do. What I couldn't help but do. I clicked the little email icon on the apps bar at the bottom of my screen. I hadn't even intended to do so, it was just habit. And, once the messages started pouring in, I couldn't stop myself from scanning them. Mostly, it was the usual stuff. People following up on business, spam advertising penis enlargement pills or timeshares, a few requests from Nigerian princes who needed my help.

I noticed Quinn out of the corner of my eye and I was about to close the laptop.

Then I saw the message.

It was from one of Innerva's old addresses, one I hadn't seen in a while. The message had no subject and no content other than an mp3 that automatically displayed as a player within the email. The duration of the mp3 was listed at 31:13.

Quinn must have seen the look on my face because she said, "Alex, what?"

I ignored her and hit "play." I still had the headphones on and James's voice was the first thing I heard. "Hey sweetie, can you hear me?"

Then Innerva's voice: "I can hear you."

James's voice: "Good. I wish you were here, though."

Innerva's voice: "Me, too."

James: "I'm sorry you're sick."

I was starting to wonder what the hell this was, and why Innerva had sent it to me, when I heard the voice of Benjamin Huang, the editor at *The Gazette*: "Can we get on with this you two love muffins? Where's the drive?"

Quinn was standing over me, pulling the headset off.

"Alex, why is your email open? You said *only* a call. If they're looking at your email, they'll be able to tell you opened it."

I shut the laptop. "Let's get out of here, Quinn. You need to hear something."

CHAPTER 16

While we were inside the store, enormous dark clouds had rolled in, greying out the sky. As we huddled together in the Thunderbird, fat raindrops began hitting the roof with a heavy patter that might have been pleasant under different circumstances.

I turned the audio all the way up on my computer, but the rain made it difficult to hear, so I held the computer up to ear level and we both leaned in as I started the recording over.

Since I'd already heard the first minute or so, I watched Quinn's expression as it played. Her face was blank until Huang's voice came through the speakers. "Was that Huang?" she asked after he'd spoken. "I've never met him."

I paused the audio. "Yes."

"Then this was recorded the morning of the shooting?"

"That's what I'm assuming, but why wouldn't Innerva have explained that in the email?"

"Innerva never likes to say more than she has to."

She was right about that. "I guess it could have been

recorded another time. There's no way of knowing for sure."

"You idiot. Date and time of recording are encoded on the mp3. I can check it later on my machine."

"Huang's voice sounds a little further away, right?"

"Yes, and Innerva's voice sounds a little clearer than James's. I imagine that James called Innerva from inside Huang's office, then set the phone on the desk or something, and Innerva was recording the whole time from her end."

That made sense, actually. I'd been wondering why James would have gone to the office alone, since he and Innerva did things together most of the time. And it was clear from the first few seconds of the audio that he'd wanted her there, too. I choked up unexpectedly. I'd spent a lot of time imagining how scared James would have been in the final moments, and it comforted me slightly to know that he'd had Innerva there with him in a small way.

But my comfort disappeared as we listened to the rest of the recording.

The initial talk went pretty much how I'd imagined it after finding out about the shooting, except that I'd had no idea Innerva had been on speakerphone. James took out the drive and showed it to Huang. James did most of the talking, but Innerva made a couple comments, mostly declining to answer questions Huang asked about the drive. After a few minutes, Huang called in Deirdre Bancroft.

From there, Innerva led much of the conversation, which made sense. James was smart, but, like I said, he wasn't big on confrontation. Years ago, James had been a stutterer, but he'd worked through it with speech therapy and dietary changes. But he never became fully confident in his speech, and, back when we were partners, I'd handled most of the unpleasant conversations. I had a hard time picturing him negotiating with a guy like Huang.

After discussing some technical specs that I didn't understand, and getting off on a small tangent about old equipment, they got down to business.

Huang: "I can help you. I know a local guy who likely has

what you need."

Deirdre: "Won't the data be all scrambled to hell, though? I mean, if there's even any readable data on this thing, it's not just gonna convert to Microsoft Word."

Innerva: "Let us worry about that. We just want to know what, *if anything,* is on there. We can unscramble whatever comes off the thing. We just don't have the hardware. Huang, what do you want for your help?"

Huang: "A story, what else?"

James: "What kind of story?"

Huang: "A big one. Something clickable. Something gossipy, and nothing about my boss."

Apparently, Deirdre had left without saying goodbye because, after a brief pause, James asked Huang a question: "Where'd you find Deirdre? She seems to know her stuff."

Huang: "Through UNLV. She just started a PhD program in computer science."

I paused the recording and said, "The news reported that Deirdre's body was found in Huang's office."

Quinn nodded and started the recording again. There were a few moments of silence, and I imagined James sitting there, fidgeting awkwardly and looking for an excuse to leave now that their business was concluded.

Huang: "What was that?"

Before James could answer, we heard what sounded like a man's voice, far away, shouting something inaudible.

Quinn asked, "Does this thing go any louder?"

It didn't, so we both leaned in, ears pressed up against the speakers on either side of my laptop.

There were a few more seconds of silence, then we heard a shot. Far away, like a tiny little pop. Two shots, actually, in rapid succession.

Huang: "Those were gunshots."

James: "What?"

Innerva: "What's going on?"

Huang: "From the back."

Innerva: "James, who's there? What's happening?"

Next came a few muffled sounds: some shuffling, a thud, a bump against the desk, maybe. Then another shot, closer this time.

James: "What's going on?"

Next came a scream that got louder over the course of a few seconds. Then Deirdre's panicked voice: "Shooting. They shot Gil."

James: "What?"

Innerva: "What's happening?"

Deirdre screamed again. Then everything was silent for a few seconds. I imagined Baxter stalking through the offices, looking for his next victim. Then it struck me. Deirdre had said "*They* shot Gil."

Unless I was mishearing, there *had* been more than one shooter.

After a few more seconds, there was a gasp, then another shot. A huge, explosive gunshot followed by a thud, possibly James hitting the floor. Another scream, which only lasted a half a second because two more shots silenced it. That must have been Deirdre.

A second later, Huang's voice: "Who the hell are—"

He was silenced by another shot, but there was shuffling near the phone. After another shot, everything went quiet.

The line crackled. I looked at Quinn, who had tears in her eyes, but I was too shocked to cry. It's a stupid analogy, but I felt like I did when Buster Douglas beat Mike Tyson, like something I knew to be a fact—that Tyson was unbeatable—had been proven false, thus shattering my view of reality. But the shattering was so sudden that my mind couldn't adjust to it in real time. Instead, the normal world took on a creeping sense of unreality. I was beyond shocked. I was treading water, barely able to comprehend what was happening. I'd been right about James being frozen with fear. I'd been right about how parts of the conversation had gone down.

But I'd been wrong about everything else.

I was about to pause the recording when I heard another voice. A woman's voice. A generic, corporate, plastic voice that meant bright red hair and a blue pantsuit: "Is that the drive?"

I stopped the recording to explain to Quinn that the voice belonged to Holly, the woman from the airport. As I did, I braced internally for the "I told you so" that was sure to come, and that I deserved. But Quinn didn't say "I told you so." She just nodded knowingly, as though the recording had proven her version of the shooting correct.

Quinn hit the play button again.

No one answered Holly's question, but then Holly spoke again: "This is it."

Then a sound, which I imagined to be the drive sliding across the desk.

Holly: "Leave everything else as is?"

There were two or three seconds of silence, then another voice. A new voice: "Yes. Back door. Let's go."

I'd been expecting the voice of Kenny, as my mind was adjusting to Quinn's version of the shooting and had placed Kenny there next to Holly. But the voice wasn't Kenny's. It was another woman. From the sound of it, she'd been further away from the door than Holly, maybe standing in the doorway or just outside it as Holly picked up the drive.

It was hard to tell, but I heard the new woman's voice as a little bit Southern. It had the same flat, robotic quality that Holly's had, but she'd swallowed the "or" in the word "door," so it sounded like, "dough." The voice also sounded a little lower than Holly's, a naturally husky voice, like she was speaking from her belly through a throat worn by cigarettes. But not *much* like that. Just a little, and it was only noticeable next to Holly's almost perfectly robotic, nondescript voice.

Quinn and I sat, listening to the crackle. Three minutes, then five, then seven. The next thing we heard were the sirens. One at first, slowly getting closer. Then another behind it. I knew from the news that Captain Payton had been first on the scene, and I imagined her tall, stocky body behind the wheel of her cruiser, racing down the road. About a minute after the call had first picked up the sirens, footsteps came into the room, then a quiet voice, speaking under her breath, that I believed was Captain Payton's: "Oh, no."

The next thing I heard was a beep, maybe a police radio or phone that had been left on. I thought I heard a voice after that, but I couldn't be sure. I leaned my head up to the speaker, but Quinn grabbed my chin and turned me toward her before I heard anything else.

"Alex, we need to get out of here. Now."

"Shouldn't we listen to the rest of the—"

"We will. Of course we will. But we're not safe. Alex, this is the Zapruder film. You have no idea how big this will get, and, whoever those people in the airport were, they're still after us. Still. They could be watching us right now. They could be—"

"Quinn, wait a sec." She was talking fast and shooting glances out the windows, not quite frantically, but something close to it. The recording wasn't enough to tell us exactly what had happened, at least not without listening to it another five or ten times. But it was enough to prove beyond a doubt that Quinn had been right, at least partially.

Baxter hadn't been there. He'd had nothing to do with it. For someone like Quinn, who had lived her whole adult life with paranoid theories swirling around in her head, having one of them proved right must have been overwhelming. And my head was spinning, too. Because the recording had answered one or two questions, but raised a thousand others. "Just wait a sec," I said, thinking fast. "If they'd tracked us here, and wanted us dead, we'd be dead."

"First," Quinn said, "we need to get that email off your server." She grabbed my laptop, slid a zip drive into it, copied the file, then saved it to my hard drive and deleted it from my email.

"Why was that necessary?" I asked.

"If they're already in your email, we're dead now that they know we have this mp3. If they're not, and they get in later, I've erased any trace that you received this. Any trace that can be accessed remotely, that is. If they find us and check your laptop, well..."

I closed the laptop, took a deep breath, and looked Quinn in the eyes. At a different time, in a different situation, I would have been mesmerized by her eyes. They were full of so much vigor, intelligence, and unpredictability. To my surprise, she met my eyes and didn't say anything. We stared at each other for I don't know how long. Thirty seconds, at least. Then I noticed her eyes making slight movements. Up, right, down, left. Up, right, down, left. And when she spoke I realized she'd been walking the thinking square in her mind.

"Here's the plan," she said. "Did you leave anything at the motel?"

"No."

"We're going back to Tudayapi's. We're going to use this recording to convince her to help us. We have to get the data off this drive, if there's anything on it. I think she wanted to help us, but was afraid. This recording will make her more afraid, but she's a good guy, so it'll also make her want to help us. If we can convince her, we get the data, we leave this town, and we don't come back. We need to get somewhere safe, listen to this recording again, and figure out what to do."

It was the opposite of what I'd expected. She was thinking clearly and speaking clearly. I'd expected the revelation of the recording to drive her further into one of her scarier head-spaces. But it had done the opposite. She was thinking a lot more quickly than I was, and though I still thought she was overestimating the physical danger we were in, I wasn't about to argue with her plan.

I was already peeling out of the *Tammen Temeeh Kahni* parking lot.

CHAPTER 17

As it turned out, we didn't need to tell Tudayapi about the recording.

When we returned to her house, Quinn marched right up to the door, the drive slung over her shoulder. I followed, and, moments later, we were back in our spots on the couch.

Tudayapi had changed back into her aquamarine pantsuit and, before Quinn could say anything, she said, "Why didn't you tell me you were Alex from *The Barker*?"

I looked at the floor, as I sometimes do when I want to avoid something negative that's about to come my way.

"Why didn't you tell me?" she continued. "Oh my God, I love, love, *love* your site. It's like if *TMZ*, *Slate*, and the *New York Times* had a threesome when they were still young and hot."

That was not what I expected. "Thanks," I said, looking up. "What were some of your favorite pieces?"

"Oh there are *so* many. I follow the shallow gossip stuff, of course. Who doesn't? But I always feel a little dirty reading it.

And your app is awesome. I only read you guys on the app."
The app was a Bird innovation. We'd known we needed one
by around 2011, and Bird had found the engineers to pull it
off.

Tudayapi got up from her chair and slid next to me on the
couch. "But the essays on race and gender have been the
most important to me. You guys were the first big site to hire
a full-time columnist to blog about trans issues. That was
huge."

"Wow," I said, "that means a lot. I mean, I know we
publish a lot of cheap crap, but—"

"You have to. To pay the bills, right?"

"That's right," I said, giving Quinn a look as if to say *see,
some people get it*. I turned back to Tudayapi. "And we try to
balance it out by doing some social good when we can."

The truth was, we'd just partnered with a blog run by a guy
named Thor Magnussen, who wrote about gender identity
issues. He provided us content, we slapped *The Barker* brand
on it. We increased his readership tenfold and split the
revenue seventy-thirty. We kept the seventy.

I was about to say something self-deprecating when I
noticed tears in Tudayapi's eyes. "There was a period about
two years ago, where Thor stopped writing about gender
issues and just did a diary thing, chronicling like twenty first
dates he went on in LA. Stuff like meeting out at a restaurant,
getting stood up, meeting a shallow girl and ripping her to
shreds, losing his lucky underwear and freaking out. Just
normal stuff. I know LA is a lot different than here, but it gave
me hope that normal life is possible, at least somewhere."

She paused, and I didn't know what to say. I was actually
surprised that anything we'd done at *The Barker* had touched
anyone so deeply. And seeing her tears made me feel her
pain. I could tell she'd gone through a lot, and I felt a tinge of
pride that our site had helped. But I still didn't know what to
say and, luckily, I didn't have to say anything.

Tudayapi dried her eyes with a silk handkerchief that
matched her pantsuit. "I know we need to talk about the

drive," she said. "But I just wanted to tell you that those stories were a big deal to me. Out here, I can feel kind of hopeless sometimes, because, even though my tribe accepts me, this is not exactly a hotbed of cultural progressivism. That series gave me hope."

Quinn had been surprisingly quiet for the last few minutes, and I could feel her itching to get back to business. It wasn't that she was insensitive, just hyper-focused on the recording, and the drive. "And all that made you want to help us, right?" I said, not expecting it to work.

"Yes," Tudayapi said.

And with that, she stood up and walked purposefully through the laundry room and into the garage. Quinn followed right on her heels, carrying the drive. "Let's keep the recording to ourselves," she whispered when I caught up to her in the hallway.

I agreed. It made sense to keep the recording to ourselves if we didn't need to use it to convince Tudayapi to get the data off the drive.

But reading the drive wasn't going to be as simple as I'd hoped. I knew Tudayapi couldn't just Airdrop the data onto Quinn's laptop, but I figured there was some solution that would take ten minutes, maybe half an hour at most. I realized that the parts that were needed to retrieve the data were rare, but Tudayapi had indicated that she had them, and I figured the task itself would be relatively easy.

I was wrong.

We spent the next four hours in Tudayapi's garage and, just like a well-structured story, the process of retrieving the data had three main parts. First, Tudayapi had to find the parts and assemble them. She poured through boxes, bins, and little jars, occasionally pulling out wires or clips or screws. She looked under and behind a few dozen other computers and monitors stored on her wide shelving. Each time she found a necessary part, she handed it to Quinn, whose job was to organize the parts on the large worktable near the garage door.

When you run a business, you're faced with a thousand decisions each day. And in situations like this, I always have a decision to make. Do I try to understand the details, or do I just take orders and roll with it? Like a few days ago, when Bird decided to trade our DVD story for the off-the-record chat. I could have gotten into the details and tried to figure out the nuances of what he was thinking, and chances are that I would have agreed with him. But I'd dropped it, choosing just to trust him. Sometimes it's important for me to understand all the details, but that wasn't one of those times. And neither was this. It was clear from watching the way Quinn took the parts, and the way Tudayapi responded to her placement of them on the table, that I had little to add to this situation.

So, what was my role? I got the iced tea. After she'd put on her overalls, Tudayapi told me to get her large McDonald's collectible cup and fill it with the sweet tea from the fridge. I'd done it, and she asked for a refill just as they finished the first part of the process. When I got back with the second iced tea, I panicked for a few seconds. The drive was in pieces, spread across the table. Each of the fourteen discs had been placed separately on a clean rag, in some order I couldn't discern. They looked like old vinyl records, and I hadn't even known they could be taken out of the large plastic case.

"How long do you expect this to take?" I asked Tudayapi.

"Another couple hours."

I walked up and leaned on the table to get a better view. Next to the discs was an object about two-by-two feet with a thick granite base covered in knobs. Dozens of wires were coming off the thing from all directions and the top looked like a record player. Quinn saw me staring at it. She said, "It's a spin stand. When computers fail, it's a way to get the data off the hard drive."

Tudayapi finished connecting wires and turned it on. A few red lights blinked. "First disc," she said to Quinn.

Quinn carefully lifted the disc nearest to her, then placed it on the stand.

Tudayapi pressed a button on the stand, and it began to spin.

"What does it do?" I asked.

"Well, normally I'd hook it up to another machine and it would essentially transfer the data from this hard drive to another. Like backing it up."

"I assume there's a 'but' coming."

"There is," Tudayapi replied, excitedly.

"Is that where this fax machine comes in?" Next to the spin stand, Tudayapi had placed a beige object that looked like an old fax machine, the kind with slick rolls of paper. The sort no one under thirty-five has ever seen.

"Yes," Tudayapi said, "but it's not a fax machine. It's an old Telex. Kind of like the things Western Union used to use."

"The issue," Quinn said, "is that IBM machines used a proprietary character encoding called EBCDIC."

"And this particular drive used encoded eighty-column card images," Tudayapi added.

They'd lost me, but they both had that gleam in the eye that people get when they're talking about something they love. They couldn't wait to tell me how they'd done it.

"Do I want to know what EBCDIC stands for?"

Tudayapi said, "Extended Binary Coded Decimal Interchange Code."

"So, no. In retrospect, I didn't."

"It's really not that complicated," Tudayapi said. "I'm surprised you know so little about computers, given that you run a website."

"You're not the first person to tell me that," I said, glancing at Quinn.

"Oh, Alex spends most of his time schmoozing at the latte stand in his fancy-pants office. Right, Starbucks boy?"

"I call it my coffice."

Quinn continued to break it down. "The issue is—since she can't transfer the data onto any of her old machines, she has to print it straight from the drive. But this Telex is based on Baudot coding, not EBCDIC, which—"

"Which is where *this* comes in," Tudayapi said. She had her finger on a thin, rectangular panel, about twelve inches square, covered in silver solder dots and little microchips connected by wires. Even I knew it was a logic board, but it looked older and more amateurish than any I'd seen.

"It's a hand-soldered antique," Tudayapi said. "Bought it off a guy fifteen years ago who bought it off a guy fifteen years before that. Only logic board I've ever seen that converts EBCDIC to Baudot."

I traced the wires from the logic board to the Telex device. "So the logic board will convert the data and send it to the Telex, which will convert it on the fly?"

They both smiled. "Awesome, huh?" Quinn said.

"Hold onto the paper," Tudayapi said.

Quinn used both hands to cradle a roll of paper, which normally would have been enclosed in a case on a spool, but the spool was busted. About a minute later, the Telex began printing.

As boring as I find computer stuff in general, I was impressed, and their excitement had rubbed off on me. I leaned in over Quinn's shoulder as the paper began coming out. She turned her head slightly and I think she may have even smiled.

The first pages looked like gibberish. Random letters and numbers surrounded by large blank spaces.

Tudayapi said, "One drawback of doing it this way is that you're going to get the raw data. It's going to be a mess."

That was when we entered part two of the process: printing the contents of the drive. It took over two hours and required a changed ink cartridge, three re-starts of the spin-stand, replacing a frayed wire on the logic board, and two cups of iced tea for Tudayapi.

While it was printing, I paced the garage. A couple times I tried to convince Quinn to hand me some of the pages, but she wasn't having it.

"It's a rabbit hole," she said. "We'll pour over this, but for now we just need to finish the printing and get the hell out of here."

I was bored, so I started a little game where I tried to walk every possible path around the five worktables. The whole time, I was nagged by a question about Innerva. The recording explained how she'd been certain James was dead when I met her at The Wynn on the evening of the shooting. But why hadn't she told me about the recording? And why had she sent the message without context or explanation?

I could come up with only two theories. The first, and most plausible, was that the recording was all she knew, and was self-explanatory.

The other, darker theory, was that the recording had been a Dead Man's Switch, a message she'd set up to send only if something happened, or didn't happen. Hackers use them all the time. Some program their machines to automatically erase all data if the owner doesn't log in for three days. Some connect their computers to their phone's GPS and set up their systems to lock down if the phone doesn't move for twelve hours. Others set their computers to encrypt certain data on their computers if an unauthorized user gains access. So, my second theory was that Innerva had been researching the recording and set it up to send to me as a contingency plan. "Send to Alex if X, Y, or Z happens." I hoped this theory was wrong, and didn't want to think about what X, Y, or Z were.

All my wondering, and the fact that Quinn and Tudayapi were only halfway through the pile of disks, made me want to get back to the recording, especially the second part, which we hadn't listened to as rushed back to Tudayapi's.

"Tudayapi, where's your restroom?" I asked.

"Off the kitchen. You'll see it."

***

I grabbed my laptop out of the car, then locked myself in her pastel pink and blue bathroom, sitting on a small wicker bench in the corner.

The first part of the recording didn't reveal any new clues during the second listen, but I did notice a few more details. The fact that my mental picture of the shooting had adjusted allowed me to hear the whole recording in a different way. On this, Quinn was right that it was like the Zapruder film. People can see many different versions of the assassination in the footage. If you believe that JFK was killed by a lone gunman, that's what you see. And if you believe he was shot from the front, by two or more gunmen, *that's* what you see. Hearing the recording for the second time, I realized that the first time, I'd heard it through the prism of believing for sure that the official media account was correct. But the voices at the end had proved that wrong beyond a shadow of a doubt.

The second time, I heard it differently.

The first voice we heard from outside the office, the man's voice, had been muffled on the first listen. I thought I could make out the words now: "Call the police." The first time I'd heard it, I'd assumed it was the voice of the shooter, Baxter, but the second time I thought it must be Gil Kazinsky, who was found dead in the back of the office. He was the only man other than James and Huang, and this further confirmed the idea that the shooters had come in through the back door.

Another detail I'd missed on the first listen was the sound of Holly's voice before she entered the office, which I'd heard as background noise the first time around. About five seconds before she came into the office, she said something like, "Almond was right," or "Damon was right," or possibly "Amanda was right." I held the computer speaker right up to my ear, but it was impossible to know for sure. I figured that with good headphones or amplifying software, Quinn and I would be able to figure it out.

Hearing Holly's voice, I was struck by a wave of shame and anger. Not only had I fallen for her and Kenny's act, I'd lead them straight to Quinn's doorstep. In retrospect, their act had been amazing. How had they managed to tailor their routine to me, my interests and background so quickly? They couldn't have. Not unless they'd been tracking me, had prepped for me. But I'd met them only twenty-four hours after receiving Innerva's email. And I hadn't been in touch with either James or Innerva for nearly a year before that.

Then there was the second half of the recording.

Captain Shonda Payton's first words came about eighteen minutes in. After that, there were about six minutes of silence, punctuated only by a few beeps from her radio. She'd walked to another room to call in the shooting, so I couldn't hear exactly what she was saying, but the beeps were loud enough to be picked up. After the six minutes, I heard two male voices discussing the scene. Then a woman saying something about blood splatter patterns.

No one seemed shocked or disturbed. Just another crime scene.

There were only two interesting moments.

The first came with about two minutes left on the recording. A man's voice, growing louder like he was walking into the office, getting closer to the phone, "Lived on Desert Road. I got called out there twice. Bastard played Clash records too loud and refused to turn them down. *Should I Stay or Should I Go, London Calling.* Neighbors complained constantly. I love the Clash, so I used to rock out in the parking lot for a minute before making him turn it down."

Then the voice of the first officer, the woman. "He has a sheet?"

"Yeah, nothing serious."

"They never do until they do something like this."

"Tell me about it. This one's gonna be a no-brainer."

They were talking about Baxter.

They were interrupted about a minute later by multiple other people arriving, and the last thing I heard was a new voice, which sounded like a young man. "Should I bag the phone?"

Then the recording ended.

I couldn't tell if Innerva had chosen that moment to end the call, or if the man who'd bagged the phone had ended the call. I guessed that if he'd noticed the phone was live he wouldn't have ended the call. Or, at least, he would have discussed ending it with the people in the room before doing so. I also guessed that Innerva wouldn't have ended the call. She was all about transparency, about data becoming public. There's no way she would have wanted to end a call that had a chance to give her more data to work with. I figured the man must have pressed "end" by accident while bagging the phone.

There was a bang on the bathroom door and I sat up, frozen. "Alex, are you okay?"

It was Quinn's voice. She needed to use the bathroom.

***

Back in the garage, I continued walking laps around the worktables, and noticed something I hadn't seen earlier. Above the garage door we'd come through, there was a little loft. I'd missed it before because the wall, the door, and the loft itself were all painted white, and a white cloth hung down, blocking the view into the loft. There was a wooden ladder leaning on the wall next to it.

"What's that?" I called to Tudayapi, who was feeding more paper into the Telex machine.

"A loft," she said, looking up briefly.

I walked across the garage and stood next to her. Quinn was cutting the pages with a large pair of scissors and placing them in what I hoped was the correct order. I could tell how hard it was for her to resist the urge to sit down and read them.

"What's up there?" I asked Tudayapi.

"Nothing."

"Really?"

"Well, nothing that would interest *you*, anyway."

Quinn said, "Give it a rest, Alex, we're almost done here."

"Should just be a few more minutes," Tudayapi said. "We're on the last disc."

"We really can't thank you enough," Quinn said. "Alex, get her some more iced tea."

I did, and, by the time I got back, the Telex was quiet.

Quinn was cutting and stacking the final pages. "Any chance you have an old binder or something?" she asked.

"Probably," Tudayapi said. She checked a few shelves in the garage, then went into the main house.

By the time the door closed, Quinn was standing under the loft, waving for me to follow her.

"Boost me up," she called out.

I really hadn't cared about what was in the loft. More computer parts, I figured, but of a slightly fancier variety than the ones down below.

"Boost me," she said again, as I walked over.

Reluctantly, I made my hands into a cup and Quinn stepped up, her grimy boot slippery on my palms. She wasn't small, but she was strong, and, after boosting her a foot or so, she was able to grab onto the ledge of the loft and pull herself up so her neck was at the bottom of the cloth. "Push."

I gave her a big push just as she swung one arm off the ledge of the loft and swiped at the cloth, ducking her head under it. "Higher."

I pushed again, to the point where her boots were resting on my shoulders, her head almost to the height of the ceiling. Just as I noticed the tracks on the bottom of her boots digging into my shoulder, she said. "Okay, lemme down."

With that, she pulled her head out from behind the cloth and slid down through my arms and onto the floor. A moment later she was back across the garage, fiddling with the stack of papers again. I brushed the dirt off my shoulders and wiped my hands on my jeans, a little out of breath.

Quinn seemed unfazed.

"What was up there?" I asked.

"Nothing you'd understand."

Now I *wanted* to know, but it wasn't worth the fight. Especially since Tudayapi was back, carrying an extra-wide 3-ring binder and a hole punch.

The instant we finished arranging the binder, Quinn bolted for the car. I thanked Tudayapi and jogged to the car, worried that Quinn might be trying to ditch me.

When I got there, Quinn was already in the passenger seat, thumbing through the pages. I hopped in the driver seat and, without looking up, Quinn handed me the keys. "Drive."

"Where?"

"I don't know, but the goal now is to get somewhere safe and figure out what's in this binder."

CHAPTER 18

Minutes after leaving Owyhee, we passed a "Welcome to Idaho" sign, and the landscape began changing. The rock formations we'd passed on the way into Owyhee gave way to long stretches of two-lane highway with flat, treeless land on either side. We passed a sign that read: NEXT REST AREA: 31 MILES

"The rest area," I said. "We'll stop there."

Quinn nodded without looking up from the binder.

A series of low hills appeared in the distance and I caught myself hoping that the rest area would be nestled between them. I knew it was silly, but I felt less safe with the binder. Somehow the thought of reading it nestled between hills calmed me.

But Quinn wasn't waiting until we got to the rest area. She was flipping through the pages erratically, stopping occasionally to glance at her passenger-side mirror. A couple times, I took my eyes off the road to look down at the pages, trying to get a hint of what we had.

I'd never seen anything like it. Whatever sorts of files had been on the drive had been sloppily converted into an unreadable mess of garbage characters, files without headers, headers without files, and segmented texts with the segments in the wrong order. Every once in a while, I'd see a word or a series of numbers that seemed to have meaning, but without context, and looking for only a second at a time, I was lost.

After about five minutes, Quinn started swearing under her breath. After seven, she closed the binder violently. We were passing into a beautiful valley with a large lake, surrounded by low brown hills, but she didn't seem like the kind of person who'd be admiring the scenery. Her eyes were trained on her side mirror and, after a moment, she tilted the rearview mirror to her side.

"Hey, I need that to drive," I said, but she ignored me and turned back to the binder.

A minute later, she was swearing under her breath again. Slamming the binder again.

"Find anything useful yet?" I asked.

"It's a mess," she said. "Worthless."

"Any way you could discuss things without judging them?"

Quinn ignored me, her eyes fixed on the rearview mirror.

I figured I'd try again because, even though I was attempting to conceal my excitement, I *needed* to know what was in that binder. "Do me a favor," I said, "Just read me a few random sections."

"Oh, read to you, why, that would be *lovely*." She said it so quickly I figured she'd had her sarcasm program loading before I opened my mouth. "Here, I'll skip to the good part. The essential clue that will tell us why we're being hunted by a couple murderous CIA thugs."

She flipped open the binder. "Slash slash slash, pound sign, pound sign, pound sign. Half a page of blank space. Is it okay if I don't read you the blank space, but just summarize it? Good? Okay then. Slash, slash, pound sign, ampersand—"

"Quinn."

"No, *don't interrupt.* We're getting to the good part: three straight pages of numbers." She cleared her throat. "Seven one two six nine four eight one one one zero zero four three eight—"

"I get the point."

She slammed the binder again, shifted her eyes back to the mirrors.

I said, "Maybe *scanning* the folder would be a more efficient way to go. Look for anything useable, anything recognizable, rather than *reading* the gibberish?" She didn't respond, and I started looking for the rest area exit. "The way I'd handle it is to make my eyes go soft, start on page one and go page-by-page, spending no more than five seconds on each page, looking for names or words or sentence fragments that seem familiar. I *know* I saw a few things that looked like names back at Tudayapi's. Just *try* it."

Quinn opened the binder again and spent the next five minutes trying what I suggested. It was actually a pretty big deal. She didn't grunt, she didn't say something sarcastic. I know it went against her nature—both using my method and the method itself, but she tried it. Every once in a while, she'd read something out loud. Some names I didn't recognize. The word "file" over and over. Some dates, mostly from the forties and fifties.

The she closed the binder. "Operation Mockingbird," she said.

"Operation what?"

"Holy hell," she said quietly. "Operation Mockingbird."

I glanced down at the binder, but Quinn's arm was covering the page. She was studying the mirrors again.

We passed a sign that read: REST AREA 5 MILES

"Quinn, what are you talking about, what's Operation Mockingbird?"

"Quiet," she said, and I followed her eyes back and forth between her mirror and the rearview mirror.

"Quinn!"

"So, okay," she said at last, "we're being followed."

She said it kind of casually, without looking at me, and I

thought she meant *in general*. As in, somewhere out there, people are following us.

Then she said, "The same gray car's been behind us since we left Owyhee."

"I'm sure it has. There are almost no exits on this road. Besides," I said, checking my mirror, "the car behind us is blue."

"I mean the one behind that. The gray car two cars back has been two cars back since we left Owyhee."

I'd gained some trust in Quinn over the last twenty-four hours, but I wasn't buying it. "Isn't it more likely that if there *is* a gray car behind us, which I can't see right now, it's just heading the same general direction we are on a road with, *again*, almost no exits?"

"I'm sure they *are* headed the same direction we are. Because they're *following* us."

"C'mon, Quinn. I'm just saying that it's more *likely*—"

"And I'm just saying, please name one thing that's happened recently that was *likely*."

I sighed, then checked the mirror again. We'd left the clouds behind in Owyhee, and the late afternoon sun was reflecting off the light blue Prius behind us. Behind the Prius, there was definitely a gray sedan of some sort, but not following closely enough to see who was in it. "Are you sure you're not just...*imagining* it. You've seemed kinda all over the place for the last half hour."

Her eyes were darting back and forth between the mirrors and the road ahead, but she was speaking calmly, like she was barely connected to what she was saying.

"I recognize patterns. It's what I do. It's why I'm good with hardware and codes, it's why I see through the official versions of stories. I've been looking at the cars behind us on this road. Not that there are a lot of exits, but there are some, and people pass each other or get passed, so there's been a kind of rotation in this mirror. A big semi, a blue minivan, a red sports car. The vehicle behind us varies. But the vehicle behind that one doesn't. The gray car stays a constant distance away. It never gets close enough that I can make out more than its color. It never drops far enough back that I can't see it. It's just there, a little gray blur two cars back, with eroded white letters at the bottom of the rearview reminding me that, however distant and half-visible it may look, *objects in mirror are closer than they appear.*"

"If they're following us, why didn't they come at us at Tudayapi's? If they're following us and they're the badass killers you think they are, why are they just following us instead of forcing us to turn down some deserted dirt road, burying us in the desert?" I was growing irritated, and the contents of that binder were nagging at me like a new text message I couldn't check because I was in the other room. Plus, I was exhausted. "I'm sorry," I said. "I'm just tired."

"You've barely *slept*. Sleep deprivation is torture. It weakens your mind. Here, look, pull over for a second, let me drive."

"But on the tiny possibility that they are following us—"

"Nah, you're probably right that they're not. Just do me a favor. Pull over."

"Why?"

"I want to drive."

"We're almost at the rest area."

"Just do this for me, please. There, next to that sign." She pointed at a large green sign with white lettering: REST AREA 2 MILES (FREE WI-FI)

I shot Quinn a dubious look, but I'd learned to pick my battles with her, so I slowed the car. The rumble strips let out a slow thrum under the tires as I eased onto the shoulder, just past the sign. When I opened the door, the heat hit me like a blow. It was four in the afternoon, but it must have been ninety degrees still.

"That sun would kill us if it had a chance," Quinn said.

"Thank God for air conditioning."

Quinn slid into the driver's seat, moved the seat up a couple inches, then started the car.

"Okay, let's go," I said, shutting my door.

The AC kicked back in, but it was weak and would take minutes to re-cool the car. But Quinn didn't pull out right away. Instead, she stared into the rearview mirror, which she'd adjusted back to her side. I turned around and looked out the back, and I was starting to get worried about what she was going to do.

The blue car that had been behind us was now passing us, and the gray car was only a hundred yards back. Quinn was mumbling under her breath.

Fifty yards away.

Twenty.

Ten.

Then the gray car sped by us. Didn't slow down, didn't do anything out of the ordinary. There were two people in the car, but they passed us going seventy-five or so, and I couldn't make them out.

"I told you they weren't following us," I said, feeling more relieved than I'd expected.

Quinn eased onto the highway. "That doesn't mean they weren't following us."

I wanted to disagree, but I remembered the way Holly and Kenny had chased us through the Fremont Street Experience. Tailing us, but never getting too close.

Quinn took the exit to the rest area and idled about fifty feet from the parking area, studying every car. The gray sedan wasn't there. She parked by a fenced-in dog park, where two or three people were watching five or six dogs. Off to the left, a small bathroom building was surrounded by dry grass and a few wooden picnic tables.

"What was it you said before?" I asked. "The thing in the binder. Operation Mockingbird?"

CHAPTER 19

"You haven't heard of it?" she asked as she turned off the car.
It did ring a bell, but I couldn't place it. "I...I might have."
"*Pathetic.*"

"Quinn, I know this might be news to you, but most people have not heard of most of the things you spend your time thinking about. And what happened to no judgement?"

She grunted dismissively. "What the hell do they do with their time, then?"

I ignored her and asked, "What is it? And—please, oh please—give me the short, unbiased version."

"Operation Mockingbird was a CIA program designed to influence media coverage. It was elaborate, international, and wildly illegal. I—"

"I can tell you want to go on," I said, grabbing my laptop bag from the back seat, "but I want to check it out for myself."

Quinn might have been the world's leading expert on Operation Mockingbird, but I didn't want her opinion on anything that involved the CIA. She was sure to filter any facts through seven layers of paranoia. "I'll read and tell you everything I find out."

"Find out from where? *Huffington Post, The New York Times,* Propaganda dot com?"

I got out of the car and stepped around to the driver-side window. Quinn didn't move. She was kind of bent over, arms wrapped around her chest, clutching at the binder. I tapped on her window three times. When she finally raised her head, I offered up my cheesiest grin. I knew that would piss her off. She frowned and turned her head towards the empty passenger seat.

Then I panicked.

The car was off, but the keys were still in the ignition, and, for a moment, I was sure she was going to ditch me. She could lock the car and peel out from the rest stop in seconds.

I tapped on the window again. She didn't turn to look at me, but after a long pause, she got out, slammed the binder on top of the car, made me promise to use the encrypted browser she'd downloaded for me, and walked slowly to the dog park, cursing under her breath the whole way.

I grabbed the binder and took a seat at a rickety picnic table near the bathrooms. The hot wind blasted my face, carrying with it the smell of stale urine. Occasionally the wind shifted and I got a hit of the mesquite trees that surrounded the dog park. Quinn seemed occupied with a friendly brown dog with a wrinkly face, and I cracked the binder and found the page she had been on. The paper had that slick, oily feel, an unpleasant glossiness.

I figured out quickly that there weren't actually any details about Operation Mockingbird in the binder. Just a one page list of names with some slightly scrambled text at the top: "MocHingb1rd Level 1 Assets." I scanned the list and thought I recognized a few of the names, but I wasn't sure. I flipped through the binder a bit, but gave up after twenty straight pages of unreadable gibberish. I was sure there was more useful information in the binder, but I decided to focus on Google instead.

Like any self-respecting Internet searcher, I started with the Wikipedia entry. It confirmed my basic understanding of Operation Mockingbird: the CIA had a controversial relationship with the press, the details and extent of which were murky.

After Wikipedia, I found what seemed to be the definitive expose on Operation Mockingbird, a cover story from *Rolling Stone* published in October of 1977 and now posted on the personal website of Carl Bernstein. I hadn't ever read the piece, but of course I knew of Carl Bernstein. You probably do, too. He's the Bernstein of Woodward and Bernstein, the guys who broke the Watergate story. Maybe you read *All the President's Men*, or at least saw the movie. Bernstein was the guy played by Dustin Hoffman. Anyway, he's the real deal. One of the great investigative journalists on Earth, at least when it comes to political stuff. If I'm the McDonald's of journalism, he's got three Michelin stars.

The piece was long and dense, and I read through it slowly while glancing occasionally at Quinn, who seemed to have made a new friend. Every time I looked up, she was petting, or chasing, or being chased by the dog.

The Bernstein story opened with a series of bullet points, which can be summarized as follows: The CIA's involvement with the American press began during the early stages of the Cold War and continues to be shrouded by an official policy of obfuscation and deception. Nothing especially earth-shattering. But as I read on, I saw that Bernstein had uncovered all sorts of details no one else had.

Operation Mockingbird had three primary functions.

First, news agencies in print, radio, and TV provided "journalistic cover" for CIA operatives posted in foreign capitals. If Agent X needed to do some work in Chile, for example, *The Washington Post* might give her a job as "Special Correspondent to South America." Journalists make perfect CIA agents. They ask questions for a living, so they are less likely to be suspected of anything shady when they start nosing around. Plus, they often travel alone or in small groups, leaving their families back in the States, so it's cheaper and easier to go undercover as a journalist than as a businessman living abroad. Plus, according to the piece, many businesses and nonprofits wouldn't cooperate with the CIA. Even the Peace Corps banned covert agents.

The second leg of the program—and the most shocking— was to build relationships with well-placed journalists who were already on the staff of key news organizations. These journalists provided a range of services: recruiting and managing foreign nationals to work with the CIA, feeding the CIA information acquired abroad, planting false information with officials of foreign governments, and parroting official CIA positions in the U.S. media.

Some journalists were paid by the CIA, always in cash, to supplement their regular income. Others helped out less formally, and for free. To many of the journalists involved, this wasn't a big deal. They did their regular reporting jobs overseas, then chatted with their buddies at the CIA when they got home. Many of the journalists and agents had served together in World War II and, under the growing post-war threat from the USSR, they viewed this cooperation as simple patriotism. It went so far that, by the late 1950s, some reporters felt miffed if they *weren't* met by CIA operatives to debrief when they returned from a trip abroad.

What kind of information was the CIA looking for?

Well, imagine you're Joe CIA, part of a 6-man unit overseeing opposition to Khrushchev in the USSR in the late 1950s. Maybe you want information about an imprisoned far-right Ukrainian dissident, but you hear a rumor that the Gulag system is winding down. There's a chance he's been moved from the Saratovsky camp he's been rotting in for the last three years, but you need to know for sure. What would *you* do? Send over a couple corn-fed agents in Yankees hats to knock on the door of the Kremlin? *Probably not.* Instead, you call your buddy, Arthur Hays Sulzberger at *The Times*. He's got a reporter in Moscow right now who'll be back next month. As it happens, he's been working on a story about

Khrushchev's reforms, and he'd be happy to help. *Just doing his duty.* By the way, want to play racquetball next week?

And this is where Operation Mockingbird gets more complicated, and more controversial.

We all know it's bullshit, but we like to think of journalists as unbiased. At least we used to. Historically, it's been one of the lies we tell ourselves to get through the day. But, we hope that they're not *literally on the payroll* of the governments or businesses or sports teams they're hired to cover. So, if a bunch of the top journalists in the country turned out to be— either formally or informally—working for the CIA, that'd be a big deal. And, according to Bernstein's article, the CIA had top people at almost every major news organization in the U.S. *The New York Times, Time, Life,* CBS News. Their list of assets was a who's who of top journalists from the 1950s to 1970s.

But journalism is rarely a one-way street. Turns out, some of the reporters Bernstein spoke to described their relationship with the CIA as a typical, mutually beneficial journalistic relationship. So, when *The Times* reporter gets back from Moscow and tells Joe CIA everything he knows about Russian plans for political prisoners, *of course* he gets a scoop or two about Korolev's burgeoning space program. Simple business.

I used to be a *real* journalist, remember? I made deals like that all the time. Just as Bird had a couple days ago. Any decent reporter covering foreign affairs would jump at the chance to have drinks with a known CIA staffer. And there's a good chance a CIA agent's view of the relationship would differ from the journalist's. Whereas a CIA staffer might puff up his importance by claiming to have control over a journalist, a journalist might think he's using the staffer to get information his competitor isn't getting.

But even more important than the foreign correspondents were the columnists and commentators. These guys—and they were all guys at the time—were the ones who shaped American public opinion about politics, war, foreign leaders, *you name it.* According to the Bernstein piece, the CIA had dozens of the top commentators in the country on the payroll. Folks who were considered by the CIA to be "receptive to the Agency's point of view on various subjects." The best-known of these columnists was Arthur Sulzberger of *The New York Times*, who, according to several CIA officials, once published a column under his own byline that was just a briefing paper from the CIA. Sulzberger called the report, "A bunch of baloney." Assuming Bernstein's story is right—and I trust him—does this mean everything in *The New York Times* is a lie? Of course not.

And that was why I didn't want to talk to Quinn about this. Luckily, she was now playing fetch with her new canine friend. She saw this type of thing in black and white, good and evil, while I saw shades of gray. Many of the CIA officials Bernstein interviewed thought of these helpful journalists as operatives or even full-on CIA agents. But the journalists tended to see themselves as trusted friends of the Agency who performed occasional favors—usually without pay—in the national interest.

One of their best assets was Joseph Alsop, a legend in the journalism business. He was a Harvard guy, related to both Theodore Roosevelt and James Monroe, who had served in the Navy in World War II before becoming one of the most influential political journalists in the country. And he had no issue with going on the record in the Bernstein piece. When asked about his role in helping the CIA, he summed up the sentiments of many of the reporters involved: "I'm proud they asked me and proud to have done it...The notion that a newspaperman doesn't have a duty to his country is perfect balls."

The third and final piece of Operation Mockingbird was to influence foreign citizens by setting up newspapers in foreign countries, paid for secretly, of course. For example, up until 1974, the CIA owned a forty-percent stake in the *Rome Daily American*, its main purpose to convince the Italian people not to become Communists. One project in the mid-sixties used high-level staffers from *The Washington Post* and CBS News—along with professors from MIT and Columbia—to figure out how to broadcast U.S. propaganda behind the Iron Curtain and into Red China. The team recommended that the CIA establish a radio broadcast run by the Voice of America and beam it into China. As apprehensive as I am about the entanglements between the media and the CIA, I wish they'd figured out something about China, because I still can't get *The Barker* past China's Great Internet Firewall.

If you read spy novels, you might picture this whole project as a group of industrious folks at the CIA managing to infiltrate the media by blackmailing reporters or getting agents placed in the mailroom. And some of that happened. But that's not the right way to think about it, at least according to Bernstein.

This was a *partnership*, and it came from the top down. Not only did the CIA have relationships with many of the top journalists and commentators, they did so with the encouragement of the publishers and owners they worked for. Top executives from most major newspapers and TV networks cooperated.

As public trust in U.S. institutions eroded during the Vietnam War and Watergate, Operation Mockingbird wound down between 1973 and 1976 under CIA director William Colby. And when George Bush took over the CIA in 1976, he immediately announced a new policy: "Effective immediately, the CIA will not enter into any paid or contractual relationship with any full-time or part-time news correspondent accredited by any U.S. news service, newspaper, periodical, radio, or television network or station." Of course, this new policy only affected one piece of the program, and the CIA would still welcome the *voluntary* cooperation of news organization and reporters.

From the 1940s to 1970s, the program was one of the CIA's most closely-held secrets, for two main reasons. First, if a journalist was found to be a CIA operative while reporting in a foreign country, he wouldn't come home. That would be bad, sure, and it led to the second reason. There was no telling how the public would react if the program leaked. Bobby Newspaper-Reader still believed that, despite its limitations, the press presented a basically truthful version of events. You know, facts. If it turned out that half of the most-trusted newsmen in the U.S. were with the CIA, public confidence would be shattered. At least that was the fear.

So, how did Operation Mockingbird become public?

A few details had already leaked when the Church Committee started looking into CIA and press relationships in 1975. But the committee, made up of a half-dozen senators, was designed as a broad investigation into U.S. intelligence services, and committee members spent most of their time searching for headline-grabbing assassination attempts, exploding suitcases, and poison pens. The investigation into the use of journalists was an afterthought. And it's not like the CIA cooperated. After months of stonewalling, the Church Committee gained only limited access to some of the files. No journalists had been interviewed. The committee's final report contained just ten pages about the program, which were agreed upon, according to committee member Senator Gary Hart, after "prolonged and elaborate negotiation [with the CIA] over what would be said."

To my mind, they were worried about nothing. As sacred as the role of the press is supposed to be—it's in the First Amendment, after all—the press is a *business*. And if the relationship between the CIA and the press were to become public, who would make it public?

The press, right?

And why would the press report something that would undermine confidence in its own product? Not to mention the fact that, if Bernstein was right about the reporters he'd named, further reporting could ruin a journalist's career. Not surprisingly, the Bernstein piece had caused a small stir, but had been ignored by the major news outlets.

One quote from "a high-ranking CIA official" in the Bernstein piece kept coming back to me. "This all has to be considered in the context of the morality of the times...There was a time when it wasn't considered a crime to serve your government.'"

There was something about the quote that got to me, and I was trying to figure out what it was. I pictured Bernstein in 1975, a long-haired Jewish reporter who leaned left, sitting across from a chiseled CIA agent with a graying crew cut and a constant frown. To the agent's generation, nothing was even slightly wrong with the program. He'd lived through the Great Depression, World War II, and the early stages of the Cold War, conflicts that *had* to be fought and *had* to be won. *Of course* journalists should help, and having a hippie like Bernstein question him must have been the ultimate insult. But, to Bernstein's generation of counterculture revolutionaries, who grew up distrusting the government and had protested the war in Vietnam, *everything* was wrong about the program. To Bernstein, the role of the press was to uncover government lies and deceptions, even when it came to war. To find out that they'd been in cahoots all along would have been shocking.

But that was forty years ago, and I couldn't help but think that the whole dichotomy between Bernstein and the CIA had somehow been erased. That the relationships between press and power had changed fundamentally.

I glanced up when I heard Quinn's steps crunching the dry grass. Her shirt was covered with dog hair and she looked closer to happy than I'd ever seen her.

I stood and tucked the binder under my arm, then gestured towards the car, tossing Quinn the keys. "Okay. Before we go through it all, I have one question. Operation Mockingbird wound down forty years ago. When the details came out, no one really cared. And I've never heard a single rumor about a journalist having a relationship with the CIA. Maybe there is more information buried in this binder and maybe not. But if the information has been public for forty years, why would it be worth killing over now?"

Quinn scoffed, like I'd asked the stupidest question in the world. While I was trying to think of something to say, she grabbed the binder from me and strode back to the car. She paused when she got to the car, staring at the dog park.

The brown dog was now alone in the fenced-in area, two paws up on the fence. He seemed to be staring at Quinn. And Quinn was staring back.

I'd lost track of the time while reading about Operation Mockingbird, but we must've been there over at hour. There were no other cars in the lot. No one had come or gone from the restroom in the last few minutes, and I knew what was about to happen.

I walked to the car. Quinn's eyes were fixed on the dog, who still had two paws on the fence, tongue out, tail wagging.

"Did he have tags on him?" I asked.

"No," Quinn said.

"He's abandoned, you think?"

"We've been here an hour and no sign of his owner. It's eighty degrees and there's no water in there."

"So, we're getting a dog?"

"I love him."

"Okay, but he rides in the back."

CHAPTER 20

Back in the car, Quinn convinced me to continue driving west, toward Oregon and the headquarters of Allied Regional Data Security, the firm where Tudayapi had once worked. I'd objected at first, but figured we'd come up with a better idea along the way. Plus, west meant I'd be driving toward Seattle, too.

In the back seat, Smedley—which is what Quinn was already calling her dog—was slobbering all over the three-day-old backpack that was holding the drive. He was a medium-sized dog, with a strong body, a wrinkly face, and a childlike enthusiasm. His fur was the color of milky coffee, and Quinn thought he might be part Shar Pei.

While she drove, I relayed what I'd read about Operation Mockingbird, insisting that she let me finish the whole story before interrupting. As usual, I was giving my balanced-journalist version of events, and I knew where she wanted to take it.

At least I thought I did.

"Three things," she said. "First, I already knew most of that. Second, if that's what Bernstein could get people to talk about, imagine how much went on that he never found."

I *did* agree with that. When stories are about to go public, companies, individuals, and governments have two options. The first is: don't comment, categorically deny it. The second is to step in and try to control the story, to minimize the story, blame it on a couple low-level officials, admit to some minor details and obfuscate the larger ones. It's fairly likely that, in this case, the CIA had chosen the second option.

"So, what's the third thing?" I asked, and this was when she surprised me.

"It's really not that big a deal."

Right when she said it, two epiphanies struck me almost simultaneously. First, I'd been pretending it wasn't a big deal while reading about it and while telling Quinn about it. The truth was, I felt disillusioned, angry, and betrayed. By the government, by the journalists involved, and by society for not caring about it when it came out. Despite being a sell-out myself, I figured that all along there had been *real* journalists out there doing real stories, keeping politicians and corporations honest. And I figured that when the big stories broke, they had effects that rippled through the years. I was ashamed and embarrassed that Bernstein's story hadn't made waves.

My second epiphany was about Quinn. It made perfect sense that she would say it wasn't a big deal. Not only had she known about it for years, she lived in a mental place where things much worse were happening all the time. Operation Mockingbird was, in her mind, a misdemeanor in a world of capital crimes. The reason I called it an epiphany is that it hit me all at once, not as mental recognition, but as a physical one. It was like a giant *whoosh* through my body. Like I could feel the world she lived in, a world where *of course* the CIA controls the media, just like they're watching us right now and are probably going to kill us any minute.

I asked Quinn why they'd be following us if it was no big

deal.

"Because it's not just about Operation Mockingbird."

"So, I ask again, why would they be following us? Why would they have killed Baxter and the others, why is the drive important?"

Quinn thought for a while, then said. "There are only three options. First, they know it's unimportant but it's a matter of principle. Somehow they found out that Tudayapi stole it from them, and therefore it must be destroyed on principle even though there's nothing of interest on it. Or, they don't *know* there's nothing of interest on it because they don't know *what's* on it. Those options are similar."

"So, what's the third option?"

"That there *is* something on the drive—in the binder— that they're trying to protect, but we haven't found it yet."

I felt like there was more to say, but we drove in silence for almost an hour. Every once in a while, Quinn would glance over at me like she was about to say something, but she never did. I'd like to say that I couldn't get my mind off the hard drive. I'd like to say that every fiber in my being wanted to get back to the binder, to channel my inner Bernstein and get to the bottom of the story. But I kept thinking about Greta, and the fact that I was supposed to be eating dumplings with her in about three days.

I was getting hungry, and I couldn't let myself get too far down that rabbit hole, so I started looking for somewhere to stop.

Quinn must have been on the same wavelength because, a few minutes later, she broke the silence with a "Hey! I've been there." She was pointing at a billboard advertising BUSTER'S TRAIN WHISTLE SALOON. "You hungry?" she asked.

***

After a quick stop for dog food, a leash, and a metal water bowl, we hooked Smedley to a shady tree in front of the Saloon, which was in an old brick building just off the highway.

179

They had a new-looking flat screen on the wall, and I asked the old man behind the bar if he could turn on CNN. He frowned at me, but pulled a sticky remote from behind the cash register. "Have at it," he said in a growly voice.

It was around seven, still early for a bar crowd, and the place was empty except for a few tables near the window, one of four men and one of four women. Both tables were littered with shot glasses, and the groups were talking so loudly I didn't think they'd mind—or even notice—if I turned up the sound. Quinn and I took a seat in a booth across from the bar, where she could watch Smedley through the window, and I could see the TV. I scanned through CNN and MSNBC, then landed on Fox News, the only one of the three not on commercial. Two talking heads were debating something or other, and I turned down the volume.

"Why the hell do you want to watch the news?" Quinn asked, dismissively, opening the binder.

"Just want to see how they're covering the shooting." That's what I always said when someone asked me why I still watched cable news. But, secretly, I was hoping I'd learn something new about the shooting. Quinn was the sort of person who was sure she knew the truth and had no interest in hearing alternatives. I'm the sort of person who, even though I know cable news is mostly infotainment, watches anyway because I can pick up kernels of truth from the way it's being presented.

All of a sudden, the windows along the far wall of the bar began to shake a little, followed by the floor beneath us. It wasn't anything extreme, and at first I thought I was imagining it.

"Do you feel that?" Quinn asked.

"I'm glad it's not just me. Earthquake?"

"Train."

The glasses on the nearby tables were rattling slightly, as well. The women at the table let out a simultaneous shriek. Then a bell rang near the kitchen, louder even than the shriek, which was still echoing in the room. A woman leaned out of the kitchen and shouted. "Dollar shot for the next thirty seconds."

Quinn tugged on my sleeve, trying to get my attention. She was pointing at a sign on the wall, next to an old Highway 34 sign.

All shots a dollar while the train passes. If the building isn't shaking, you're paying full price.

The men and women by the windows all had their hands up and Quinn thrust hers up as well. The rattling slowed, then ended, and the old man poured refills for everyone at the tables, then stopped at ours. "Brown or clear?" he asked Quinn.

"Definitely brown," Quinn said.

A minute later, she was staring at a chipped shot glass of what I assumed was whiskey of some kind. "Don't do it," I said. "Or, if you must, have some of the free peanuts first."

She pondered this for a moment, ate a few salted peanuts from the bowl the old man had brought, then began studying the binder.

The news was back on, leading with new developments in the shooting at *The Gazette*. An LVMPD spokesman named David Matterson had given a press conference that day at a small wooden podium with the seal of the department taped crookedly to the front. Behind him, a half dozen officers and supervisors stood, looking concerned. It was the same setup they'd had the morning after the shooting, when I'd seen coverage in the airport.

The only difference was that Captain Shonda Payton wasn't standing to the left of Matterson as she had the previous day. On that first morning, when a question came up about the crime scene, Matterson had deferred to Captain Payton, who then approached the podium and said a version of, "That detail is part of the ongoing investigation and we won't be able to comment."

But Captain Payton was nowhere to be found. Instead, to Matterson's left stood Captain Diego Vasquez, who was stepping in occasionally to offer the same refusal to comment that Captain Payton had.

"Weird," I said to Quinn, whose nose was buried in the binder. "The police officer who's been there every day isn't there. There's a new guy."

"Same suit and lie, different face."

When I covered the courts back in New York City, I had multiple sources inside the police department and often had to stop by different precincts. I realized quickly that all the same office politics and competition that happen in other organizations also happen within police departments, so I couldn't help but wonder why Captain Payton had disappeared from the podium. She spoke well, was personable and photogenic. She was a good look for the department and, having been first on the scene, added credibility to everything said on the podium. Plus, she added diversity, which police departments are usually sensitive to. So there's no way they would've replaced her unless there'd been some conflict.

I explained all of this to Quinn, who dismissed it. "Maybe she's out sick. Maybe she just doesn't want to be part of the charade."

"But that implies that she *knows* it's a charade."

Quinn finally looked up from the binder, staring at me like I'd just said the stupidest thing she'd ever heard. She held up the shot glass, said "To sheep everywhere," and threw back the whiskey. "*Of course* she knows," she continued, setting down the glass. "First on the scene. You think she didn't notice any details that don't fit into their perfect little story?"

"Are you saying you think she knows what happened, because—"

"Not at all. Not even *I'm* that paranoid. It's more likely that she noticed a few inconvenient facts that got swept under the rug because they couldn't be explained by the Baxter theory."

"Maybe so," I said.

I flipped off the TV and looked for the old man. I needed to order some food, but he was chatting with the table of men. Then the walls started rattling again and Quinn's hand shot up.

***

An hour later, we'd eaten burgers and fries, Quinn had downed her second and third shots, and I was studying a section of pages that were, according to Quinn, the only other interesting portion of the binder.

"It's a table," she said, her voice a little loose.

"What did you mean, 'a table'?"

She explained that on old hard drives—or "disc packs" as she preferred to call them—data was often stored in tables, just like the ones we use today in word processors like Microsoft Word. They're basically just columns and rows of information set off by thin lines or spaces. "And what happens when you make a table that's too wide for the margins of your page?"

"I call Bird," I said. "He knows how to fix that sort of thing."

"It splits it up to another page. The whole thing turns into a mess."

I put my hand on the binder. "A mess like this?"

"Exactly." She stacked our plates, then slid the binder to her side of the table and pulled out four pages, lining them up left to right.

I moved to her side of the booth and leaned in. She said, "It looks like a table of names that got split between pages, probably because of unreadable data in some of the columns. But look, there's a pattern on these four pages." She dragged her finger across the four pages, starting on the top left of the first page, connecting what appeared to be parts of words across the pages, while skipping over the blank spaces and gibberish in the middle and right side of each page. "Ba. Ker. Gold. Stein." Four sounds. Four pages. "Ba-ker. Gold-Stein. *Baker Goldstein.* In the original, this would have just been two columns with Baker in one column and Goldstein in the other."

"It's not a name I recognize."

"But they have to be names, right? Look at the next one down."

Again, she started on the top left of the first page and drew her finger across. "The. Odo. Rep. Etrov."

I stared at her. "That doesn't sound like a name."

"Put it together." She held a finger over the last letter on the third page and all the letters on the fourth page.

"Theodore?"

"Right," she said.

Next, she covered everything except the last six letters.

"Petrov?"

"Right!" She looked at me expectantly.

"I'm supposed to know who that is?"

"Theodore Petrov? The Brighton Beach Six?"

I had no idea what she was talking about. "He was a CIA asset during the Cold War. And no, not just in my head. The Brighton Beach Six were a gang of men—all of whom had parents that fled Russia during World War Two—who spied on Soviet nuclear programs from the late-forties to the sixties."

"And you learned about this—"

"It's fact. Public record. Even the CIA-mouthpiece newspapers *you read* acknowledge it."

"Okay, then who's Baker Goldstein?"

"I don't know, but I plan to find out."

The bar started shaking again and Quinn's hand shot up, but I gently pulled it down before the old man noticed. It was almost seven, and the bar was starting to fill up with a pretty rowdy crowd. The last thing I needed was a plastered Quinn Rivers, so I tried flattery. "Skip this round, okay? I need you to explain this to me."

She frowned, but said, "*This* is what they don't want us to know. I'll bet you anything that every name on this list is a CIA asset connected in some way to Operation Mockingbird. And I'll bet you anything that some of them have already been outed, like our friend Petrov, but some of them *haven't.*"

"And that's what they're protecting?"

"Exactly." I gave her a raised-eyebrow look as she shoveled a handful of peanuts into her mouth. At this point, skepticism was my default with Quinn.

As the bar grew louder and louder around us, we went through the names, one by one, pausing after each name to research it on Quinn's laptop. We even looked up the people Quinn thought she'd heard of, which she agreed to despite being offended that I didn't trust her. But it *did* give her the opportunity to gloat when she was right.

And she *was* right. Every time.

Benjamin Daudet was a low-level minister in the French Government in the 1950s who'd been outed as a CIA asset and effectively exiled. There was no clear connection between him and Operation Mockingbird, but Quinn noted that he'd studied at Harvard in the early 1940s, which would put him in the same time and place as others who we already knew to be connected.

Chandler Willingham was the owner of Central Paper, a pulp producer and paper supplier that had cornered the market back in the late 1800s. He wasn't mentioned in Bernstein's article, but he supplied paper to half the newspapers in the country in the mid-1900s. When Quinn proclaimed that the CIA had used his paper supplies as leverage over any newspapers that wouldn't cooperate, I asked her to stick to the facts.

Elisa Gunderson was a student at Harvard's Russian Studies Institute when the CIA began recruiting her. She died in an airplane crash in 1979, and her connection to Operation Mockingbird had been reported in one obscure book published in the late 1990s.

Then we hit a few names I knew right away, including Barry Bingham, Sr., a Harvard grad and former Navy officer who'd controlled much of the media in Kentucky, especially Louisville, in the forties, fifties, and sixties. His newspapers had won a half dozen Pulitzers under his watch. He was also listed in the Bernstein piece as a CIA cooperator, though the extent of his involvement was unclear.

Near the end of the list, we hit a name that surprised us both. He was someone we both knew of, and, of all the people on the list, he was the only one who still held a position of significant influence in the world. And he hadn't been mentioned in the Bernstein piece.

Dewey Gunstott.

CHAPTER 21

I knew Gunstott as the ninety-year-old CEO of International Family Media Holdings, one of the largest media-entertainment conglomerates on Earth. IFMH is a little like Disney, but focused on acquiring and selling media assets, rather than producing and branding their own. They're the most-powerful media organization you've never heard of.

Gunstott had been interviewed frequently and profiled at least a dozen times in the major business magazines. Though he hadn't been mentioned in the Bernstein piece, a few searches allowed us to make tangential connections between him and Operation Mockingbird.

He'd grown up just outside of Louisville, Kentucky, then attended an elite Connecticut boarding school and Harvard. He'd flown Douglas A-26 Invaders in the Pacific and, in 1947, had returned home to work at the *Louisville Courier-Journal*, one of the papers owned by Barry Bingham Sr. We couldn't find any records of Gunstott's reporting work, and in all the interviews we found, he never mentioned his time there. In fact, it wasn't clear that he'd written a single word for the *Courier-Journal*.

Three years after returning from the war, he was back on the east coast, moving from job to job at CBS, first in marketing and communications, later in programming. He ascended rapidly for about ten years before jumping ship to become the first CEO of IFMH who wasn't born into the company. He'd been CEO for over forty years and had grown the company into a behemoth.

IFMH had its fingers in everything. They owned three movie studios, a comic book company, a special effects studio, and music companies that controlled about one-fifth of the music ever commercially published. And that was just their content divisions. Their distribution included newspapers, cable companies, radio stations, theme parks, movie theaters, and more. Then there were the archives. They'd seen the streaming revolution coming and, according to reports in various business magazines, had toyed with the idea of starting a Netflix rival themselves. Instead, they'd started buying up archives, anticipating that old content would find new life on streaming digital services. So they'd bought up old movies and shows spanning the globe, specializing in Asian content for the Asian market. Specifically, China.

For the last thirty years, China had been Gunstott's obsession. Over the years, he'd made dozens of attempts to crack the Chinese market, most of which had failed. Since all media in China is government-controlled, it's not an easy task. But as the Chinese middle-class grew and Disney gained a foothold, China became an essential market, not a luxury, for IFMH.

In 2017, China became the largest movie market in the world, a title the United States had held since the medium was created. Selling TV, movies, and other content to China's growing middle class was the goal of every media company in the world. It was the largest market for potential growth left on Earth.

Of course, Gunstott's biggest competition was Disney, which had its own difficult history of trying to break into the Chinese market. But lately, things had been getting better. In 2016, they'd released three of the top films in China, including *Jungle Book* and *Captain America: Civil War*. Not to mention the $5.5 billion Disneyland Shanghai that opened that year. Disney had improved at navigating the financial and legal issues, but there were cultural conflicts as well, and Disney had made multiple missteps along the way. They'd released the film *Kundun* in 1998, for example, then apologized for its sympathetic portrayal of Tibet. Many other movies had been banned or limited:

Back to the Future: banned for "disrespectful portrayal of history."

Avatar: the 2D version was banned because of fears it would intrude on the market and because it "May lead audiences to think about forced removal, and may possibly incite violence," according to Hong Kong's *Apple Daily*. The 3D version was allowed a limited run.

Noah: banned for religious themes in the secular country.

The Da Vinci Code: banned for religious themes after a limited release.

A quick scan of the current business news results for IFMH revealed that Gunstott was on the brink of closing a massive deal with China, a deal that might finally open up the market to his movie, music, and television products.

On its face, the deal was boring. The kind of thing you wouldn't even notice or care about. But you should. Deals like this re-shape the world while you're sleeping. The basics of the deal were that China would let a lot more of IFMH's content behind their Great Firewall in exchange for greater control over that content globally through a partnership with Shanghai Pictures, a movie and TV studio that had flirted with Disney for a few years before backing out of the deal.

Gunstott's deal, which would be his crowning achievement, was set to come before the Senate Subcommittee on International Trade and Finance sometime in the next month. If it passed, IFMH profits could exceed a trillion dollars over the next ten years.

"That's it," Quinn said, knocking back her fourth shot. "The deal with China is big enough that it could have caused Gunstott and his people to go through records, to make sure he was as clean as can be."

"The deal is huge, sure, but that's the craziest thing you've ever said."

"Don't you see? They're polishing Gunstott's past?"

"He's one of the most powerful businessmen in the country. Don't you think his past has been polished?"

"Do you know *anything* about China?"

I didn't know much, which I was ashamed of, but I didn't admit it to Quinn. I just gave a noncommittal grunt. Right out of her playbook.

"China and the CIA go WAY back. In the states, news that Gunstott is a CIA asset—"

"*Was* a CIA asset. We don't know if he still is."

"Fine. Whatever. But if people in the U.S. found out, it wouldn't even make page one of the business press because half of the higher-ups are *also* friendly with the CIA. Same reason the Mockingbird revelations didn't get any play outside of the alternative press, which *Rolling Stone* used to be."

"But in China?"

"In China, a revelation like this about Gunstott might be enough to derail their approval of the IFMH deal. It's the kind of affront that could sway them."

It was possible, but not plausible, and I wanted to get out of there before another train passed. "Let's get a hotel, okay?'

"I'm not leaving until we're on the same page about this. I know that massive global conspiracies are *inconvenient*. But you've gotten a lot smarter since I met you. You've got to see my point."

I waved at the old man behind the bar, who quickly brought us our check. "So, lemme get this straight. You think that Gunstott was tracking down any records that could have outed him as a part of Operation Mockingbird, he found out about the drive, somehow learned it was stolen by Tudayapi, then tracked it to Baxter, then—"

"Yes, and we already know what happened at *The Gazette*. At least part of it. My bet is that the shooters got to Baxter's, made him admit to giving the drive to James, then tracked James to *The Gazette*, and brought Baxter with them."

"Why not wait until James was alone to kill him?"

"Well, two *obvious* reasons. First, James was going to a *newspaper*. They probably thought he was going to leak the contents of the drive. The ultimate disaster. Second, a mass shooting is the perfect cover. From their perspective, taking out six people as opposed to one or two is just collateral damage."

Even when sober, Quinn's mind was like a drunk driver— full of confidence and bravado, but likely to fly off a cliff and crash on the rocks below. And, after four shots, she was moving way too fast for me. My mind wanted to sober up, slow down, and go step-by-step.

"Okay," I said. "If I grant that. Here's a question: if the CIA somehow found out that a drive marked for destruction *hadn't* been destroyed, that would lead them to ARDS, then to Tudayapi, right? But she'd already traded it to Baxter. So how could the CIA have found Baxter, how could they have learned he had the drive, without contacting Tudayapi? She would have told us if they'd—"

"How stupid are you?"

"Fairly stupid, apparently."

"Tudayapi would have posted about it on message boards, collector sites."

"So the CIA just happened to be looking around on the message boards she happened to be posting on?"

"They have search tools, bots. And they have hackers as good as James and Innerva working for them, combing the Dark Web and doing jobs for them as needed. This one would have been easy. 'Hey, Jimbo, we need to track down a 1968 IBM 2314 that was supposed to have been destroyed but wasn't.'"

"And it just so happened that Tudayapi was posting about it, or selling it, at the same time? Okay, I buy it." I didn't buy it, but I wanted to hear the rest of her theory. "But how would the CIA have been alerted to the fact that it wasn't destroyed in the first place?"

This stumped her, and Quinn rose suddenly to use the bathroom. Though she hadn't been slurring, I realized immediately that four shots were hitting her hard. At first, she seemed steady, probably a combination of sheer will and leaning her hip on the table. But the first step towards the bathroom caused her to stumble, then crash into the bar stools three feet away.

I jumped up to steady her, but she waved me off and used the backs of the stools as props, walking sideways and crossing one hand over the other until she made it to the end of the bar. From there, she had the walls of a narrow hallway to prop herself up as she made her way to the restroom.

I told the old man I was driving, paid him, and asked him not to serve her any more. He just nodded and frowned. I was guessing he didn't like out-of-towners.

Quinn returned from the restroom on slightly more solid footing.

"I splashed some cold water on my face," she said.

"I paid. Let's get out of here, okay?"

Her words were sloppy and she was exuding a quality I wasn't used to. Sweetness. A kind of flirtatiousness and openness I had never seen from her. She said, "Did you bring me here to get me drunk, Alex?"

"You'll recall, Ms. Rivers, that I objected to each and every one of those shots."

"Are you gonna try to sleep with me?"

I didn't say anything at first. It was one of those awkward moments where a realization hits me faster than I can form it into words, and I have to translate it from my body to my brain and mouth. The realization was: I had never thought of Quinn sexually—not once—even though, by any standards, she was strikingly beautiful. It wasn't like me, either. Even when I was with Greta at our happiest, I thought about having sex with other women. And she thought about having sex with other men. This was the kind of thing we could talk about, though she was always more comfortable with it than I was. Thinking about something and doing it are two totally different things, she assured me.

So, under normal circumstances I would have been sizing Quinn up from the moment I met her. But the combination of confusion, adrenaline, and fatigue had all taken precedence. Now, even though there was no piece of me that believed Quinn and I were a good match, I couldn't help but think about Greta and the fact that she might be in bed with some hotshot right now.

Even if Quinn *were* interested, there was no way I was going to sleep with her after four shots. To be honest, even thinking about it kind of made me sick to my stomach. I felt protective of her, like I had about Greta and Rebecca during the pregnancy. It sucked to admit it to myself, because she drove me crazy, but I cared about her.

"No," I said. "I am *not* going to try to sleep with you."

I studied her face to see if I could read disappointment or relief, but she just looked confused, and I thought she might have forgotten her original question.

"Let's go," I said.

CHAPTER 22

I paid cash at a cheap motel three blocks away from the bar. It was closer to the center of town and still within sight of the tracks, but the manager assured me there would be no rumbling.

The room was small, but clean, and Quinn collapsed on one of the double beds as I stowed the bags and turned around to sneak Smedley up the external staircase. By the time I returned, Quinn was asleep, and snoring loudly. Even when Smedley jumped onto the bed, licked her face, and cuddled in next to her, she didn't budge. Not wanting to move her, I fetched an extra blanket from the closet near the bathroom and covered them up. Then I took off her shoes and tucked her feet into the blanket. Smedley poked his head out from under the blanket as if to check that everything was okay, then closed his eyes.

On a whim, I called the non-emergency line of the LVMPD from the motel phone. When I asked for Captain Shonda Payton, I was told that she wasn't in—which I expected—then transferred to her voicemail. Though I didn't trust my read completely, when I'd seen her on TV I got the sense that she was a good cop, an honest cop. If Quinn was right that she knew something, I wanted her to know that someone else out there did as well.

"Captain Payton, hello. This is Alex Vane from *The Barker*. A close friend of mine died in the shooting at *The Gazette*. The story that's being reported in the media is false, and I can't help but wonder if you know that. I can't tell you where I am or how to contact me, but please, when I call again, take the call."

I just hoped that she would.

I lay on the second bed, staring at the ceiling.

Quinn's minor flirtation had me thinking about Greta. It had been three days since I'd left Seattle. Our anniversary was three days away, and it felt more important than the slow-motion chase scene I was in the middle of.

When your life is threatened, or may be threatened, your survival instincts kick in right away and you act. You run. You swap cars. You drive 600 miles with a stolen hard drive and a paranoid recluse.

But right after you land in a safe space, even temporarily, you start to think about what you're staying alive for in the first place. What matters. Of course, I wanted to get home. I wanted to figure out who killed James, but most of all, I wanted to get back to Greta. And get *her* back to me. Without her, I really didn't care.

I must have read a dozen times that, when you lose someone you love, you're supposed to remember the good times. Better to have loved and lost, and so on. But that's not how my mind works. I was fixated on the period since she'd kicked me out, the dark times. The time she'd told me the truth about myself three months ago.

She'd agreed to meet me for coffee and, after two postponements, I sat in a hip coffee bar near *The Barker*, planning to sell her on number five on my stupid list: *Don't Be Lazy About Your Body*. It was about how men get comfortable and lazy in marriage. Once the thought of finding mates passes from their minds, they just kinda give up. I'd lost five pounds since the last time Greta and I had met, I'd worked out that morning so I had that healthy glow, and I'd arrived early to order a cold brew with coconut milk, which, she'd been assuring me for years, was "full of healthy fats."

She strolled in wearing a yellow spring dress and a smile that nearly melted me. She looked better than ever, like she could stop traffic or make the clocks run backward. My heart sank. As pathetic as that sounds, I felt unworthy. You have to understand, when she and I got together back in New York City in 2002, I was a bit of a playboy. We'd met at a bar, hooked up in what I thought was another one night stand, then reconnected and *stayed* connected. She was the first woman I ever lived with.

She was beautiful, smart, and honest enough with me to keep me from becoming too full of myself. As much as I was into staying fit at the time, she always ripped me for not "inhabiting my body." One time she told me that I danced like the uptight white guy that black comedians make fun of. And she was right.

Greta, on the other hand, was a bonafide dancing queen, a sex goddess. Whatever *IT* is, she had it.

There are just people out there who spend their lives in their bodies, men and women both. Greta couldn't name the Chancellor of Germany, where her mother was from. And she didn't know the currency they use in Japan, where her dad was from. She inhabits her body. For her, being in her body all day was a good use of a day. At the time, she was a massage-therapist, working mostly with elite athletes, and I learned quickly that she knew things I'd never know.

So, the sex was transcendent, of course, but it really wasn't about sex. She affected everyone the same way. Gay men and straight women at my office noticed it, too. When she walked into a room, everyone looked up from their phones or laptops. And they didn't *stop* looking until she was gone.

Then there was the dancing. She danced like a slow-burning fire. I don't think she was an especially *good* dancer, technically, but you couldn't take your eyes off her. When she moved, it was like she'd sprung from the earth only to drag you into the central, molten core. Or maybe it was just me. Maybe that's how all men feel when they watch the woman they love dancing.

But, on that morning, when she strolled in wearing the yellow dress, I felt she was out of my league. She spotted me, got a cup of water, and sat. I had a plan. I wasn't going to play it cool or act removed. I was going to explain how *The Barker* was buying a green lifestyle blog, how I'd been eating better and working out. Then I'd express my love from a position of strength, not desperation.

But I didn't do any of that. When she sat down, the first thing she said was, "Alex, you look good. Are you finding out what happened to you these last few years?"

It took me by surprise, and it wasn't as condescending as it might sound. She seemed genuinely concerned for me. "Kind of, I guess, what do you mean?" She just looked at me, but I knew that opening up was a big deal to her, so I said, "What do you think happened to me?"

And she told me.

I already knew about half of what she said. Another thirty percent I recognized as true as soon as she said it. It was the last twenty percent that hurt.

The first eighty percent—the things I knew or kind-of knew—went something like this: about three Christmases ago, Greta and I had gone on a weekend getaway to The Cascades. Neither of us ski, but we rented a little cabin in the snow so we could reconnect. We'd had a wonderful weekend and, long story short, on our drive back into Seattle we'd decided it was time: we'd try for a baby.

But *The Barker* had been hit by another lawsuit the next day, one that sucked me back into the site. And working on the lawsuit felt good. I'd been feeling down and it gave me something to focus on, something to win at. When we settled the lawsuit, we had a lot of ground to make up. I hired Bird. The site started growing again. We'd always been early adopters, but we got out ahead on social sharing, live video, and using memes to promote stories. I even got an army of interns who each had hundreds of fake Twitter handles so, when we wanted to, we could get a story trending quickly.

At the same time, I let myself go a little. Remember how I told you that James had lost and regained the same twenty pounds over and over? For me, it was thirty. I also got less interested in sex, and, of course, in the thought of parenting.

It's a cliché, I know, but work was something I could control. I'd sit at my desk with a bag of peanut M&Ms and watch the traffic spike after a big story hit. I'd compare the number of Facebook Likes our story on Ben Affleck's divorce got compared to TMZ's story, or I'd see how fast our team of interns could get something trending on Twitter.

But, worse than getting out of shape, I got distant. According to Greta, not a day went by when I wasn't buried in my phone, darting from crisis to crisis, many of them self-created.

The last twenty percent was a total shock, and I remember it perfectly. She'd tossed her long black hair back, sipped her water, and said, "Lately, Alex, you got sad. Some men get mean or bossy or controlling. You got sad. Like you were just done being a person. One of the things I loved about you was that you had a core that wanted to do what was right. A sense of fairness, a value for the truth."

"What do you think happened?" I asked, trying my best not to sound as crushed as I felt. My head was stuck on her use of the word "loved." I could change actions and attitudes. But I knew I couldn't make her love me if she didn't any more.

"Your work," she said.

"It can't be all about how much I work."

"No, not that. That's a little thing. I know I've complained about it a lot, but it's more about what the work did to you. To your values. To your sense of what's right. *The Barker* has corrupted your *soul*."

She held the "L" in "soul" in her throat for a few seconds.

She just let it roll. It had never been about how much I was working. It was about what I'd become.

Quinn was snoring loudly now, and even Smedley was wheezing a little, so I balled up two shreds of tissue to use as earplugs and got under the covers, still thinking about what Greta had said. That day in the coffee shop, I'd been devastated, but mostly because what she'd said made it less likely she'd take me back. But now I was devastated for a different reason: I knew she was right.

I didn't like what I'd become, either, and I fell asleep wondering whether it was too late to do something about it.

CHAPTER 23

Friday, June 16, 2017

After walking Smedley in the pink morning light, we grabbed a continental breakfast and began driving west, toward ARDS.

I'd come up with an idea in the middle of the night, and I figured I'd convince Quinn on the way, and we'd never actually end up there. So, as I drove out of southwestern Idaho into eastern Oregon, I laid out my plan.

We'd go to a Copy Center and scan the contents of the binder, then send them to Bird to post on *The Barker.* He'd write a short accompanying piece, noting that the pages came from an authentic CIA hard drive from the late 1960s. He wouldn't make any attempt to synthesize the information or comment on it. And he wouldn't draw any special attention to Gunstott. He'd just post all the pages in their raw form.

In a separate article, I'd have him post the audio from Innerva, citing "a person close to the investigation" as the source. I'd dictate a bare bones story over the phone, just pulling out the highlights from the audio that most clearly called the official version of the shooting into question. We wouldn't need to go into too much detail because, within hours of publication, an army of Internet researchers and police would be analyzing every second of the audio.

Mark Twain said that a lie can travel halfway around the world while the truth is putting on its shoes. In the Internet age, a lie can travel much faster than that. But so can truth. The shooting at *The Gazette* had fallen off the front pages in the last twenty-four hours, but it was still being discussed on talk shows, and updates were still being run in many papers. The audio would thrust the shooting back to the number one topic of discussion in the country. In my view, this would keep us safer. The LVMPD would be mortified. Public pressure would force them to find out what really happened. In the end, it would lead to the real killers. To Holly and the other woman. To Kenny, if he was involved. Maybe they'd get called off our tail, if they were still on it.

And when Internet researchers started poring through the contents of the drive, someone would find Gunstott's name within an hour. He'd deny everything, of course. He'd claim that the documents were fake, and no one would be able to prove him wrong. But it was also possible that the Chinese already suspected him, or that someone out there was sitting on more evidence. With stories like this, sometimes all it takes is a trickle of information to open the floodgates.

And there was another reason I liked my plan. If I put out a story like this, Greta would respect it. Pitching it to Quinn, I liked it, too. Like I was returning to what I'd loved about journalism in the beginning.

When I'd finished pitching her my idea, Quinn was staring out the window. At first, I thought she'd stopped listening, but I was wrong.

"Your idea assumes three falsehoods," she said. "One: that we're not being followed right now, that they don't know that we haven't yet shared the information with anyone, that if they see us copying the binder they won't just shoot us, that—"

"But—"

"Don't interrupt. I let you talk. Let *me* talk."

It was the longest she'd let me talk without interrupting, and I owed her a chance.

She said, "I *know* your objection. It's that if they wanted us dead, we'd be dead. That if they *were* following us, we'd know. But you're wrong. Remember the Fremont Street Experience, Alex? They *were* following us, but they *weren't* trying to kill us. They were keeping us in their sights. You have to remember that people are sometimes more valuable alive than dead, as long as they're under control." She paused, waiting for me to object, but I didn't say anything. "Okay, two: you assume that leaking that audio wouldn't immediately get us killed. Think about it. They almost certainly don't know we have it. If we leaked it, that's like declaring war on them. On the CIA. You don't do that and live."

"What if we leaked it to a different site, so it couldn't be tied to me?" It hurt me to say it. Even there, driving with conspiracy-theorist Quinn Rivers and her dog, Smedley, and possibly being followed by the CIA, my journalistic instincts had kicked in. I wanted that audio on *my* site. *I* wanted to break the story.

"Doesn't matter," Quinn said. "If they wanted, they could have been in your email before it arrived, which is why they *might* already know we have it. The only reason I assume they don't is because we're still alive. If it leaked, they'd figure out quickly that it had been recorded over the phone. They'd likely end up at Innerva, who has disappeared. Eventually, they'd end up at you."

"What's your third problem?"

"You assume people will care."

"But—"

"No, Alex, seriously. You live in a world where things tend to go right, where, despite setbacks, things come up roses. Where you can be an asshole for a decade and your wife stays with you. Where you can sell out and become a major player in the end of journalism, but publish just enough real stuff to sleep at night on your bed of cash. If you told me the truth, you'd probably admit that, on some level, you believe all of this is just a misunderstanding, that in a few days you'll be back at *The Barker* drinking coffee. Everything back to normal. And I bet you still think Greta will come back to you." She paused. "You do, right? I mean, you may have to work at it, you may have to make a slight effort, but you're tall and rich and white and handsome. Things tend to just work out for guys like you. It's not your fault. You've had a pretty good life. You're lucky."

"What does any of that have to do with my assumption that people will care about this story?"

"You like to believe that, if you just put the raw facts out there, *the people* will somehow kick into gear, find the truth, and so on. That an army of truth seekers will expose the corruption, harness the intelligence of their deepest selves, and expose the real enemy."

"And you don't?"

"It could happen. *Could.* But it usually doesn't. Remember the WMDs in Iraq? What happened when it turned out they weren't there, and the evidence had been fabricated, largely by the CIA, on orders from Cheney?"

"Well the—"

"*Nothing.* Nothing happened. Conservatives and hawks thought, 'Well, we needed to go to war, so it's okay to manufacture the evidence to get us there.' Liberals thought, 'Damn Cheney! I think I'll post about it on a message board, eat a salad, then go buy a Prius so I can feel superior as I suck the remaining juice out of the earth at a slightly slower rate than conservatives.' But do you know what most people thought?" She turned to pet Smedley, who was now resting his paws on the divider between the two front seats. She sounded resigned. "Nothing. They didn't even notice."

We drove along in silence for a good ten minutes. I didn't mind her thoughts about me. Hell, I'd had half of them myself. But I didn't agree with her about anything else. To me, it wasn't as black and white as she was trying to make it. And I was starting to believe that there was a deeper reason behind her pessimism, one she didn't want to admit. Or one she wasn't even aware of. As much as Quinn's paranoia had been proven right over the last few days, she had no instinct to share the truth with others. The opposite was true: she wanted to keep it to herself.

The same paranoid state of mind that had concluded that the CIA was after her—especially *her*—also assumed that she was the *only* person who could make the situation right. And my guess was that that's why she wanted to go to ARDS. She'd finally gotten a piece of real, verifiable information, and she wanted it to be hers, to horde it. In that moment, she reminded me of Gollum. But instead of an all-powerful ring, she had a binder, a hard drive, and a 31-minute audio clip.

Finally, I said, "So, what's *your* plan? I still don't get what we would actually *do* at ARDS."

"We have to finish this ourselves. We are only half a day away. When we get there, we'll be able to find out what's really going on, who's really after us. Then we connect the dots, send all the info somewhere safe, and disappear."

There was no way I was going to disappear, but I didn't tell her that. And I was starting to get pissed. "But *how* will we find out what's really going on? Why *in God's name* would we go there?"

"Where else would we go?"

"What...I...anywhere."

"Think about it," Quinn said, and, clearly, she had. "Allied Regional Data Security is the biggest data security firm in the west, outside of California. Tudayapi said over half of their contracts come from government or intelligence. They're a major player. It answers the question I've had since the minute Baxter was framed for the shooting."

"What question?"

"When Gunstott ordered that his past be scrubbed clean, how did the CIA know the drive *hadn't* been destroyed? How did this come to the surface *now*, of all possible times? If Tudayapi stole it years ago, why now?"

I'd wondered that, too, but dismissed it as something I wasn't going to be able to figure out. But Quinn had a theory.

"At first, I thought that maybe they'd been patrolling message boards or antique computer resale sites, looking for old CIA stuff. But they couldn't have found the drives by chance. There are hundreds floating around, and they'd have no reason to believe these particular ones were special. Tudayapi never posted photos, and the sticker would have been the only identifying mark. So somehow they found out that these particular drives hadn't been destroyed."

I knew where she was going with this. "An audit?"

"Exactly," Quinn said. "A *huuuuge* part of government and intelligence budgets goes for audits. Whole companies that just follow paper trails to make sure something that was supposed to happen actually happened. The way I see it, Gunstott somehow ordered his team to double and triple check every bit of his past. Track down the paper trail on everything he's ever done. Opposition research on himself, essentially."

"And you think there was some record somewhere of an audit of old CIA data or data destruction, and they found a discrepancy?"

"And that discrepancy was the two hard drives."

"That makes *no* sense. If that was the case, they would have just gone straight to Tudayapi. Taken the drives, killed her, whatever."

"But she no longer had them."

"Right, but even if she'd sent them to Baxter, they still would have ended up at her house first. And they..."

I trailed off, knowing what Quinn was going to say. I didn't want to have to listen to her say it.

I opened my mouth, but nothing came out.

Well, not nothing, but not the well-reasoned objection to her faulty thinking I'd planned. "Oh no," I heard myself whisper. "Oh God, no!"

PART THREE

CHAPTER 24

They *had* visited Tudayapi.

Before we got there.

That was the only possible explanation, and Quinn had figured it out somewhere back in Idaho, through what I imagined was a bit of a hangover. She watched as my mind raced. Someone—the CIA or Gunstott's goons—had found out that the drives hadn't been destroyed. They'd traced the drives to Tudayapi's job for ARDS, then to her. They'd shown up at her door, but she'd already sold the drives. Rather than kill her, they'd used her to locate Baxter. They'd probably planned to kill her after killing Baxter, but once things got out of hand, once I got the drive and escaped, they'd figured out we were heading for her, and they'd used her again.

It explained why we hadn't been followed out of Las Vegas. Or, it explained that we *had* been followed, but that Tudayapi had been reached before we got there. It explained why she'd been willing to help us. Whoever was following us used Tudayapi to try to find out what we knew.

But the revelation raised more questions than it answered.

Quinn saw the look on my face, and she read me right. "They were there. *Before* us. They got to Tudayapi."

"I'm there," I said. "But, why? If they were willing to kill Baxter, to kill James and everyone else at the Gazette, why..."

I trailed off. My mind was dancing around from theory to theory. I was bordering on panic. If they'd been to Tudayapi's before us, they could have bugged her house, even our room, our car.

Quinn said, "For some reason, we're more valuable alive than dead."

"How'd you figure it out?" I asked.

"The loft."

"Do I want to know what was up there?"

"At this point it's too late anyway—"

"Too late for what?"

"Anything. I just mean, knowing or not knowing won't help you."

"So?"

"She has a Dark Web data center. She stores data for criminals. Knowing what I know of her, it's probably Chinese gangsters, hackers, or Bitcoin miners."

"So?"

"My guess is that she got flipped. Whoever is after us got to her first and let her stay in business as long as she helped them. Helped them with us and, probably, agreed to help them with others. Someone like her is valuable."

"So, back to the original question. Why in God's name would we go to ARDS now?"

"They're messing with us, Alex. And it's the only way to take back the power."

***

ARDS was about twenty miles northeast of Eugene, Oregon, and we had two possible routes.

I argued that we should take Interstate 84 northwest, then cut south on Interstate 5. We'd probably have more consistent cellphone reception that way, which would be good if we needed to use Quinn's laptop. Plus, we'd be around more people.

But Quinn wanted to take the more-direct route through Central Oregon. Small highways. Small towns. But slower speed limits and more isolation.

Our disagreement made me think of my fights with Greta. In my mind, when deciding on a driving route, you start with time. What's the quickest route? All other considerations are secondary. But Greta lives her life like a work of art, and timing would be one of the last things she'd consider. Greta might base an entire route on a single factor that appeared dubious to me. I could see her next to me, in Quinn's spot, staring at the map. "Oooohhh, if we take State Highway 73, we can go through a town called Lavender. I wonder if they have lavender fields there? Let me check." She'd Google it while I grabbed the map, only to find that State Highway 73 was a hundred miles out of the way. It might sound like I'm complaining, but it's one of the things I love most about her.

Quinn was closer to Greta on the spectrum, but she didn't treat life like a work of art. I was beginning to think that she treated her life—or at least these last few days—like a movie she was starring in. Sure, interstates are efficient. That's what they're there for. But they are boring. Small highways, small towns, a huge forest that we'd be passing through at dusk: these were things that Quinn could get behind. If she was going to get nabbed by the CIA, it should be at a lonely gas station bordering a small artichoke farm in rural Oregon, not at a sprawling rest stop on Interstate 84 surrounded by SUVs and moms and dads and kids.

I thought it would be better to be surrounded by people. If we were being followed, we'd be safer around people. But Quinn argued that, if we were on smaller roads, it would be easier to tell if we were being followed.

"Why do we need to know if we're being followed? Why is that the deciding factor? Don't we just want to get to ARDS and find out what's going on?"

But I knew the answer before the words came out of my mouth. To Quinn, finding out *was* the goal. Proof she was being followed was what she wanted.

She said, "We need to know exactly who we're dealing with."

And that's when it hit me. Quinn didn't think we were going to make it out of this. She viewed the whole world as a web of powers outside of her control. Credit scores. Big tech companies. ARDS. The CIA. You don't beat those powers. And if you're not going to make it out alive, the best you can hope for is to be proven right.

"Quinn, do you think you'll be alive in a week?"

She shrugged, like it didn't even matter, and I knew I was right. I also knew I'd give her what she wanted. We took her route.

***

Highway 20 passed through a dozen tiny towns like Burns, Riley, and Brothers, then cut through the Willamette National Forest and its nearly two-million acres of mountains, canyons, winding streams, and endless evergreens. We'd filled up the tank before entering the forest, and stopped around nine to catch a few hours of sleep at a turnout.

We figured that ARDS would open early, and we planned to be there first thing.

I woke up around 4 am with the first light, and got out of the car to pee and take Smedley for a walk. The air was wet and rich with the smell of cedar, which reminded me of my hometown, Bainbridge Island.

When we got back on the road, I drove and tried to talk to Quinn about a plan for our arrival. But she was quiet. A couple times I even tried to make small talk, but she just ignored me. For a while I thought she was sleeping, but each time I tried to talk to her she kind of flinched and almost looked at me. It was an active kind of ignoring.

We exited the forest just as dawn broke, a faint yellow-pink light sneaking through the trees. And we were only twenty miles from ARDS. The wireless signal on Quinn's laptop was working again and she decided to look up ARDS online so we'd know what we were looking for.

And that's when Quinn freaked out.

We were coming out of a deep valley at the edge of the forest when she started shaking. The laptop was on her lap, but I couldn't see the screen. Her arms were wrapped around her, like she was hugging herself, and her shoulders were shaking in what looked like an involuntary twitch.

"Quinn, what's wrong."

Nothing.

The shaking slowed and eventually stopped. I went back to watching the road. "Look," I said, pointing at a road sign. "Ten miles to Coburg. Let's talk about how we're going to approach this. I think you should do the..."

The shaking was back, but worse this time, and she'd closed the laptop. I kept one eye on the road while watching her out of the other. Her eyes were closed and she was shaking, subtly but steadily, her whole body moving in little ripples from her legs all the way to her head.

"Quinn?"

Nothing.

"Quinn?"

Smedley was sitting up in the back seat, staring at her. He had that concerned look that dogs sometimes get when their owners are in distress.

I just kept driving, saying "Quinn" every minute or so to make sure she knew I was there. Her shakes didn't seem to be getting worse, so I just kept going. I wondered whether she'd read something about ARDS that had scared her, but I doubted she could have found anything especially interesting in the couple minutes she'd been online.

I saw ARDS from a few hundred yards away. It was located about a hundred feet off the highway, up on a hill. It was a low, hulking series of rectangular buildings surrounded by a surprisingly high fence, and, as we got closer, Quinn's shaking increased to the point that I was genuinely worried. I pulled into a little turnout, from which we could see ARDS above us and to the right. Building after building, more than I could see, all flat-roofed and grey, some surrounded by small fences within a larger perimeter fence. The outside fence was dotted with tall lights every ten yards and, as I watched them, they turned off as the sky lightened.

An entry gate sat about fifty yards out from the main fence and, for the first time, I realized that they probably weren't going to let us in.

"Quinn. I don't know what's happening. But I'm about to call an ambulance. I—"

"I'm not going in," she said.

"Well, judging by that gate, neither of us is going in."

I was trying to be funny, but it didn't land the way I thought it would. She turned and met my eyes. Her whole face looked hollow, terrified, like she'd just witnessed a crime.

"Quinn, what happened?"

"It looks just like the picture I found online. It reminds me of...where I used to stay."

"Where?"

"Seven Homes Rehabilitation Center. It's a psychiatric hospital in Texas. I spent time there years ago. The fence, the buildings. It looked just like this. The psychiatric state, the prison system, the military industrial complex, they must have the same architects."

She hadn't mentioned spending time in a psychiatric hospital, but it didn't surprise me. The shaking had steadied into a slow rocking, and it was clear she was in some sort of shock. I reached back and gave Smedley a little tap on the side. He took the hint and climbed into Quinn's lap, though he was big enough that his tail landed on my arm.

Quinn wrapped her arms around him. "You have to go in, Alex. I can't."

"They're not going to let us in anyway."

"They might."

"They won't."

"Try."

I looked at the entry gate, where it seemed like a shift

change was underway. Two men had parked a golf cart at the gate, and two others were stepping out of the structure behind the gate. They seemed to chat for a minute before the two who had been on the cart stepped into the structure and the two who'd been in the structure drove down the road toward the complex of buildings.

Quinn reclined the seat all the way, closed her eyes, and lay back. Smedley took the opportunity to start licking her face, and the absurdity of the situation struck me all at once.

I knew what I had to do.

CHAPTER 25

Saturday, June 17, 2017

I drove Quinn to a friendly-looking coffee shop in town. She took her bag and said she'd tie Smedley up on the post out front, grab a coffee and a scone, and read through the binder. She had settled down as I drove away from ARDS, and assured me she'd be fine for an hour or so. Plus, the coffee shop had a big water bowl for dogs right outside, next to a couple metal tables on the sidewalk.

I promised to be careful, and drove back to the security gate alone.

As I slowed the car, a middle-aged guy with short black hair leaned out of the structure, which looked like a toll booth. His green uniform seemed too big for his thin frame. Before I could launch into the speech I'd planned, he said, "ID, please." He didn't even look up.

"N-n-no," I sputtered. "I don't work here or anything.

I'm—"

"ID, please!"

It wasn't a request. I handed it to him and, as he inspected it, I noticed another man in the booth. He was taller, filled out his uniform with thick arms and a bulking chest, and had a phone pressed to his face. His eyes were locked on mine.

The first guy handed me back the ID. "Mr. Vane. They want you in building three. Pull up there, to the right." He stepped out of the booth and pointed at a small structure set off to the right of the main complex. Like the other buildings, it was a dull gray square.

"Wait, who wants me? What are you talking about?"

"I have no information about that, sir. They are expecting you, though."

"Who?"

He stepped back into his little booth. I glanced at buff guy, who was no longer on the phone. I got the sense that he knew more about what was going on than the first guy. I leaned my head out the window. "Hey," I called to him, past the first guy. "Can you tell me what's going on? I just—"

The gate bar lifted. The man took a seat as if he hadn't heard me, and the first guy closed the sliding window of his booth. They were done with me.

I eased the car forward, checking my rearview to see what they were doing in the booth, but they didn't seem to be doing much of anything. The small building wasn't marked in any way, but it had a dozen parking spots in front. Just like the other buildings in the complex, it was a gray square, but it had a couple cosmetic touches the other buildings didn't: two small windows, both curtained, and a clay pot of dead flowers on the porch. At least they'd tried.

Three cars were parked right up against the building and I took an empty spot next to them, grabbed the backpack with the drive in it, and strode up to the building. The door swung open as my foot hit the first step.

It was Kenny, smiling down at me.

He was wearing a suit much like the one he'd been

wearing at the airport. Beautifully cut, tan linen. Completely out of place in the moist morning air of central Oregon. He looked like he should be drinking champagne on the deck of a yacht off the coast of Dubai.

He took my hand and shook. "Alex, I'm Amand. Please come in."

"I'm not coming in," I said. "I just came to bring you this."

I swung the drive off my shoulder and set in on the top step. When I looked up, Amand offered an amused smile.

"That's very kind of you, Mr. Vane, but don't you think we would have taken the drive from you if we'd wanted it?"

"I don't know what you're doing. I know *we* don't want it or need it."

"Do you think we don't know that you have the printout?"

That pretty much confirmed what we'd figured out about them getting to Tudayapi's before us.

"How did you get her to flip?"

He just smiled, studying me.

"It doesn't matter that we printed it. There's nothing on it that isn't already public. For the life of me I have no idea why it was worth killing over."

"We haven't killed anyone."

I stared at him for a moment, trying to figure out what kind of lie he was telling. There were three options. First, he could have known I had the recording. So, lie number one was, "I have to lie, but we both know the truth about the shooting." The second was that he knew about the shooting, but didn't know *I* knew. So, lie number two was, "I really want to convince you that I'm telling the truth." And the third option, which I immediately dismissed, was that he *didn't* know about the shooting, that he'd been brought in later, and sincerely believed that no one had been harmed in pursuit of the drive.

Amand was wearing a constant smile, like he was such a phony that he had a fake look of sincerity plastered across his face at all times. When he insisted that they hadn't killed anyone, his cheeks had tightened a little. He said it with a little more emphasis than he would have if he knew that I knew the truth about the shooting. My best guess was that he was selling me the second type of lie because—and I had to agree with Quinn on this—if they knew we had the recording, I didn't think this would be going so smoothly.

And since the recording was the only thing I had going for myself, I was glad he seemed not to know about it.

"Why'd they let me through the gate?"

"Please, why don't you come in?" He stepped out of the doorway and onto the top step, avoiding the backpack, which he hadn't even acknowledged. He gestured toward the open door like he was inviting me up for coffee and cookies. His smile was so phony, so fixed on his face, you could mistake him for a mannequin. But I realized right away that I hated him because he reminded me of myself at my worst.

I stepped up and he headed back into the building.

I grabbed the backpack and followed him in.

***

The inside of the building was nicer than I expected. Amand led me through a foyer and down a wide hall into what I assumed was his office. The first thing I noticed were two large pictures on the wall. The first was of a boy with a cheesy grin and a baseball uniform, kneeling on a patch of the greenest grass I'd ever seen. He was 10 or 11 and, judging by his uniform, he played for *Eugene Lumber and Paint*. "Your son?" I asked, gesturing at the photo.

He nodded, but I already knew it was.

The second picture was a close-up of a beautiful little girl with curly black hair—his daughter, I assumed. She was leaning into a water fountain, the water spraying her nose as she giggled.

"Do you keep pictures of your kids here to make people think you're a regular guy?"

"Alex, please," he said, sitting down in a black ergonomic chair, the same kind we have at *The Barker*. I sat across from him in a matching chair, a smooth, black-lacquered desk between us. "You're treating me with such suspicion."

As I was staring at him, I flashed to our conversation in the airport. I'd known that something was a little off about it. But, in retrospect, it was quite impressive. Assuming that Innerva handing me the drive had been the catalyst for this whole thing, he and Holly had researched me and concocted a story that I'd believe in under twelve hours. They'd learned enough about me, my business, and the happenings in our field to be able to convince me they were corporate headhunters. Sure, I'd been exhausted and in shock from James's death, but still, it was an impressive feat of bullshitting. And, in a sense, they *were* corporate headhunters.

"Look," I said, "I just wanted to give this drive back to you. You followed me to the airport, you chased me through Las Vegas for it, you—or someone—chased us through Nevada and into Idaho. I don't want anything to do with this anymore. I'm leaving it here, I'm catching a bus back to Seattle, where I want to get on with my life."

"Alex, you asked earlier why we let you through the gate. Would you still like to know the answer?"

"Yes."

He leaned over and reached a hand under the desk. I flinched, thinking for a half-second that he was going to pull out a gun. His hand came back up with a sparkling water. Perrier in a little green bottle.

But he'd noticed my flinch. "Alex, you really need to calm down. We are the good guys, like you." He slid the water across the table, then retrieved another. "They switched to plastic bottles a while back," he said. "But it's still good. I keep a mini-fridge under my desk. I quit drinking ten years ago." He twisted the cap off the bottle and it gave a little hiss. "These are my new booze."

"Why are you telling me this?"

"I want you to trust me, Alex. I truly do." His shiteating grin was gone. He'd grown warm and friendly. "You don't strike me as a fundamentally cynical or paranoid person, Alex. Give me fifteen minutes and I think you'll see that we're on the same side here."

"Why'd you let me in?"

"I'll tell you, but I think maybe you already know."

"Quinn?"

"Yes, you had the sense to leave her elsewhere. She's not the type we welcome here. You, on the other hand..."

"Why me?"

"We figure you might be reasonable."

"About what?"

"You run a business in America. A very successful business. A very *influential* business. We exist for the purpose of protecting American business—and thereby, protecting Americans—from foreign and domestic threats."

"Who is *we*?"

"Allied Regional Data Security."

"But who do you work for?"

"It's complicated, Alex. How familiar are you with post-9/11 U.S. security systems?"

"Not very."

A smile flashed across his face. He leaned forward in his chair. "'You sleep under the blanket of freedom that I provide, and then question the manner in which I provide it.'"

It was a line from *A Few Good Men*, a bad Jack Nicholson impression. But I chuckled because, I had to admit, I loved that movie. I was softening on him slightly, and I decided to play along. "And you would rather I just said *Thank You*, and went on my way?"

He gave a little fist pump, pleased that I'd recognized the line. "Actually, Alex, we'd rather you *join us*."

I said nothing.

"By bringing the drive here, by not bringing that unfortunate woman, and through years of actions big and small, which I've learned about only in the last few days, you've shown yourself to be a great candidate."

I was playing it cool, and I gave him a look like I didn't know what he was talking about, but I was afraid that I did.

He said, "A candidate for *what*, you're probably wondering.

Alex, we'd like you to partner with us at ARDS. Our job is to protect the security interests of the U.S. We have partners all over the world, and we'd like you to join."

"Is that why you haven't killed me?"

"Alex, you have the wrong idea entirely. We don't kill people except in very rare circumstances, and only when authorization has been given and grave national security risks are present."

"Define *grave*," I said, but he just resumed grinning.

I wanted to dive across the desk and wipe the smile off his face. But besides the fact that he could probably kill me with one hand, I didn't want to let him know what I knew about the shooting at *The Gazette*.

He continued, "The contents of that drive are unimportant in the overall scheme of things. We know what's on there now, and we know it's not enough to do any damage to anyone. As far as we are concerned, that case is closed."

I was beginning to trust this guy, and I hated myself for it. "If it was a CIA hard drive, why were you chasing us? Why not them?"

"Ha! Now that's a *complicated* issue."

"But there must be someone in charge, someone giving the orders."

He smiled at me like I was a child. "Alex, do you know how many people work directly and indirectly for the U.S. security system?"

"I don't know, twenty thousand total? Not counting the military."

"One point two million. And over two-thirds work for private contractors."

That didn't sound right, but my read on this guy was that he was relaxed, knowing he was in charge, but he was also trying to convince me of something. Back when I was a journalist, my editor loved to remind me not to have "bad guys" in a news story. Even the criminals, the drug dealers, the murderers, are the heroes of their own stories. Society might not like what they do, but journalists have to understand their motivations if they want to write about them accurately. I thought of my old editor while talking to Amand because, while it was clear to me that he was the villain, the longer we spoke, the less I felt that Amand saw *me* that way. To him, I was a naive kid who needed to be educated. And, once I was, *of course* I'd agree with him.

He continued, "I'm one of 800,000 men and women servicing American security interests from within a private company. Alex, the world of security the government created in response to 9/11 has become so massive, so unwieldy, and so secretive, that no one knows how much money it costs, how many people it employs, how many programs exist within it, or exactly how many agencies do the same work. And no one is in charge."

He paused for dramatic effect, stood, did a lap around the desk, and sat back down. "And this is a *good* thing, Alex. A great thing. You know the saying, 'To kill a snake, cut off the head,' right? U.S. security doesn't have a head, and therefore it can't be killed."

He was growing excited as he talked, like he was pitching me a story I just couldn't pass on. "Don't you feel safer knowing that there are men like me protecting your interests? There's a reason we're called Allied Regional Data Security. It's all about data these days. For centuries, we spoke to people, built relationships in foreign countries. *Diplomacy.* Now, half of U.S. intelligence is gathered by listening to recorded cellphone calls and reading emails. Most of this information, known as signals intelligence, or *sigint,* is funneled into a steel and glass building twenty-five miles north of the State Department in Fort Meade, Maryland, the headquarters of the NSA. I've met some of those losers. They get off on eavesdropping on phone calls and reading emails. They know who's sleeping with whom, who has a sick kid, who's pissed at his in-laws. As long as you're not hurting America, you're safer than ever. Guy like you should love what we do."

"I guess whether one loves it depends on your definition

of 'hurting America.'"

"It does, but my bet is that you and I have similar definitions. You're no activist, Alex."

He was right, of course. I was aware of all sorts of problems in the world, but I'd never set about to fix them. "I'd say I'm conscious of many of the things I choose to stay unconscious of."

"Perfect, Alex. And you help millions of Americans remain unconscious, as well."

It was clear he meant that as a genuine compliment, but it hurt like hell. "That's the exact opposite of what journalism is supposed to do," I said, defensively.

"Please, Alex. Let's be grown-ups here. We're partners, or about to become partners. We both know that journalism hasn't served that purpose much lately, if it ever did. We both know that most of what goes on is not fit for public consumption. Information is a game. It's always been a game. Journalists play it, intelligence agencies play it. Is it even slightly surprising that there'd be back and forth there? That there always *has* been? Why do you think we don't really care about the drive? Because Americans don't care, either."

On this point, he sounded like Quinn, but I still didn't agree. Bird and I were quite good at making people care. And though we usually used those powers to get them to care about nonsense, I still believed that we could get them to care about the drive, about Gunstott. And I *knew* we could get them to care about the shooting.

Amand continued, "As pissed as people would be to know about half of what goes on in the name of national security, they'd be much more pissed if it didn't happen and we became a minor power."

I finally opened the water and downed it in three long swigs. I shook the few remaining drops around in the bottle and asked for another. I was buying time. My sense of Amand was that he was genuine. He wasn't going to hurt me. He really didn't care about the drive.

"Alex, do you know who I was before I came to ARDS?"

"Should I?"

"Well, my story got a lot of press. Your site even did a piece about me. I've been waiting to see if you recognized me, though I do look *a lot* different now."

I'd thought he looked a little familiar in the airport, but only in the way that a generic-looking person always looks a little familiar.

He smiled again and cupped his hands under his chin, as if to say, "C'mon, you really don't recognize me?"

I frowned at him.

"I was a CIA contractor in Pakistan, posing as a diplomat. Killed two guys."

"You're *that* guy?" I remembered the case. It was three or four years earlier and had gotten a lot of attention in the U.S. Amand had been arrested and charged under Pakistani law for killing two civilians. The conflict had escalated tensions between Pakistan and the U.S., but I couldn't remember the details.

"You know the story, right? I'd been there two years when I got into a scrape. I was driving through Lahore in the Punjab region, just going about my business. I was going to get a tea on my way to a meeting. I stopped at a red light and two guys came up to my car, told me to get out. They were trying to rob me, Alex. I was packing, of course, and I shot them both."

"How'd you end up getting out of that one, anyway?"

"We paid them off." He said it looking straight into my eyes, like he wanted to study my reaction.

"It's that easy?"

"They knew they'd never actually convict me, of course. It was a Pakistani stickup. Their way of lodging a protest against our covert actions there. The drone strikes, the Bin Laden killing—in which we illegally invaded their airspace—and so on. They were being the kid who won't put his damn shoes on until you give him a candy bar. Anyway, the candy bar was about $3.5 million to the families of the deceased, but you can bet that local police and judges and officials got a piece of that. Officially, it was *diyya*, which is blood money. In Islamic Law, you sometimes pay *diyya* and you sometimes pay *qisas*, which basically means an eye for an eye, or physical retaliation."

"And we wrote about this?"

"One of your blogs ran some stupid Huff-po-esque liberal shit-think about how Americans should be subject to the laws of the lands they're working in, how diplomatic immunity shouldn't apply in this case. Normal useless drivel that makes some people feel a little less evil after reading it, but, of course, changes nothing."

"So why are you telling me this?"

"Because the whole story was a lie, Alex. Of course those two guys never tried to rob me. I *murdered* them, and I'd do it again. It's *why I was there.*"

"Who were they?"

"That part I can't tell you, but let's just say they had interests adverse to those of the United States."

I shook my head in disbelief. "The whole thing of you getting robbed was a lie?"

"Listen, I want you to understand something. It doesn't matter that you know. The truth doesn't matter. We live in a post-truth world—I read about it on your site, Alex. The point is, no matter what you do, the fact that you have that information can't hurt me. There's just too much information out there and the official story is too firmly etched in the public mind."

I finished my second water and he handed me another, then said, "In a few minutes, you're going to walk out of here, with the drive. You can keep it as a souvenir. That's how much I trust you, and how much I want you to trust me. We don't care about it. All I ask is that, over the next few years, if I call you, you take the call."

"That's it?"

"Well, I'd also ask that you answer the questions I have when I call."

"What sort of questions should I expect? I don't know

anything about anything important. Anything security related."

"I agree with you on the 'security related' part, but not the 'anything important' part."

"Gossip? Stuff we know but don't print? Info you can blackmail people with? What would you want from me?"

He leaned forward, like we were conspiring together. He said, "In my business, there are formal assets and then there are 'hip-pocket' sources. People who work elsewhere but are happy to share info from time to time. We'd like you to become the latter."

I didn't like the thought of being in anyone's hip pocket, of course, but it was dawning on me that this was real. This could be over in a few minutes. He seemed not to know that I had the recording, and he was offering me a deal, and all my mind could do was calculate how long it would take to get back to Greta. "If I say yes, what happens to Quinn?"

"People like your companion can't do any real damage," he said. "She's been right that someone has been watching her, but it was never the CIA. Those guys make twice as much money as we do, so they farm people like her out to people like us."

"You didn't answer my question."

"I assure you that she'll be fine. You head back to Seattle, let her go wherever she goes, and we'll pretend like this whole thing never happened."

"Can I go back and see her? Just let her know what's going on?"

He stood and walked around to my side of the desk. "That won't be necessary, Alex. We already have people outside the coffee shop. They'll tell her."

I leapt up. "You what?"

He stepped back. "Oh, don't *worry*, Alex. We're not going to hurt her. We'll be taking her back to Vegas."

"Her place in Vegas burned down."

"Yes, we know."

"So—"

"Look, Alex, this is the *real* world. We know that you had no intention of joining the likes of her. She's not...our kind. She's crazy. She's paranoid. We will *not* hurt her, but we need her back in Vegas where we can keep an eye on her."

I wanted so badly to believe him. I mean, he had two beautiful kids who played sports. He seemed to genuinely care about America, about safety. Plus, he was just doing his job, and we've all done things we didn't feel great about because it was our job at the time. Lord knows, I have.

"How did you know where Quinn was?"

"We've been tracking you since Duck Valley."

I felt like a fool. "Do you already have her?"

"No. Like I said, two of my guys are outside the coffee shop where you left her. Cute dog, by the way."

I don't like being played. But Amand had played me and won. I was way out of my league. And then the full weight of what he'd been saying hit me. He was asking me to become a source, the twenty-first century version of the journalists who were part of Operation Mockingbird. Instead of newspapers, it was the web. And instead of the CIA, it was ARDS.

But I wasn't going to go down without a fight. "Tell you what," I said. "If your guys approach her, she might run, or be violent. She'll be more receptive if I explain this to her. We'll drive over to the coffee shop, you give me two minutes with her, and we'll part ways once I know she's gonna be okay. Like you said, she's a little crazy."

But that doesn't mean she's wrong, I thought.

CHAPTER 26

Amand called his men at the coffee shop and told them to wait for us. We took separate cars because I told him I wanted to leave straight from the meeting. On the drive over, I was trying to figure out what I'd tell Quinn. The whole situation was beyond screwed up.

Quinn had been right about Baxter being framed, but wrong about who had done the framing. I knew America had a vast web of private security contractors. But I didn't know they could be authorized to carry out a shooting like the one at *The Gazette*, at least not within the United States. Which led me to the thought, maybe they *hadn't* been authorized to do so. Maybe they'd been tasked with bringing back the drive and had tracked it to Tudayapi, then to Baxter. And when they'd reached Baxter, maybe they'd panicked. If they had been ordered to get back the drive, only to find it in the hands of two notorious data hackers, they might have panicked. Obviously, they were ex-military or ex-police. Those private security firms were a revolving door to the military and the official intelligence agencies. So, I could see the possibility that the shooting at *The Gazette* had been a last-minute thing, an on-the-spot response to learning that James and Innerva were involved. Then, probably by tracking Innerva, they'd found me and the second drive.

At first, I'd assumed that the drive had something to do with ending up on the No Fly List. But Greta had been behind that. So the whole show in the airport had just been a feeling out, of sorts. Amand and Holly had fully intended to let me get on the plane all along, to head back to Seattle and live out the rest of my life in peace. Clearly, they knew who I was, they knew what kind of stuff we published, and felt like the drive would be safe with me. Or, more likely, they had planned to have another member of their team meet me in Seattle and get the drive from me then. Not that it mattered now.

It was around nine in the morning and the coffee shop was bustling. Couples with dogs and strollers sat at outdoor tables in the morning sun, and a steady stream of customers came and went, holding paper cups and bags of pastries. But Smedley wasn't out front, as I'd expected.

I parked in the last open spot across the street, and leaned on the car while waiting for Amand to find a spot. When he emerged from around a corner a couple minutes later, he looked like he should be boarding a private jet, headed for Tangiers. He wore a long, tan coat, and was way too handsome to be a private security contractor outside Eugene, Oregon.

He gestured across the street, where two men in cheap suits were waiting, trying and failing to look casual. I had just one more question for Amand, but I had to ask it in a way that didn't let him know that I knew about the shooting. "If the drive was important enough to follow me to the airport, why are you letting me go with it now? How'd you find out what was on it?"

He frowned at me, like he was disappointed, then started crossing the street. I followed him, and it hit me as I stepped onto the curb in front of the coffee shop. "Tudayapi?"

"Sure," he said, patting me on the shoulder like we were old bros walking into a bar on a Friday night before the big game.

"She somehow made a copy?"

"She was just doing what we told her to do."

"But she said she couldn't back up the data."

He shot me a look, disappointed that I could be so naive.

"But how?"

"You don't need to know how, Alex."

I stepped up onto the curb, wondering how Quinn had failed to notice if Tudayapi had somehow backed up the data on the drive. But I wouldn't use my two minutes to ask her. My plan was to help her escape. As much as I trusted Amand to leave me alone, I didn't trust him, or any of his goons, to be as gentle with Quinn.

Amand shook hands with the two guys in front of the coffee shop, then tried to introduce me, but I was already at the large window, looking in. I didn't see Quinn, so I turned to Amand and said, "You're gonna give me two minutes, right?"

"Sure."

The coffee shop smelled like muffins and fresh roasted coffee, and they even had a bearded guy in the corner, hand-roasting coffee in small batches. It was a magical smell, and it brought me back to reality in a way nothing had for days. I missed Seattle.

I scanned the tables, which were full of older folks drinking coffee and young people drinking fancy, coffee-like beverages and staring at phones. But I didn't see Quinn.

I found two single-patron, unisex bathrooms in the back. Both were occupied, and I waited until the people came out. No Quinn.

I scanned the coffee shop again, making sure there wasn't an upstairs or a separate seating area I'd missed. But toward the back, next to the guy roasting coffee, there was a red door with a silver handle marked "Emergency Exit."

"Does an alarm go off when someone opens that door," I asked the guy.

"Uh, no. We use it for breaks and stuff. Boss doesn't like us smoking out front."

I speed-walked back out to the sidewalk, trying to conceal a smile. "Did you ever see her in there?" I asked the two meatheads next to Amand.

"Well, no," one of them said. "We just figured—"

I made a quick calculation that I should pretend to be shocked, but the truth is, I wasn't. Right when I'd realized she wasn't there, it seemed like the most obvious thing in the world. *Of course* she wouldn't wait around for me.

I turned to Amand. "What the hell?" I said. "I thought your guys knew what they were doing."

Amand just stared at them. I got the sense that he didn't like surprises, but he wasn't going to rip these guys a new one in front of me. But I could tell he wanted to. "This is unfortunate," he said. "You two start a scan of the area, talk to the people inside. Find her." Then to me, "Alex, walk with me to the car."

I followed him back across the street and he leaned on my old Thunderbird like he was posing for the cover of *BMW Owner Monthly*. "This is too bad, but it really doesn't matter. You're free to go. Head back to Seattle. We'll look for her, just to let her know what's going on. But if we don't find her, well...it's no biggie."

"But she has the binder. The print out. You know that."

"We do, but, like I said earlier—"

"You said you trust me with the information. You never said you trusted her."

"I'd recommend that at this point you just head home, Alex. Your anniversary is tomorrow, right?"

I wanted to tell him to go to hell. But, for Quinn's sake, I bit my tongue. "I'll go home, and I'll take your calls, if you promise nothing bad will happen to Quinn."

He held out his hand for me to shake. I shook it tentatively, slowly, looking him in the eyes. I believed that he wouldn't hurt Quinn. Maybe I was misreading him, but I believed that *he* believed we'd struck a deal. He smiled broadly, then gripped my hand with a strength I hadn't expected. The kind of handshake that is meant to intimidate. He said, "And you promise *never* to speak of this again."

"Yes," I said, and he let go of my hand.

With that, I got back into the car. Quinn had taken her duffle bag, so she had at least a few hundred bucks, a friendly dog, and a fake ID. Not to mention a pistol.

She'd been planning to disappear for years, and I guess she'd decided that now was the time. She was probably in some big rig truck, halfway to Canada by now. At least I hoped it was something that benign. I knew she could take care of herself—she'd been doing it for years—but I was concerned about how she'd freaked out when we arrived at ARDS. I honestly had no idea what she'd do next.

I got into the car quickly, waving at Amand as he walked back across the street, probably to give the two staffers a good dressing down. I hoped they wouldn't find Quinn. I really did.

But there wasn't much I could do about it, and Eugene was only four hours from Seattle.

CHAPTER 27

I was energized as I left town, but I crashed soon after. Halfway home, I had to stop at a rest area and sleep for a few hours because I was nodding off behind the wheel. Before I left, I got a few cups of coffee from one of those ridiculous coffee machines, and was pretty wired for the final push north.

Of course, I was eager to get back to my apartment, eager to see Bird and Mia, and eager for tomorrow. For my date with Greta. But I was preoccupied with Quinn.

We were bound to go our separate ways eventually, and I was surprised we'd stayed in the same location for as long as we had. Almost four days, altogether. Probably more continuous time than Quinn had spent with any one person in fifteen years. And more than I'd spent with anyone other than Greta. But Quinn wasn't the kind of person who would just quit and disappear. She had the binder, and my guess was that she'd try to get it out somehow.

I just hoped she wouldn't do anything to get herself in trouble.

With Quinn out of the picture, my biggest struggle during the last couple hours was resisting the urge to check my phone while driving. It was strange to be back to not looking at my phone for the ordinary reasons—safety, responsibility—rather than because it could get me killed. But I did pull off the road into a rest area once to check it, and was happy to discover a note from Mia, who wrote to confirm the plan for tomorrow.

Everything was still a go for my meeting with Greta. Mia fully expected her to show up at 10 am, expecting to meet a new client for an all-day, hands-on coaching session. She assured me that things were going fine at the office, too. Bird has mastered the art of the image-based listicle—the sort where you promise a reader a list, but the list turns out to be made up of image cards you're forced to scroll through one by one. In case you're wondering, we do that so we can sell more ads. She assured me that website traffic was up, and the office was running smoothly. She wanted to know what was going on, of course, and I wrote back promising to fill her in when I got back.

By the time I reached Tacoma, the nap and coffee had caught up with me and I felt like a new man. I passed the car dealerships, the casino, and the outskirts of the somewhat depressed, post-industrial city, and loved every billboard and building along the way. Then I saw the lights of Seattle in the distance, twinkling at me like they were welcoming me home.

The evening was gray and dreary, but the air was warm enough to roll my window down. The smell of Seattle started to fill the car: moist air, tinged with salt and exhaust fumes. I felt I'd lived a thousand lives since I'd smelled it last, and I became filled with memories and memories of memories. It was the finest smell in the world, and I was nearly in tears.

By the time I stumbled through my door, I was in love with the city again. I still have the king-sized bed I bought back when I lived in New York, which Greta and I used to keep in our guest room. As I flopped down, the bed felt softer and more supportive than ever. I pulled the thick comforter over me and knew I'd be asleep within minutes. But, as I often do, I decided to check my phone one last time, just in case anything had happened in the last couple hours.

I opened up Twitter and Facebook. A few notifications, but nothing interesting enough to keep me awake. I was no longer trending on Facebook and, with no new quotes from Greta, and no one else who would go on record, the story of my impending divorce had dried up. People were tagging me in stories here and there, but nothing major and, most importantly, nothing new.

I was about to close my phone when the little endorphin rush hit me. A new Facebook message. I swiped over to the Messenger app and saw that it was a "Message Request," a Facebook message from someone who wasn't on my "Friends" list. I got a lot of those, so I was about to ignore it. Then I saw who it was from.

Smedley Vegas.

If the name hadn't tipped me off, the link would have soon enough. I clicked it and landed on a Chinese site, *The Dissident Blog*. I couldn't understand any of the characters, of course, but I was so tired I started scanning them like I was reading in English.

根据自由新闻中国收到的文件，一个美国首席执行官，接近达成一项协议，将媒体内容提供给中国，已经是CIA最重要的资产超过50年。这些文件列出了美国中央情报局计划对 美国媒体系 统的秘密控制 -一个已经公开四十多年的 计划-家庭媒 体控股公司 CEO Dewey Guntstott 是中央情 报局的资产。 在过去 六年里，他一直在谈论将他的公司的电影，音乐和其他财产投入市场。中国现在必须问自己是否想让中情局管理 他 们的媒体。

I noticed the name in the center, a knot forming in my stomach.

I tapped the "Translate" button at the top of the page, a new option from Google that I barely believed would work.

The text on the page changed quickly, and I read the poorly translated article.

According to Liberty News China, received the document, a US chief executive, close to an agreement to deliver media content to China, has been CIA's most important asset for more than 50 years. These documents list the CIA's plans to control the US media system - a plan that has been in public for more than 40 years - Dewey Gunstott, CEO of the home media holding company, is the CIA's asset. For the past six years, he has been working to putting his company's films, music and other properties on the market. China now must ask whether it wants the CIA to manage their media.

Despite the bad translation, I picked up enough words to understand that Quinn had somehow leaked the story to a rogue Chinese website.

Below the summary story there was a link to the full piece. I followed the link and clicked translate. It was hard to tell, but there didn't seem to be any more details than in the summary on the front page. Just more background about Gunstott, about Operation Mockingbird, and more references to a "secret source." Thankfully, there were no quotes from Quinn.

It made sense that she would have leaked it to China, rather than the U.S. She was banking on the fact that, in the U.S., the news that Gunstott had once been on a list of CIA assets wouldn't make much news. But in China, it was possible that it would cause a much bigger stir. For starters, Gunstott's deal was already on shaky ground. But the bigger reason was that the citizens and government of China don't believe that the CIA is out to serve their interests, as most Americans do.

Quite the opposite.

Starting with the failed attempts at arming a Third Force against Mao in the 1950s, and continuing through the multiple American attempts to spy on Chinese nuclear facilities, the Chinese were famous for their distrust and loathing of the CIA. And having this news reported on a dissident Chinese site was sure to piss people off because it would involve national shame in a way that didn't figure in American news stories.

One thing I couldn't figure out was how Quinn had managed to get the documents past the Great Firewall, and how she'd managed to do it so quickly. She'd assured me that it was nearly impossible. I imagined I'd find out soon enough, but tomorrow morning was what mattered, and I needed to sleep.

*

CHAPTER 28

Sunday, June 18, 2017

I slept hard, harder than I had in years. The kind of blackout sleep where you wake up and don't know who or where you are or what day it is.

But I only slept until four in the morning. I'd fallen asleep around eight, so that gave me a good eight hours. But instead of getting up, I lay in bed and stared at the ceiling, wondering where Quinn was. I hoped she was okay, and was growing more impressed that, somehow, I'd been scooped by a paranoid recluse who hated the media.

I showered and dressed and, by the time I was ready to go, the light was streaming in through my large windows.

Greta was often late, but I showed up at Mee Sum at a quarter to ten, just to be sure I beat her there. I bought a plate of pork buns and, for ten minutes, I watched the shoppers stream in and out of Pike Place Market. I walked down the block to watch the guys throw and wrap fish for tourists. Then I paced, checked my phone, and paced some more.

At ten I started getting nervous.

By ten after ten, I was freaking out, wondering if she'd figured out the meeting was a setup. Then Mia called.

"What's going on?" I asked. "She's not here."

"That's why I'm calling. Mark got a call from her office, canceling the meeting. They said they can't reach her."

Mark was the guy we'd used to set up the fake meeting. "She wouldn't have gone into the office before a Sunday morning client."

"They said they haven't been able to reach her since *last night*."

"What are you talking about?"

"She's gone."

"She's not gone, she probably just got distracted or forgot or something. She's always late to—"

"Alex, they checked her apartment and she's not there. She's not answering her cell or anything."

I didn't know what to say. "I'm sure it's nothing...I...you'll let me know if you hear anything else?"

"Of course."

"I'm going to head to the office to check on some things. I'll see you Monday."

But I didn't go to the office. I went to a fancy coffee shop above Mee Sum, the kind that's crowded all day, where the baristas draw superheroes in your foam. I took a seat in the back and pulled out my phone. I knew Greta better than anyone, and had a few ideas about where she might be.

First, I checked her social media. She hadn't posted any updates since Thursday night. Her last Facebook post was a picture of a beach, opening on an expanse of water. But not one of our local, pebbly beaches. It was a vast, sandy beach. An ocean beach. The Pacific. The caption read, "Hoping to cross this soon."

My mind went to the possibility that she was moving out of the country, but I realized right away how paranoid that was. As I read through the comments, I figured out that she was planning a visit to Japan because various aunts and cousins had commented with dates they'd be available for a visit. On Friday morning, she'd written her last comment, "Hope to come out this winter," followed by a smiley-face emoji.

Okay, so she wasn't leaving the country, but maybe she—

My phone rang. A number I didn't recognize from a 458 area code. I usually ignore calls from numbers I don't recognize, but I answered it just in case it had anything to do with Greta.

"Hello?" I asked tentatively.

"Morning, Alex." A man's voice, but hard to hear because of the background noise. People talking and music.

"Who is this?"

"Don't you recognize my voice? We had such a nice talk." Amand.

"I'm busy," I said. "What do you want?"

"Just calling to check in. How's your morning going? I'm out at my favorite breakfast spot. I usually get the waffles with local berry syrup, but today—"

"Look, I don't have any info on anything about anything. I haven't even gone to work yet."

I was about to hang up when he said, "Alex, you didn't let me finish telling you what I'm having for breakfast."

"Why would I..." My stomach sank. It knew something my head hadn't yet figured out.

"Like I said, I usually have the waffles, but I'm trying to cut carbs and bring more healthy fats into my diet. Today I'm having the organic chicken sausage, a small fruit plate, and a coconut milk latte."

He was taunting me.

"Coconut milk is the new big thing. It's being lauded by nutritionists, yoga teachers, life coaches. Back in Kuwait, we don't drink it, but it's not half bad."

"*You* have Greta."

He didn't respond.

"Listen you son-of-a—"

"I just wanted to tell you about my breakfast. I'm sure she'll turn up any minute."

"You *dirtbag*. Where the hell is she?"

"I have to go now. I'm going to go do some yoga. Better on the knees than running, or so I hear."

"Amand, please, I—"

"Oh, I'm sure she's fine. Like I said, I'm sure she'll turn up any minute. Or, more precisely, I'm sure she'll turn up in exactly nineteen minutes."

The line went dead and I looked at the clock on my phone. It was 10:41 a.m.

The next nineteen minutes were the worst of my life.

I called the police first, but they weren't going to file a missing person's report until twenty-four hours had passed. I told them about the call, about Amand, but it sounded ridiculous coming out of my mouth. "A guy at Allied Regional Data Security called me. He was messing with me. I know they have her. He said…coconut lattes."

Greta's staff had already called the police twice and, unless I had new information, they'd be filing a report later that night. For now, there was nothing they could do.

I did an online search and a search within apps to see if Greta had been mentioned on anyone else's social media feeds, but nothing came up. The last five minutes I just sat, staring at my latte, clenching my jaw and cursing every second I'd taken her for granted.

11 a.m. passed, then 11:05.

The call came at 11:07. It was Mia, who was smart enough to lead with, "She's fine, Alex. *Totally fine.*"

"What happened? Where was she?"

"I don't know all the details. Her secretary called. She was taken by a couple men, but nothing at all happened to her. She wasn't hurt, wasn't robbed. Two men took her and then dropped her off at her apartment at exactly eleven this morning. That's all I know. Alex, what the hell is going on?"

I hung up without replying, Amand's smarmy smile

floating in my mind like a target.

I called Greta on every number she had, then texted her cellphone. Nothing.

Assuming Mia was right, and that Greta was fine, Amand had taken her just to show me he could. To prove to me that this was his world, and I was just living in it. When I'd left Eugene, I'd planned to let everything slip away. To string him along, pretend to help him a little, but offer up nothing of value until he forgot about me.

I slugged my latte in two sips, vowing to make it my last lactose-full beverage, and strode out of the coffee shop. I knew I couldn't live with Amand hanging over me—over Greta. By the time I got to street level, I had a plan. One man had set this whole thing in motion, and he was the only one who had the power to stop it.

CHAPTER 29

Monday, June 19, 2017

Dewey Gunstott.

It took the rest of Sunday, and every connection Bird, Mia, and I had, but I landed a meeting with Gunstott at 9 a.m. Monday morning. After finally reaching his press secretary, I'd tried to lie my way into the meeting, then finally told him about the drive, about Operation Mockingbird, and about the story I planned to write, connecting the dots to the shooting at *The Gazette*. Then I demanded five minutes with Gunstott to give him a chance to comment on the record.

It was a threat, a shot in the dark. But it worked.

Dewey Gunstott worked on the top floor of the Murray Building in downtown Seattle, only a half mile from my office. For years, I'd probably been walking past him in Pioneer Square or buying from the same fruit stand at Pike Place Market. Not that he was the kind of guy who bought his own fish. He had people for that. Just like he had people to hunt me down.

The Murray Building was surprisingly modest to serve as the home of such a powerful company. Thirty stories, but old fashioned. Boring gray stone, too few windows, a standard marble lobby, a slow elevator. I guess you could call it classy, but compared to the offices of *The Barker*, it was archaic.

When the elevator opened on the thirtieth floor, a young man in a brown suit was standing there, looking as old-fashioned as the building. He had short brown hair, the same color as his suit, and flashed a fake, business-like smile. "This way," he said.

He led me down the hall and through the open door of Gunstott's office, which was nothing like I'd imagined. First, it was wedged between two other offices, not in an expansive corner. Second, it was surprisingly small, less than half the size of my office. But more than that, I was surprised that it was empty.

"Take a seat," the kid said. "Mr. Gunstott will be right back."

The kid left and I sat on an overstuffed couch covered in old brown leather. The kind you run your hand over just to feel how soft it is. The whole place reminded me of my grandpa's office from when I was a kid. The couch, the cheap art on the walls, the scratchy-looking curtains, the mahogany side table with a single decanter filled with brown liquor. If there was a theme to the room, it was brown.

After a couple minutes, Gunstott appeared in the doorway looking confused, then lumbered up to me. I stood quickly to shake his extended hand. He was taller than I'd pictured him from the headshots I'd seen online—maybe six foot two, a little overweight, but less than I'd imagined. His face was disproportionately fat for the rest of his body, and his cheeks were red and puffy. All in all, he didn't look bad for a ninety-year-old man.

He poured himself about a quarter ounce of the brown liquor without saying a word, then took the tiniest sip possible. He repeated this twice, like he was trying to drink a drop at a time.

"So," he said, sitting behind the desk, "what do you want?"

It was strange, because, from his tone, I got the sense he might not know why I was there. "I'm Alex Vane, from *The Barker.*"

He sipped his drink. "Are you the guy from the editorial board at *The Seattle Times*? That hit job you did on my stadium bid was *horseshit.*"

He sipped his drink again.

"I'm *Alex Vane. The Barker*, the online magazine. Your assistant didn't tell you who I was or why I am here?"

"The kid? That's my nephew. He's a glorified doorman. I didn't have a chance to talk to my press secretary today. He sets these things up, I knock 'em down."

"Are you honestly telling me you don't know who I am or why I'm here?"

"He said something about China, but that's half the meetings I take these days. And I have a standing rule: I'll talk to anyone in the press for five minutes a year, and you're down to four minutes."

I ran my finger along the crease in my jeans, trying to think. If he was lying, he was a damn good liar. "I have the Mockingbird Drive."

"The what?"

"The hard drive. From the CIA. You're on it."

"Son, where did you say you're from?"

"The Barker."

"Never heard of it."

He picked up a hunting magazine that—no kidding—had a big brown bear on the cover, and started flipping through the pages.

"Mr. Gunstott. I have the hard drive."

He lowered the magazine slightly. "You say you have a hard drive? Is that like a computer?"

He seemed distracted. Like I was wasting his time. He was *not* acting like someone who was confronting a powerful journalist he'd been chasing for a week. One who could cause him embarrassment and possibly derail his China deal.

Until that moment, I hadn't known for sure whether I'd publish the audio of the shooting, but I was ready to go all-in. "Mr. Gunstott, you worked at the *Louisville Courier-Journal* in 1952. While there, you were approached by a CIA asset, one either already at the paper or one from outside. My guess is that it was the senior editor, since he was also an asset. You've been a CIA asset ever since. For the last six days, I've been followed. You, or someone you control, ordered the shooting at *The Las Vegas Gazette*. Six people died to protect your secrets. My website has proof of this and will publish it tomorrow."

He put down the magazine and stared at me, like he was seeing me for that first time. "What in tarnation? I...I worked at the paper in Louisville, sure. That was a long time ago, that—"

"1952."

"Okay, but what were you saying about a shooting, being followed? What the hell are you talking about? And the CIA thing? Are you talking about my boss, what was his name?"

He was looking straight at me now. His eyes were wet, his cheeks blotchy. He didn't seem drunk, just genuinely confused. Like an old man, lost on a golf course.

The realization came first in my chest, then spread through my whole body. He truly had no idea what I was talking about. Of course he hadn't ordered the shooting at *The Gazette*. He probably hadn't even known about it. And of course he didn't consider himself a CIA asset. He just had some friends who happened to work for the government, people he shared information with, and who shared information with him.

I said, "At some point in the last few months, did you ask anyone to do a background check on you, to look into your past, to destroy any records?'

"I don't know why I'd answer that question."

"Six people were killed in Las Vegas!" I was almost shouting.

"What does that have to do with me?"

"I'm sorry," I said. "I think I've made a bad mistake. Are you...you're about to finalize a major deal with China. Is there any chance that the deal started a new process of looking into your background, of..."

He stared at me for another few seconds, then said, "Sure, it's possible. My background gets poured over a hundred times a day. Would everyone involved do some due diligence before we break into China? Sure. Would I pay even the slightest bit of attention to it? No."

He was telling the truth. Someone had decided to look into Gunstott's background—maybe someone on his staff, maybe a business partner. Somehow that had led to ARDS, to Tudayapi, to Baxter, to Innerva, and then to me.

I didn't know what to say. All I could think about was my talk with Amand, who'd been right about everything. It was a system of perfected security. Depending on your position in the world, it was either a system of perfected good, or a system of perfected evil. No one was in charge.

I was up against a snake with no head.

But most of all, it was a system that was too big to fail. A system that protected itself. Sometimes slowly, sometimes awkwardly. But it protected itself. And sometimes without the protectees even knowing they were being protected.

"Let me just ask you this: are you regularly in touch with anyone in the CIA?"

"This interview is over," he said, shaking his glass gently, like he was rattling an invisible ice cube.

I tried a few more questions, but he wasn't having it. A minute later, the young man in the brown suit was escorting me out of Gunstott's office.

***

Riding the elevator back to street level, I came up with a theory. Gunstott was most likely one of the agents of Operation Mockingbird who didn't see himself as a CIA asset. He was buddy-buddy with some agents, was happy to share information and often received information that was

246

helpful to his business interests. Coming out of World War Two and heading into the Cold War, he was the type of guy who viewed Russia as an existential threat, both personally and to U.S. business interests. And, fundamentally, he viewed the government as a mechanism to protect U.S. business interests. *His* business interests.

I stepped out onto the sidewalk and looked up at the sky. It was one of those mid-summer gray skies we sometimes get in Seattle. A light mist was falling, the kind that might fall all day without getting anyone wet. I wandered down the street in a daze.

I've never been a crusader, and I wasn't about to become one, but I knew what I had to do. I had to publish the contents of the drive, I had to publish the audio, and let the chips fall where they may. But first I had to see Greta. I'd knock on her door, stand outside her window with a boombox, or whatever the modern equivalent of that was. I'd confess my sins, pour my heart out, and promise to get back to real journalism. I'd reclaim my soul.

I was contemplating all this when I saw a headline flash by on a TV through the window of a sports bar.

Audio of Gazette Shooting Leaked.

The story had just ended, but I was pretty sure I'd seen an image of *The Gazette* building on the screen. By the time I was inside the bar, the TV was on commercials.

The bartender was just setting up his station for the early lunch crowd, and I got his attention. "What was that last story about?" I asked. "Did you hear it?"

He looked at me like I was an idiot, kind of like Quinn used to look at me. "The sound is off."

"The captions? Did you read any of the captions, the subtitles, the...." I pointed up at the screen.

"Something about that shooting in Vegas, I think."

"What? What was it?"

"Man, we're not even open yet. Can you just—"

"I'll leave, just tell me what it said."

"Don't you have a phone? Look it up."

Stumbling toward the door, I opened the CNN app, and there it was, right on the top of the page:

Audio of Mass Shooting Calls Official Story into Question.

I stepped under the canopy of an empty bus stop so the mist wouldn't wet my phone and scrolled down to the story.

> *CNN has obtained exclusive audio purported to have been taken by the girlfriend of James Stacy, one of the victims of the mass shooting that took place at The Las Vegas Gazette last Tuesday. The recording is thirteen minutes long and appears to contain a conversation between Mr. Stacy, Gazette editor Benjamin Huang, and a woman, whose identity CNN is attempting to verify.*

> *Next of kin to Mr. Stacy and Mr. Huang have not been reached to confirm the voices on the recording, but voice experts at CNN have confirmed that there is a 99% likelihood the voices are those of Mr. Huang and Mr. Stacy based on analysis of recorded interviews with the two men.*

> *If authentic, the recording would rock the six-day-old investigation into the shooting, which, in addition to Mr. Stacy and Mr. Huang, took the lives of four others.*

> *Police have reported that the shooting was committed by Baxter Callahan, a reclusive political activist living just outside Las Vegas. But the audio suggests two gunmen, possibly more, and may also indicate a different chronology than the official police version.*

The story was total amateur hour. But when news this big breaks, it's often a matter of minutes until you get scooped, so you just throw something up on the web. In italics at the bottom of the story, I read: *Details unfolding by the minute, watch CNN for live updates.*

Only three people on earth could have leaked the audio, and I was one of them. The other two were Innerva and Quinn, and there were decent reasons to believe it had been either of them. If it was Innerva, it meant that she was

248

somewhere safe and was sick of waiting for me to break the story. But that wasn't like her. She never sent information to reporters herself. James had always handled that. I guess in this case, she could have used an intermediary, but I doubted that she had someone else she trusted who could be reached so quickly. The other consideration was who the story had been leaked to. In ten years together, James and Innerva had never leaked a story to CNN. When you're out to smash the system, you don't give massive scoops to TV stations that are part of one of the biggest media empires the world has ever seen. Of course, they leaked to corporate newspapers from time to time, but never to a TV station.

Quinn, on the other hand, had no contacts, no idea how the media really worked. Furthermore, she was on the run. I could see her sitting in a parking lot of a Starbucks, hopping on their free Wi-Fi and uploading the audio to CNN's online tip forum. What I didn't understand was why she'd only leaked the first ten minutes of the audio. If I remembered correctly, the ten minutes covered the shooting, but not the voices of the shooters in Huang's office.

I scrolled back up to watch the video. But, as I was watching the ad—a commercial for a new line of Fords, of all things—I felt a hand on my forearm. When I looked up, I saw a big beefy face, too tan to be natural. Just behind the face, I saw Holly's bright red hair. She was leaning out of the window of a silver SUV, idling in the bus stop.

"Alex, there you are," she said. It was her voice, her real voice, and it was just like I'd imagined it would be back in the airport. A beautiful Irish accent. Half leprechaun, half mermaid, like a gurgling brook on a moonlit night.

But I didn't have time to savor it.

The beefy man was gripping my bicep, and the last thing I felt was a sharp sting as he stuck a needle in my arm.

CHAPTER 30

"Up!"

I came to with two large men standing over me, one white and one black, and the stench of cheap minty aftershave. The white one was the beefy guy from the street, but, looking up at him, I was mostly aware of his bushy mustache and abundant black ear hair. His head was bald, doughy, and bright white, the rest of his face soft and clean shaven. His face was only a couple feet from mine and he kept saying "Up" in a stern, booming voice.

I had no idea where I was.

I stood, but immediately tumbled into a wall. The black man grabbed my arm and held me for a few seconds as my gelatinous legs established themselves. He had long dreadlocks tied into a neat ponytail and a thin, angular face that didn't match his hulking body. We were almost exactly the same height, and he looked like he wasn't just "in shape," but might be an amateur bodybuilder or professional athlete. He had one of those bodies that assaulted you with its symmetry and definition, even through his black suit.

I felt right away that neither man would hurt me, and I looked around as I felt the energy and control returning to my legs. I'd been lying on a cot in the corner, one of only five objects in the room, the others being three swiveling office chairs and a desk that looked like it belonged in a college dorm room. The walls had been painted an ugly off-white, the carpet was thin but new-looking, still emitting a chemical stench that reminded me of the adhesives in Quinn's house.

The men watched me but didn't say anything. When I'd gotten my legs, Dreadlocks walked me over to the desk and pushed me down into one of the chairs. Ear-hair nodded at him and walked out.

"Where am I?"

I said it more as a statement to myself than a question. The sound of my own voice scared me. Somehow it made the whole thing real in a way I wasn't ready for. Like when you see a photo of yourself posted by someone else on Facebook, and then the memories of last night come flooding back.

A minute later, Ear-hair returned, but I wasn't focused on him. Holly's bright red hair was peeking out from around his thick shoulder, and, a second later, she appeared as he stepped to the side of the desk. Behind Holly, another woman. Like Kenny back at the airport, I couldn't tell her nationality, not that it mattered. She had black hair pulled up in a tight bun, so tight it was like her forehead was being lifted and stretched back. She looked like the "After" photo in a Botox ad. She was short, maybe five foot two, and thin. Contrasted to Holly's affable face, her look could best be described as *severe*.

Holly and the new woman sat in the swiveling office chairs across from me while Dreadlocks and Ear-hair stood sentry on either side of the desk. Holly said, "Well, Alex. This is unfortunate, isn't it?"

I wish I'd said something sarcastic and awesome. Something like Mel Gibson would have said in Lethal Weapon or, for the older folks, like Clint Eastwood would have said in pretty much anything. Something like, "Unfortunate for *you*, maybe," but cooler than that, and with a better accent.

But I didn't. I said, "Your name's not really Holly, is it?"

"Sure it is."

"And who's that?" I asked, nodding toward the other woman.

"My name doesn't matter," the woman said.

Holly smiled. "She's right, it doesn't. What matters is you, Alex. You've been on quite a road trip."

"Why'd you drop the accent?" I asked.

"Amand said you could be trusted. Your friend, not so much."

"Where is Quinn?" the other woman asked.

"At least give me something to call you," I said, trying to sound light.

"You can call me Bonnie."

"Do you all have names ending in y or ie?"

She ignored this. Said, "Alex, look around you."

I thought she meant it metaphorically, but she didn't say anything else so I glanced around the room again.

"Do you know where you are, Alex?"

"No."

"Do you know how long you were sleeping?"

"No." I usually have a pretty good internal clock, but the sleep had been a blackout. Might have been a few hours, might have been a day or more.

She continued, "This is either going to be one of the best days of your life, or one of the worst. We aren't into long, protracted interrogations here. We prefer to just access the information we need, do the job, then move on. If you were someone else, we might be using *other* methods, but you're not. I think you can understand that, right?"

"I can."

"So where is Quinn?"

"I don't know. You guys must have looked into her background. She's *crazy*. Unstable, unreliable. I didn't want to go with her in the first place. At the security place in Oregon, she freaked, she bolted. She's *paranoid*."

"We know about your talk with Amand," Holly said.

"And?"

"It's clear from that conversation that you don't want to do anything stupid. That you're willing to let this whole thing go, not to press it."

"I am." I was lying, and assumed they knew it.

Bonnie leaned across the table. Her eyebrows were perfect black arches and I could see that they were touched up. "So, where's Quinn?"

"Why do you need Quinn?"

"Do you know what she did yesterday?"

I shrugged, but Bonnie wasn't buying it.

She slid my phone across the table. "Swipe it," she said.

I did, and it opened to the CNN article I'd been reading the day before. This wasn't a situation I was going to be able to talk myself out of.

"Here's the deal," Bonnie said, standing and walking around the table. She stood right behind me and I looked back, but my muscles still felt weak, too weak to keep my neck craned back. I stared at the table in front of me as she spoke. "We had a job to do. It was to destroy the drive and any copies of any data that might be on it. From the time you met Holly and her associate in the Las Vegas airport, that's been our *only* aim. Once we learned what was on it from that freak—Turdaylapi—or whatever *its* name is."

"Tudayapi," I said.

"Once we learned what was on it, the matter was closed. Your friend has caused…complications."

"She's absolutely screwed you over," I said, relishing the fact a little too much. "Why didn't you just kill me there, or when you found me at Quinn's house, or outside ARDS?"

"Be quiet," Bonnie said. "Let me finish. You and Quinn were going to be free to go. Now it's too late for her."

I swiveled my chair just a little so I could stare into her black eyes. She squinted at me, grimaced, then looked away. I don't believe in all the stuff Greta says, stuff like hate just being congealed animal aggression in people. But I did feel like I could feel the hate coming off Bonnie's body. She genuinely wanted to hurt me.

Holly stepped between us. "Some of our performance has come into question recently. We're on a tighter leash than usual. Alex, you can trust us. If we were allowed to kill you, we would have."

She was trying to sound reassuring, and I bought it. Between Bonnie's clear frustration and Holly's warm smile, I was convinced that, for some reason, they weren't being allowed to dispose of me as they normally would. "Amand? He's your boss?" They didn't respond, so I said, "It's because you screwed up the job at *The Gazette*, right?"

It was a gamble. I assumed they already knew that I knew the official story was bullshit, but I wanted to be sure.

"We had nothing to do with that," Holly said.

Bonnie was pacing behind me. I swiveled all the way around and she stopped. I said, "You want to tell me the truth, right? You want to tell me why and how you did it. But you can't."

"Shut up."

"It pisses you off that you can't brag about it. You know what pisses me off? That you killed six people to protect an asshole like Dewey Gunstott."

Bonnie was staring at me, blank faced. But I was on a roll. "And it pisses you off even more that somehow you botched the job."

Holly said, "Alex, we—"

"Don't say anything more," Bonnie interrupted. "He doesn't need to know anything."

A silence hung in the room, and I needed a minute to think. "Can I have some water?" I asked.

Holly nodded at Ear-hair, who walked out.

Something was feeling off about this whole situation. Not that I knew much about security operatives or interrogation practices, but this had an amateurish vibe. An informality.

The suits the two goons were wearing didn't match. Holly's accent was fading in and out.

And then there was Bonnie herself, who was clearly the ringleader, but also seemed to be at odds with Holly, and not just in a good-cop/bad-cop kind of way. They almost seemed to be competitors.

I was playing it as cool as I could, but I doubted they were buying it. Remember when I said that to read people you need to be really present in yourself? I was having a hard time reading Holly and Bonnie, but I don't think it was because they were especially good at concealing their thoughts. I was rattled. Besides the lingering effects of whatever drugs they'd given me, I was nervous. And I knew it was showing.

But I also knew something they didn't: that there was more of the recording than Quinn had leaked to CNN. I decided that my best chance to stay alive was to let them know what I knew, to use it as a bargaining chip.

Ear-hair retuned and set a little paper cup in front of me, one of those four-ounce deals that comes in stacks of 100 and goes in the rack attached to a bottled-water dispenser. I drank it in one swig and said, "I'm still thirsty."

Ear-hair looked at Bonnie, who nodded toward the door. He returned a minute later, and I drank again. "Another, please."

Again Ear-hair walked out, but this time he left the door open behind him.

"Shut the door," Bonnie called after him. She swallowed the "or" in "door," so it sounded like, "Shut the dough."

I'd suspected it, but that's when I knew for sure. Bonnie was the second shooter.

When Ear-hair returned, I just left the water in front of me.

"Aren't you going to drink it?" Bonnie asked.

"Not thirsty anymore."

"Alex, it's not a good idea to mess around with us. We'd really like to kill you."

"But we don't *want* to do that," Holly said. "We really

don't."

"I do," Ear-hair said. "I'd love to."

"Shut up," Bonnie said to him. Then to me, "Where's Quinn?"

I met her eyes and made my voice hard. "Were you the one who shot James?"

She just stared at me.

"Were you holding Baxter's shotgun or his handgun?"

Nothing.

"You're smaller than Holly, so I figure you had the smaller gun, though you're more insecure than her so maybe you needed the larger gun to, you know, feel like somebody."

"Shut *up*," she said again, putting her tiny, cold hand on my forearm. "Shut. The. Fuck. Up."

"The first shots came from the back alley," I said. "From the *back* alley."

Her grip tightened on my shoulder and the two meatheads inched closer to me, probably anticipating that I'd do something stupid. As it turned out, I already was. Something much stupider than I knew at the time.

"From the *back* alley," I repeated. "Esperanza didn't die first. Baxter did. You shot him before you even walked through the door. Or was it Holly? Doesn't really matter, I guess." I paused, letting it hang in the air. Holly's face was blank and pleasant, but I knew she was thinking hard.

I glared at Bonnie. "I'd like to think that Holly had the shotgun, that *she* killed James, not you. I'd like to think that Holly's was the last face my friend saw, not yours."

Her fingers were digging into my forearm, her long fingernail breaking the skin. "Not because she's prettier than you. Just because she's more...I don't know...pleasant."

I felt her move behind me and noticed a glint in Ear-hair's eye just before he slugged me on the cheek. My head shot back and struck Bonnie. "Again," she said.

This time, Dreadlocks hit me across the other cheek, and much harder. His fist was like a brick dropped from a tall building onto a marshmallow. I lurched sideways, only staying on the chair because Ear-hair held me up.

Bonnie said, "Alex, stop making up stories."

"I heard your voice," I said. "You were in the room. With Holly. Amand wasn't there, was he? Was he in the car? Waiting outside? A two-woman team. Very progressive of you."

"Again!" Bonnie shouted, and a fist came down on the back of my head, smashing my face into the desk.

"You were in the room," I said again. "I have the recording, and a dozen of my journalist pals will share it if I die."

My head was pounding, like it was being compressed from all angles at the same time and fighting to expand outward. I heard movement but didn't look up. A few seconds later, I peeked out and saw that Holly and Bonnie had left the room.

Ear-hair said, "That was a bad idea."

I was about to ask why, but, the next thing I knew, I was woozy. Everything faded to black.

CHAPTER 31

I didn't know how long I'd been in the box. Could have been an hour, could have been a day.

I woke up sitting in the most compact position my body would take, chin over my knees, arms along the outsides of my legs, hands taped to my ankles. I jerked my arms to try to rip the tape, but my head immediately hit a hard ceiling. I leaned to the left and the right. On each side, I hit a wall within a few inches. The only light came through a dozen small holes on each side.

I was in some kind of a box, roughly three feet square and made out of smooth plastic or acrylic.

Next, I noticed the pain. It started in my lower back, a dull aching. A throbbing on the right side of my neck that ran down into the shoulder blade. I felt nothing in my legs. Maybe because they were asleep.

But beyond the pain was the discomfort, the claustrophobia. It was like my whole body was an itch I couldn't scratch. Like my skin was crawling from the inside.

I panicked.

I pulled my arms out as hard as I could. Nothing. I scooched all the way back, pressing my back against the box, then thrust my legs forward as hard as I could. But I only had a few inches to move and couldn't generate any thrust.

Finally, I screamed. It started as a deep, animal groan. Pure pain. But my mind raced and raced and the scream got higher and higher until it faded out as a pathetic squeak.

I collapsed in on myself for a few seconds, then bashed my head against the top of the box until I passed out.

***

The process repeated itself a few times. Wake up, pain, terror, panic, smash around, pass out. My pants were soaked with urine, too, having no other choice but to relieve myself where I was.

These episodes alternated with brief periods of strange lucidity. I thought of my old friend Camila Gray, who'd helped me break a couple big stories over ten years ago. For a while, I'd also been infatuated with her, but we weren't meant to be, and she'd been back in Des Moines for years, writing books about the media and teaching at a small college. When we'd drifted apart, I told myself we'd just lost touch, as people do. But, in the box, the truth came all at once: I was ashamed of where I'd let my career take me. I feared her disapproval.

And, of course, I thought of Greta, dancing through a crowd of people like a woman possessed. Imagining her was the only thing that brought me any comfort and, for a few seconds at a time, I even forgot that she'd filed for divorce. Then, I'd remember in an agonizing jolt. Hunched over in the box, body screaming in pain, I began thinking that I'd done something to deserve it.

When I awoke, a blinding light was streaming through the top of the box, which had been opened. The first thing I saw was Holly's bright red hair and freckles.

Then the light hit my brain, causing a coursing pain like a high-pitched screaming on the morning of your worst hangover. I blinked furiously as my eyes adjusted. Dreadlocks and Ear-hair were back, lifting me out of the box into a small room with bright white walls and three simple oak chairs.

Before I knew what was happening, I was on a wooden plank, tilted such that my head was below my feet. I was looking straight into a bright light until a black cloth was tied over my eyes and secured in some way I couldn't see. Ear-hair jammed my head between a lightly padded restraint. Dreadlocks strapped my feet, chest, and arms to the plank.

Then I heard Holly's voice. "Alex, I know you're scared. But you have no reason to be. We're here to help you. Bonnie and I wouldn't be doing this if it wasn't necessary. We just have a few questions for you. Is that alright?"

Her voice was back to the generic tone. Her lovely accent gone.

"I know you might be afraid," she continued, "but just say yes, or even grunt if you understand. I just need you to answer a few questions and then you'll be heading back to Greta, okay?"

"Go to hell." Kind of a weak response, I admit, but at the time I really meant it. I hated her more than anyone in the world. Despite the blindfold, I could see her face in my mind. Creamy skin dotted with freckles. A smile that could start a war. But as I listened to her I imagined myself not just hurting her but inflicting pain. Running her over with a car, but just clipping her so she couldn't move, then backing over her limbs until they were mush.

"Alex, please. This could take ten minutes if you were cooperative."

"I won't be," I said.

"Did you make any copies?" she asked.

I said nothing.

"Did you make any copies of the recording?"

I thought of Greta.

"Where is the drive itself?"

It was stowed in my closet, but, again, I said nothing.

Next I heard rapid footsteps, someone walking across the

room. Then I heard a slight splash of water on the floor. A few drops hit my hand.

My heart twisted in my chest. I screamed, "Nooooooo," but it wasn't going to do any good. I was about to be waterboarded.

"Go easy on him," Holly said. "He's soft. His heart could stop."

"Wouldn't be the end of the world." It was Bonnie's voice. The last I'd hear for three minutes.

There really aren't words for it. The water started slowly, flowing through the rag across my mouth and dripping and trickling down my throat. I've heard it's like drowning, but I don't really know what drowning is like. I felt the water pooling in my throat. I tried to spit it out, to gag or cough, but the angle on the board and my inability to move made that impossible.

Fifteen seconds of water, then about a minute of nothing. Silence from Holly and Bonnie as I gagged and panicked. I knew what Holly meant. My heart *could* stop.

Almost as bad as the physical part were the thoughts racing through my head. The closest thing I've ever experienced was when I'd stayed up all night drinking Red Bull and coffee, then taken one hit of some potent strain of legal weed that Bird had. At first, I'd had some paranoid thoughts, but the caffeine and stimulants kept speeding them up until they moved through my mind so fast that I crashed, literally. I blacked out and fell into a table.

But with waterboarding, there's no blacking out. Every time I came close, Bonnie stopped.

"Where did you get the recording?" Bonnie screamed, inches from my face.

The next thing I knew, Holly was crouching next to me, whispering in my ear. Her accent was back. "Alex, you have the wrong idea about us. We're not even slightly mad at you. We don't care about you at all. We are paid professionals. Security experts. We're just doing our job here. Don't pretend like you don't know stuff like this goes on all the time. Please don't pretend that. It's utterly disrespectful to the men and women who have to carry out tasks like this to keep you safe."

Of course I knew that things like this happened. I'd donated twenty bucks to the ACLU after Abu Ghraib. I knew about Guantanamo. But I'd always imagined stuff like this happening to *other* people. People *elsewhere*. Maybe not all of them were guilty, but it didn't happen to people who weren't putting themselves in bad positions.

When you're being tortured, your mind starts doing gymnastics, trying to find a way out of what's happening. In the span of twenty minutes, I went from hating Holly's guts, to loving her and deeply regretting anything I'd done to offend her. At one point, my mind started playing scenes from movies with strong, authoritarian speeches, like *Full Metal Jacket*: "If you ladies leave my island, if you survive recruit training, you will be a weapon. You will be a minister of death praying for war. But until that day you are pukes. You are the lowest form of life on Earth. You are not even human fucking beings. You are nothing but unorganized grabastic pieces of amphibian shit!"

I think this was my mind's way of putting what was happening in some kind of context. You see, people like me, whose problems in life have mostly been psychological, or philosophical, don't know what to do when the threat becomes existential.

Holly was still speaking. "The thing is, Alex, there are two kinds of people in America. People who understand that things like this are necessary to keep things from devolving, and people who look to a bright, utopian future, and think things like this *shouldn't be*."

I said, "I swear I don't know where Quinn is."

"Have it your way," Holly said.

Bonnie resumed the water, this time for longer. Twice, then three times, then five, and I lost track after that.

I didn't get used to it, each time was worse than the last. Waterboarding isn't a simulation of death. It is your body actually approaching death.

After the last time, Holly was back in my ear. "I'm sorry about that, Alex. Truly. It wasn't necessary."

I loved her in that moment. I really did. It was the most transparent good cop, bad cop routine ever, but it didn't matter. I loved her and would have done anything to make her happy. The thing about being close to death is that it makes other things not matter. If they were trying to manipulate me, it was working.

"Where did you get the recording?" Holly asked.

Without thinking, before my mind could even process a thought, I said, "Innerva." It was like my body shot the word out before my mind could hold it back. Like as a kid, when I'd intend to lie to my mom, but she'd look at me so sweetly that I'd just admit the truth.

"Good," Bonnie said.

"And where is Quinn Rivers?"

"I don't know," I stammered, but as I finished the last word a blow struck my solar plexus, causing me to gasp for air.

Holly said, "That really wasn't necessary, Bonnie. Alex is one of the good guys. He's just misguided right now."

When I got my wind back, I said, "She left me in Eugene. I haven't heard from her since. I swear."

"Where's Innerva?"

"I don't know." I tightened my abs as I said it, anticipating a blow. But it didn't come.

Bonnie said, "You met with her at The Wynn."

"I did. She gave me the drive. Said she was disappearing. If you know anything about her, you'll believe me. She would never have told me where she was going."

"Is there any more to the recording?"

"No."

"You're lying."

As much as I loved Holly, I still hated Bonnie. "Screw you."

I could share all the grisly details, but I won't. I'd long

since realized that they didn't care about the drive, about the fact that Quinn had leaked the story to the Chinese press. They only cared about the recording.

We went back and forth for another hour, two hours, five hours. I don't know how long, but it felt like an eternity. Punching, waterboarding, then a break. Sometimes, everyone would disappear for a few minutes, maybe to give me a break, maybe to communicate with Amand or others. Then they'd come back and we'd do another round.

But I guess that they never got the authorization to kill me, because, after I'd passed out for the tenth or eleventh time, everything stopped.

CHAPTER 32

Wednesday, June 21, 2017

When I woke up, the room was black and silent. Terror.

I could still feel the water in my throat and I gagged. But there was no water. Then I thought I was in the box again. I tried to move my hand, but couldn't. I crinkled my nose and puffed out my cheeks, which seemed to be moving alright. I wriggled my toes.

Within a minute, I could move my arms and legs. I wasn't in the box.

I pushed myself up by the elbows and tried to sit up straight, but my stomach and back muscles wouldn't contract, so I collapsed in on myself and tumbled to the floor.

I was in my apartment. The grain of the wood floor was familiar and I could see the light coming from the living room through the crack under the door. I scooted over to the door and opened it. Morning light streamed in from the living room, brighter than I expected. It was late-morning sun.

I propped myself up on the arm of the couch until I felt confident enough to take a step, then stumbled toward the built-in phone on the wall. I dialed the front desk.

A familiar female voice answered, but I didn't know her name. "Hello, Mr. Vane, how can I help you?"

"What time did I get home?"

"One of *those* nights, huh? I've been there. The overnight desk clerk told me you were brought up to your apartment by a couple of friends. Middle of the night. Dead drunk, he said."

I hung up without saying anything. I knew that, when I asked Dexter, it would turn out that my two bros were Dreadlocks and Ear-hair.

Once I knew who and where I was, and that I was safe, my first thought was of Greta. She'd been taken, and released. It was my fault. I saw myself standing on the sidewalk after the meeting with Gunstott, waiting for the CNN video to load, the needle in my arm, the box.

And the torture.

It didn't come back in the form of memory. I certainly *could have* remembered it, in the sense that, if I'd tried, I could recall the details. But instead, it came as a series of bodily sensations—creeping, crawling feelings of discomfort, asphyxiation, and, from time to time, uncontrollable panic.

I dialed Greta, not knowing what I'd say if she picked up, but I didn't have to wait long to figure it out.

"Alex, what happened? Where are you?"

"I...I was taken. How are *you*? I know what happened. I mean, I heard what happened."

"I'm okay. The police have no idea who took me, or why."

"They didn't say anything or...do anything?"

"Nothing. The cops think it may have been some horrible prank or something."

I didn't know if I should tell her the whole truth right away. The phone felt like a hunk of lead in my hand, and it was taking everything I had just to stand there and talk. I would tell her, just not now. I listened to her breathing and, out of nowhere, my eyes started watering. I rarely cry, and when I do, it's usually the result of a long string of thoughts that make me sadder and sadder until a few tears squeeze their way out. But standing there in the kitchen, between the long silences, hot tears began rolling.

I said, "I was going to meet you Sunday morning. I was the new client."

"I know."

"You...how?"

"I figured it out a couple days ago. My assistant thought it was weird that a new client would book me for a full day without ever having worked with me. It wasn't hard for her to figure out what was going on."

"I feel like an idiot. It was...I don't know. I was trying to..."

There are awkward silences and comfortable silences. And, as I looked around my apartment, I knew that this was one of our old, comfortable silences. A silence in which she could see through me, but I didn't care because I knew she loved me anyway. It hung in the air for a long time, until the warm sun gleaming off the floors blurred my vision. My head screamed with a piercing pain, but I didn't care. I looked out at the Puget Sound long enough to see a ferry boat make its way into the ferry terminal, leaving a low wake behind it as it cut through the water.

I was still crying, but I wasn't sad. I felt broken, ashamed, and grateful to be alive. "Can I ask you something?" I said to Greta.

"You want to know if I was planning to show up, right?"

She knew me. Despite everything, I needed to find out if I had any hope with her.

"I wasn't going to at first. At first, I was pissed. But then I thought about how I got you added to the No Fly List. About how some of the things that went wrong with us were actually my fault. Did you really call Dexter Park?"

"I did. Well, I had Mia call him. Yoga. Couples counseling. And pork buns from Mee Sum."

The line was quiet for a while, then she said, "I was going to show up."

What hit me then was that I didn't know if we'd live together again or stay married. But I knew that I was royally screwed up, and I would need her help to get myself right again, if that was even possible.

She said, "Alex, what's been going on? My assistant said that Mia said you'd been out of town. And now the news about the shooting not being what they said before. Did something happen?"

"Can we get together tonight? No pressure, no expectations. But can we?"

She agreed, and I promised I'd explain everything, but first I needed to make sure this thing was over. I searched for my cellphone, which Dreadlocks and Ear-hair had been nice enough to leave on my kitchen counter, then fell onto the couch and turned on the news. CNN and MSNBC were on commercials, but FOX was talking about the shooting. What I wanted to find out was whether anyone was connecting the leaked documents on the Chinese website to the shooting.

I listened to the report as I swiped to open my phone. Fox was doing one of the bits where, after a minute-long report from a stringer in Vegas, they spend an hour debating the information. A scruffy looking professor-type sat on the left, across from a youngish blonde woman in a chic black pantsuit on the right. A bored looking host "moderated" the discussion behind a glass table.

Host: But the recording, if authentic, does seem to imply that the first story we heard was...

Chic Woman: That's exactly the point. The first story we heard may or may not be correct, but we need to give the officers the time to—

Professor-Type: Can I get...can I get in here? I'm sorry, but why are we giving the Las Vegas police the benefit of the doubt? No...no, let me finish. They botched this case from day one, when they announced, "case closed," and told us the chronology of the shooting. It's not our fault they got it wrong. Why should we trust them now?

Host: So, what do you recommend?

Professor-Type: This case needs to be federalized, taken over by the FBI.

Chic Woman: Just what we need, more federal intervention in the business of the states.

Host: What about that? If the original version has been called into question, we don't know if this is a deranged loner or radical Islamic terrorism. We don't know if...

Professor type: Wait a second, how can you make that leap if—

Chic Woman: We don't know, we don't know yet. If there's any chance this was radical Islamic terrorism, then yes. Bring in the FBI, DHS, the CIA. Bring in the Marines. But until there's some indication of that, can't we let the local police officers do their jobs? Until then, aren't we just speculating?

Host: Well, we are coming up against a break, and until we receive additional information, speculation is all we have.

Professor-type: It's what we do.

Chic Woman: It's what we do.

They all laughed, and I felt like reaching through the screen and shouting at them, "It's *all* you do!"

I wanted to tell them that if they want to claim to be a news station, maybe they could put some resources into reporting the news, rather than hosting staged arguments about pseudo-facts. I considered checking the other networks, but I knew they wouldn't be much better. I'd always thought that the cable news setup was a little surreal, but today it was like watching the performance of two children fighting for mom's attention. It was such a petty distraction in a world full of serious topics, such a waste of resources, such a...it was a lot like my website, actually.

I'd been browsing my news apps and social media feeds while listening. The shooting was trending again on Facebook and Twitter, but there was no new information and the LVMPD hadn't responded to the release of the audio except to issue a one paragraph statement indicating that they could not yet verify the authenticity of the recording and they would look into the matter further, but, for now, they had no reason to believe that Baxter Callahan had not acted alone.

From what I could tell, Captain Shona Payton had not made another appearance on behalf of the department, and she hadn't been quoted anywhere that I could find.

Meanwhile, the Gunstott story had picked up a little steam in China, though it appeared to have gone unnoticed by the American media. A follow-up article on *The Dissident Blog* quoted three unnamed Chinese officials, all saying some version of the same thing: China had long suspected that America would try to spread its propaganda though the media, and, if these allegations turned out to be true, Gunstott's deal could not be allowed to go through. It wasn't much, but it might be enough to get people digging.

In my mind, there were three questions to answer. The first was, why had they let me go? I couldn't be sure, but my guess was that they believed that I didn't know where Quinn was, and that there was no more to the recording, which, according to the news I'd read, had given no indication about who the shooters were, other than the fact that there may have been two. They had also probably spoken with Amand, who believed he had me under control.

And that was my second question: was there a way to escape from this web? Could I go to the police, or anyone, and tell them what happened without bringing more trouble on myself?

My third was simple: what could I do to stop Dewey Gunstott?

I walked to the bedroom and changed into a pair of gray jeans and a black t-shirt, which felt looser than normal. I ran my hands over my stomach. Definitely a little flatter. I realized I'd been running on coffee and snacks for a week, and hadn't eaten in at least twenty-four hours. As stupid and vain as it was, it put a little spring in my step as I slid my phone in my back pocket and headed out the door.

CHAPTER 33

As surreal as watching the news had been, being back at *The Barker* was the opposite. I'd expected it to feel weird, but, as soon as the elevator opened, I felt better than I had in years. The bright green and blue cables, the shiny computers, the gleaming floors, but mostly the people. Typing, chatting, sipping coffee, reading through papers, hurrying to and fro.

Bird met me at the elevator. He'd seen me from across the room and drifted over.

"You live!" he said, leaning in to hug me. It struck me that he had no idea what I'd been through.

I hugged him back, awkwardly because of the size difference, then gestured to his office. "I don't have time to tell you everything," I said as we walked, "but I'll give you the headlines, then we need to get to work."

We took our usual spots in his office, Bird behind the desk, sipping a Red Bull, me on the other side. But instead of pacing, I sat stiffly in a red chair made of shaped hard plastic. My body ached.

Other than Greta, Bird was the only person I trusted completely. I told him a short but true version of the shooting, the meeting with Innerva, the airport, Quinn, Duck Valley, Tudayapi, Quinn's disappearance, the torture. I didn't look at him as I told him the last part. He was a genuinely good guy and I knew he'd be concerned and want to talk about it, but I wasn't ready for that. Plus, there was something I wanted him to do.

"I need a listicle," I said. "The greatest listicle of all time. A listicle that will go so viral it will take over the world conversation for a few days. Can you do that?"

"Well, what's the topic? I mean, what's the story?"

I slid the plastic chair around to his side of the desk, opened his laptop, and pulled up *The Dissident Blog*.

He scanned the two stories about Gunstott, then said, "This is from the binder? From the drive?"

"Right."

"And this is real? I mean Operation Mockingbird was real?"

"Yup."

"And Gunstott, that's the *real* Dewey Gunstott. Of IFMH?"

"Yup."

He smiled, relishing the challenge. "Just to be clear, you want me to create something that will get people paying attention to this story?"

"Right now, I just want something that will get the whole country talking about Dewey Gunstott and his deal with China. That will be enough to get the ball rolling."

Bird took a long, slow sip of his Red Bull, then cracked his knuckles one by one. "Come back in a half hour," he said, smiling.

***

I opened my laptop, only to find it running a program I'd never heard of. One I hadn't installed.

It was called Collude, and seemed to be just a white text box surrounded by an orange frame. As I stared at the white space, trying to figure out what was going on, words began appearing.

Quinn did a good job upgrading your computer security, but it was nothing I couldn't get around.

The words were disappearing as I read, almost as though I was erasing them as I scanned.

From now on, this app is the only way you'll hear from me, and the only way I'll hear from you. Messages are protected by military-grade encryption. They are as untraceable as messages get.

Amand will not bother you again. I've uncovered enough dirt on him to keep him quiet for good. And he knows it. That's why they let you go.

I have left the country, and there will be no funeral for James. But there will be revenge.

Stay safe,

Innerva Shah

After sitting in stunned silence for a few seconds, watching the last of the words disappear, I tried to look up Tudayapi's phone number, but of course she wasn't listed under that name. I managed to reach the young man at the front desk of the motel in Owyhee, who remembered me and gave me her number.

It was all surprisingly easy until he said, "What's the deal with your friend?"

"What?" I asked.

"The woman you were here with."

He was talking about Quinn. "Wait, she's there?"

"You mean you're not with her? Well, she...I probably shouldn't say anything more."

He hung up and I dialed Tudayapi, who picked up after three rings.

Before I could say anything, she said, "I thought you'd be calling."

"Because you knew I'd found out that you sold us out?"

"I helped you, Alex. I could have done much worse."

I didn't have time to feel betrayed, so I said, "Look, I need to know something."

"Sure, Alex, anything for you." She said it like I should just forget her monumental betrayal.

"What's in your loft, behind the curtains?"

"Quinn said you'd figure it out eventually. Yeah, I leaked the story to China for her."

"Is she there?"

"She's here, or, well, she was. She left a little while ago."

My mind was racing. "Start from the beginning," I said.

"Apparently, Quinn and you—you bad boy—snooped while you were here. Quinn discovered my offline servers in the loft. She assumed, rightly, that they were my China servers."

"Your China servers?"

"I work with a few businessmen in China."

"Hackers?"

"Call them what you want, but it's important to them to be able to store information in a way that is only accessible at certain times."

"And she brought the binder back to you to upload?"

"Well, as you may have heard, I already had the contents of the binder backed up. But she told me what to send. She was embarrassed, too, that she'd missed the backup drive connected to my logic board. Anyway, she showed up in a broken-down old Ford F-150. Carjacked some poor grape farmer in Oregon. Showed up at three in the morning, saying all sorts of stuff, but basically implying that the fate of the world rested on scanning and uploading the binder and sending it, along with an explanation, to some resisters in China."

"And you just did it? And she forgave you for—"

"Look, Alex. She and I have lived similar lives. We've lived on the outside looking in. Lived in a place where *you do what you need to do to survive.* Where you know that everything can be taken away at any time, so you do what's necessary. Quinn knew that I'd done what I had to do when those two ladies showed up at my door, but that I'd done the bare minimum to help them."

I had a thousand questions, but no time to ask them. "The guy at the motel. I called him to get your number and he mentioned Quinn. Where is she?"

"She stayed around for a day, but left early this morning, don't know where she was going."

"She didn't say anything or do anything about—"

"I don't know what she was planning. Only thing she did was make me crack her new cellphone, so it couldn't be tracked."

"What kind of new phone?"

"Not sure. Samsung or something. But brand new. She had it when she got here. Only other thing was, she asked me how to use Facebook Live. Told me you said it was going to be the next big thing."

I thanked her and hung up after promising to be back in touch soon.

A minute later, Bird was in my doorway. "Alex, it's done."

CHAPTER 34

The story he'd come up with was the finest clickbait I'd ever seen. And it was a shame we were going to run it advertisement free. Ads slow down the speed at which a story loads, and decreases the chance that someone will click through. And I wanted as many people as possible to see his masterpiece.

The headline read:

Communist Censorship: Coming Soon to a Theatre Near You

Actually, that was one of five headlines Bird had written to appear on different users' phones, depending on location, age, gender, and other demographics. He was using every tool in the box to maximize the chances someone would click. About fifty percent would get the main headline, but five to fifteen percent would see one of the following gems:

Did Mao Hate Jesus?

Who Ya Gonna Call? Not the Ghostbusters if You're in

China.

Why There Will Never Be a Gay Kiss in Star Wars.

China Won't Air Duck Dynasty Because They Hate Freedom.

Of course, the headlines had been optimized to hit all sorts of keywords that our subscribers had clicked on before, as well as the Google, Facebook, and Twitter algorithms.

But no matter which headline you clicked, the same article appeared. The article consisted of ten slides, basically photos with a small caption under them and a little control bar to make it full screen.

Slide number one was a picture of Gunstott, standing in a group with three Chinese men, all wearing matching dark suits. "Is that him making the deal in China?" I asked.

Bird chuckled with a little more disdain than usual. "You still think like a newspaper person. I couldn't *find* a recent picture of him actually *in China*, so I just grabbed one from a few years back. It really doesn't matter, and the story doesn't say when the picture was taken. It's all about what it *signifies*."

I read the caption under the image. *Dewey Gunstott, the CEO of International Family Media Holdings, is about to partner with the leaders of China in a deal that may kill your favorite TV shows.*

I could see where this was heading, and I scrolled through the next images more quickly.

#2: A graph comparing the revenue from movies and TV in China and the U.S., which showed a rapid increase in Chinese spending and a flat line in U.S. spending. The caption: *By 2022, China will be the biggest customer of U.S. media holdings on earth.*

#3: A black slide with no image, just covered in red text: *As China becomes our biggest customer, U.S. TV and movie studios will engage in self-censorship to protect their business interests.*

#4: Another black slide with red text: *And it's not just liberals who will suffer.*

#5: Phil Robertson from Duck Dynasty, his gray and black beard taking up half the image, with a snippet of one of his speeches about democracy and freedom and communism across the lower half. The caption read: *Yup, they even banned Duck Dynasty for being "Overly supportive of capitalism and critical of China."*

#6: Mel Gibson, long haired and suffering, a still image from *The Passion of the Christ*, a big red X across his face. The caption under the image read: *Religious freedom? Nope. Banned for being religious in secular China.*

#7: Another black slide with red lettering: *And we saved the best for last.*

#8: An image of the two male leads from the Star Wars: The Force Awakens, Finn and Poe, sitting in the cockpit of the fighter jet. The caption read: *Despite assurance from JJ Abrams that Star Wars will soon see its first gay romances, we expect the bottom line to win out. If these guys kiss, China won't air the film. Therefore, these guys will never kiss. Because...*

#9: Another black slide with red lettering: *IF THIS DEAL GOES THROUGH, DISNEY WILL BE NEXT INTO CHINA.*

#10: A white slide with phone numbers, addresses, and some official-looking seals of government agencies. The caption: *Speak out today! Let your congressman and the Senate Subcommittee on International Trade and Finance know that you oppose the IFMH deal.*

When I'd finished reading I walked a small circle around Bird's desk. "Once we publish this, things could get ugly," I said, already dialing our legal team in my mind.

"It's nothing that new. I mean, writers have questioned this deal before, and for some of the same reasons. Most people didn't notice, but—"

"That's what I'm saying. People are going to notice this. Plus, because we're not reporting anything new, it's like a late hit when the guy has gone out of bounds. Gunstott is going to sue the hell out of us."

"Maybe, but he won't win."

Bird could tell I was apprehensive. He said, "Alex, you *asked* me to put this together."

"It's just...I just wish I knew where Quinn was. There's a chance this could endanger her, as well as us."

Bird was staring at his laptop, the way he sometimes did when I was using his office to think out loud. He looked up at me suddenly. "Wait, what did you say her last name was?"

"Rivers. Quinn Rivers."

"Curly black hair, kinda tall, smoking-hot in an *I-haven't-bathed-this-month* kinda way?"

"Yeah."

Bird spun his laptop around on the desk so it faced me. "I don't think you're going to have to worry about her."

CHAPTER 35

Quinn was streaming live on Facebook.

The video was of her face, but I could see the top of a seatbelt and the back seat of a truck in the background. After a few seconds, it became clear that she was driving. She wasn't speaking, but the audio was on and I could hear the unmistakable whoosh of tires on highway.

Bird said, "There are two hundred thousand people watching this live stream. It's being shared all over Facebook."

"The phone must be on the dashboard, propped up somehow."

"This is the woman you just spent five days in a car with?"

I didn't respond because I was scrolling through the comments on the video, trying to figure out what was going on.

But Bird was faster and he'd already found it on his phone and figured out the context. "Basically, she started the feed twenty minutes ago by announcing that she just killed two people and is going to take her own life."

My stomach twisted, hardened. "Did she say who she killed?"

"Checking."

I watched Quinn's face, her striking eyes and freckles, trying to read her through the screen. I couldn't tell right away whether she was bluffing, or lying, or if she'd gone over the edge. If she *had* killed someone, maybe it had been in self-defense.

I said, "Did she say where she is?"

"Northern Nevada. Heading toward Vegas."

"See what else you can find out."

But I was already imagining what had happened. Quinn returned to Owyhee to have Tudayapi upload the contents of the binder behind the Great Firewall. My hunch was that Amand, or possibly people who worked for him, had followed her. Maybe Bonnie and Holly had chased her after letting me go.

"This says she went live outside an Indian Reservation in—"

"Owyhee."

"Right, and she's being chased by the CIA, she says, and possibly others. She gave out her name and social security number, as well as the name of a couple of the group homes she grew up in. Said she dropped out of MIT and was institutionalized for a while. She basically gave her whole bio. Her Facebook name is Smedley Vegas, and she has no posts and doesn't even have a profile pic."

"She's new to social media," I said with a chuckle, trying to calm my fears.

"It's up to four hundred thousand viewers."

Quinn started speaking, and Bird and I huddled over his laptop. "If you missed the beginning of this, my name is Quinn Rivers. I just killed two armed, extra-military or possibly CIA operatives at a gas station outside the Duck Valley Indian Reservation. I killed them in self-defense, but I am now being pursued. I am on the run, driving south toward

Las Vegas. I will not be taken alive."

Her eyes darted up to the rearview mirror.

Bird said, "If she's being pursued, why aren't there sirens?"

"She could be imagining it."

"Is she *that* nuts?"

"Yeah, but that doesn't mean she's wrong."

Every few seconds, Quinn checked her rearview mirror, and I wished she'd angled the camera a little differently so we could see out the back of the truck.

"This is gonna end badly," Bird said. "I'm on Twitter right now and people are saying that the shooting happened at the Fuel Stop gas station, police are pursuing her."

"Publish your listicle," I said.

"Why now?"

Bird was right. There was no good ending to what Quinn had started, but I wasn't going to sit back and watch. "Quinn is at the edge of the cliff, and we might as well jump off with her."

CHAPTER 36

Back in my office, Bird was leaning over my laptop. He had made the listicle the lead story on our homepage and app. Within minutes, it had been shared across our social media feeds, our newsletter, and in every other corner of the Internet. He'd sent a message to every *Barker* employee, encouraging them to make sharing his piece their priority. It was on its way to going viral.

"Done," Bird announced.

I sat in the swiveling chair next to him and turned the laptop toward me. It now showed Quinn's video in the upper left and a browser tab open to a blank page on the right.

"Just type in blank box," Bird said. "Then click 'Post' each time you're done with a thought, and it will post."

"Good, let me see how it'll look on our site."

He pulled up another tab, a special page he'd created that had three elements. On the top left was Quinn's live video. On the top right, a blank text area with the header, "Live Commentary from *Barker* CEO Alex Vane." The bottom third of the screen had links and previews of the listicle he'd just published and the story from *The Dissident Blog,* plus links to a few summaries of Gunstott's China deal.

"How'd you get the Facebook video onto our site?"

"You don't want to know."

"Is this going to get us shut down?"

"Probably not in the next hour, but it's bad. You can't just get the video to show up, so I had to set up a screen capture on my personal laptop, and beam it to our site. There will be a second or so of lag time since what you're seeing on our site is essentially a live video of my laptop screen, which I've set to full screen playing Quinn's live stream."

We could deal with the fallout tomorrow, but now Quinn was speaking again. "What are all those little blue thumbs and hearts going across my screen?" She was staring at the phone and I smiled, knowing just how clueless she was about the impact she was having.

The video was now being watched by 700,000 people, and growing. I tried sending Quinn a private message to the account she'd used the day before, but I knew she probably wouldn't see it.

"I'm heading down a long stretch of straight, flat highway," Quinn said. "I'm about six hours outside of Las Vegas, and I drove the opposite direction on this road only six days ago. Until then, I'd been living quietly and happily— well, not exactly happily—but living, anyway, dammit, in a small house in Las Vegas. That's when Alex Vane, the CEO of *The Barker* showed up on my doorstep with a hard drive."

From that point on, she spent about twenty minutes telling the story, step by step, of our trip. While she did, I added notes, essentially a running commentary on her narrative, hitting "Post" after every comment. When I clicked "Post," the text would go live to the page with a little time and date stamp. Usually I just confirmed what she'd said, sometimes I added details she omitted. It was when she got to her disappearance that I had to listen out of one ear while typing my story.

"Outside of Allied Regional Data Security, I came apart. All the stuff that had happened to me since 9/11—and really since birth—just came crashing down. Sitting outside of the embodiment of the secret security state, I just lost it. Alex dropped me at a coffee shop and I went in, fully intending to stay there, to ride it out. But I couldn't. I had someone bring my dog, Smedley, into the coffee shop. Then I bolted."

I hadn't even thought of Smedley, but he must've perked up at the mention of his name because I heard a little whimper and Quinn glanced up at the rearview mirror and smiled slightly. I thought of him fondly, slobbering in the back seat, keeping Quinn company.

"I came back to the home of Tudayapi, and convinced her to upload the documents behind the Great Firewall. I sent ten minutes of audio to CNN, the ten minutes you've no doubt heard already. And I'd planned to leave it at that. The next day, as I refilled my tank on the way out of town, two plainclothes officers or CIA agents or gestapo goons approached me. Well, they didn't actually have time to approach me. I shot them before they got close. Up until the shooting, all of it had been orchestrated by Dewey Gunstott to protect his deal with the Chinese government."

Quinn was a little bit behind on the facts, so I began correcting her in my posts. Not that she could see it, but I liked to think that she would have appreciated the end result, which was the two of us having an argument in real time. It was a multimedia, live-streaming, breaking news story the likes of which the world had never seen.

When she got to the end, her eyes grew wet, and she said, "I doubt I'll make it back to Las Vegas."

The video now had over a million viewers and had been airing for forty-five minutes. The entire staff at *The Barker* was watching, while sharing our page everywhere they could. Bird's listicle had already surpassed a million page views, and was being retweeted a thousand times a minute. It was the definition of viral. And he'd updated the list to include a link to the special page he'd created, so a quarter million people were now watching Quinn's feed on our page while reading my posts.

#TheBarker was trending on Twitter, and so was #QuinnRivers.

In the silence, I thought of Tudayapi and called her from my cell. She picked up after one ring and said, "Alex, I'm already doing it."

"What?"

"Are you calling me to see if I'll route your page and Quinn's video through my servers to China?"

"How'd you—"

"I'm telling you, Alex, I know you. From your articles."

Five minutes later, I got a text from Tudayapi. "It's up in China."

The Dissident Blog was mirroring our page, carrying it live so their Chinese readers could see Quinn's video and my comments, neither of which would be visible on regular Chinese platforms.

Then the sirens started, and I started fearing for Quinn's life. Getting all the facts out in the open was one thing, but I still didn't believe this could end well.

"Sirens have started behind me. I'm not sure who it is, but I intend to keep this video live as long as I can, to make you see how non-conformists are treated in this country. Luckily, I am a woman, so they might not shoot me immediately. But since they know I killed the two back in Owyhee, they might anyway."

Bird had been running around the office, checking stats and making sure the page was as viral as possible. He glided in and leaned over my shoulder. "The thing has exploded, Alex. CNN just broke in with live coverage. They mentioned us and are trying to get permission to carry the video live across their network, but for now they're just showing screenshots. If Facebook won't give them the permission to air it live, we are going to get absolutely reamed for what we're doing. We—"

"Don't have time to consider it now. Bird, look." I pressed

my finger into the screen. Quinn was crying, lightly and almost imperceptibly.

I wracked my brain, trying to figure out how to help.

Suddenly, I lunged at my desk phone and buzzed Mia. "Can you find me the number of Captain Shonda Payton of the LVMPD right away?"

I only had one card left to play.

CHAPTER 37

As she often did, Mia over-delivered.

After being told that Captain Payton wasn't on duty that day, she did a quick Google search and learned that she had been put on temporary paid leave, for undisclosed reasons. Two minutes later, she'd found her home number and connected us.

"Hello?" I recognized Captain Payton's voice from her appearances on TV just after the shooting.

"Are you watching the news?"

"Who is this?"

"Sorry, this is Alex Vane. CEO of *The Barker*. My friend is about to get shot about five hours north of you. I'm the guy who had the audio. The one of the shooting."

There was a short pause, then she said, "I shouldn't be talking to you."

"Captain Payton, ma'am, please. Turn on the news, open up Facebook. The woman in that car is about to be killed because she leaked the audio of the shooting. I have the rest of it. Now, I don't know exactly what happened, and neither does she. But I think *you* do."

She was quiet for a moment, then spoke again, her voice weaker. "I've been watching. I...I've been trying to figure out what to do. I—"

"Please," I said, "we don't have much time. I need you to help me keep her alive. Do you have a camera on your computer?"

***

Captain Payton went live on Facebook about ten seconds before she dialed the Nevada Highway Patrol. Bird shared her Facebook stream on the official *Barker* page, and had his army of interns share it to their personal pages as well. By the time she got connected with a staff sergeant, Bird was posting the full audio recording to our site, and 5,000 people were watching her call live.

"Colonel McGuire," she said. "I need to tell you now that this call is being broadcast live on Facebook. This is Captain Shonda Payton of the LVMPD. Are you aware of the chase on Highway 45 right now?"

"I took this call as a courtesy to a fellow officer," he said, his voice gruff and irritated. "I'm getting calls from news networks as we speak."

"Please, Colonel McGuire. I swear to you, I'm not trying to embarrass you or your troopers. The woman who is being followed down Highway 45 right now is mentally unstable. She also has evidence regarding the shooting at *The Las Vegas Gazette*. I've been put on temporary leave for questioning the official story of that shooting. That story is false. Please, step in, call your men or women in uniform. Make sure they take her alive."

"Is she armed?'

"Yes."

"Did she kill two people?"

"Yes, but they were not police officers, and she says it was self-defense."

"My troopers are well trained, and I'm sure they will do everything they can to end this safely."

He hung up without another word.

Within minutes, Bird had updated our page to include an archive of Captain Payton's video. He'd also added a mirror of her live stream, which she was continuing.

I was going back and forth between her video and Quinn's, muting one while listening to the other. Quinn had slowed down to fifty miles per hour. I could see that she was thinking—walking that little square with her eyes—but she'd been silent for over fifteen minutes. The sirens still wailed faintly in the background.

Meanwhile, Captain Payton was ending her career.

Over the course of five minutes, she displayed eight different photos in front of the live video. The first four were of bullet holes in the walls of *The Gazette*. As she displayed them one by one, she explained how the kill shots on each of the five victims had been perfectly placed. "Death on impact," she said. "The kind of shots a professional executes. But then there are about five holes in the walls, in spots not very near victims. Either the shooter was perfectly accurate, then wildly inaccurate, or the shooter—or shooters—were perfectly accurate, then added a few random shots around the office to make the shooting look more amateurish. If you've listened to the audio leaked three days ago, these four bullet holes correspond with shots eight through eleven in the recordings."

The next two photos were of the drive. Or the remaining pieces of the drive.

"There was one more bullet fired, twelve shots in all. And this is what tipped me off to begin with. I found these fragments next to the body of James Stacy on the floor of the office where three of the bodies were found. At first, I made nothing of it. Just some old piece of junk that got caught in the fire. But further inspection uncovered a one-ounce slug embedded in the floor under Benjamin Huang's desk. My theory? The shooter shot the drive separately, the bullet passed through the desk and lodged in the floor."

She showed pictures of the desk and the floor.

"I will lose my job for this, no doubt. But when I brought these facts to the attention of my superiors, I was told to move on. 'We have the killer,' I was told. 'No need to go over what he did with a fine-tooth comb.' Now, let me go through these again."

I switched off her video and turned on Quinn's. Her head was tilted slightly back and I could hear noise from outside her car. "They're saying something to me," she said. "Through a bullhorn. They want me to pull over. To throw any weapons out of the car. They say that they have a tire slasher set up ten miles ahead, and this is my last chance to be taken safely."

I wanted her to live, but, at the same time, I didn't think she'd make it in jail.

"Pull over," I whispered to myself. "Pull. Over."

Quinn said, "I don't believe they will take me peacefully. They'll torture me, to find out what I know, and I'm not going to let that happen." She moved out of the frame, and seemed to be turning the wheel. A light screech of the tires, then the phone wobbled. "I've turned off the road, onto the desert flats."

Just then Bird burst through my door, waving for me to come out. "They've got a live shot."

I grabbed my laptop and followed him into the open area of the office. Every screen in the place was playing CNN, which had a shot of Quinn's red truck from a helicopter above, but muted so we could hear Quinn's audio.

Over three million people were watching her live stream, and now millions more were watching the view from above on TV. One way or another, Quinn's story was going to be told.

The CNN shot panned out and showed the area around the truck. Quinn had turned onto a patch of flat, cracked desert that seemed to go on for miles before ending at some craggy hills.

"I don't see any way out," she said. "There are low mountains a few miles away, and this patch of land is getting bumpier. I don't...I don't know what to do. And I'm almost out of gas."

I started thinking about suicide by cop. I don't pray, but, in that moment, I started asking a higher power I don't believe in to please not let her get killed on TV. I figured that different parts of her brain must be fighting one another. The part that so desperately wanted to believe that everyone was out to get her would want to get shot, would want to have the cops end it. I just prayed there was another part. A part that wanted to survive.

She drove on for another couple minutes, slowing as the land got rougher. Her phone jostled up and down, causing her to come in and out of the shot. The CNN helicopter was still showing the truck, and Quinn seemed to be nearing the hills.

Then, just like that, her truck stopped.

She slammed on the brakes and her head shot forward, so, for a moment, all I could see was the seat. On the overhead shot, I watched the truck stop, dust swirling behind it.

Quinn grabbed the phone, turning it on her face as she got out of the truck. She spoke quietly. "I have a friend named Alex Vane, who is part of all this. I already mentioned him, I think. I did, right? He has more faith in the system than I do. If I get shot, I'll blame him. If I get tortured, I'll blame him."

She turned her head and let out a quick whistle, then crouched down. "Good boy," she said. The video caught a quick shot of Smedley running to her side. "And if anything happens to Smedley, I'll find Alex and kill him."

The helicopter camera was locked on her now, slowly zooming in as the dust settled and the police cars raced toward her.

"Put your hands up," I said to myself.

Quinn trained the phone on the police cars, which were only a hundred yards away. The last thing she said before she stuck her arms up was, "Take care of Smedley, Alex."

She dropped the phone and her live stream went light blue, but didn't end. Just a static shot of the sky. But from the helicopter camera, we could see what happened next.

Four police cars rolled up, two on either side of her, stopping about thirty yards away. Smedley was running in circles around Quinn, dust flying everywhere, as eight officers jumped out and drew their weapons.

"Don't shoot," I said to myself.

For a full minute, the standoff continued. Quinn's hands up, officers pointing guns at her, Smedley running circles around Quinn as if to protect her. Both Quinn's phone and the helicopter camera were too far away to pick up audio, but I could see Smedley snarling as the officers shouted at Quinn to drop to the ground.

Then Smedley stopped circling Quinn and lay down at her feet, brushing her left leg. Quinn lowered her left hand, reaching for him like she was going to pet his head, to reassure him. But to one trigger-happy cop, it must have looked like she was reaching for a gun. He fired, and Quinn collapsed like a rag doll alongside Smedley, face down in the chalky desert.

I thought she was dead, but no.

Holding her right leg, she inched in the direction of the truck as two officers ran toward her.

Then I realized that she wasn't crawling toward the truck. She was crawling toward her phone. The static shot of the light blue sky switched suddenly to a close-up shot of her face, covered in dust. "They shot me, Alex. Right leg. Come get me."

Her live stream ended and, from the helicopter shot, I could see her throwing the phone aside as the two officers reached her. I never would have imagined that I'd be relieved to see a friend carried off in handcuffs.

CHAPTER 38

Thursday, June 22, 2017

Greta and I landed at the Boise airport the next morning and drove straight to the jail where Quinn was being held, which was the city jail of Jackpot, Nevada.

I'd love to tell you that we held hands on the airplane, that this whole ordeal brought us right back into each other's arms. But you and I both know that things don't work out that easily. Because we'd booked last-minute flights, we didn't even sit next to each other on the plane. In the rental car, she complained about "new car smell," and we almost got into an argument when I assured her it *couldn't possibly* be "new car smell" because the car had 60,000 miles on it. We agreed that it must be the air freshener, and moved on. But I could tell she'd enjoyed the spat, and so had I.

I spent most of the ride from the airport on the phone with my lawyer, who had flown in from Seattle and was already at the jail where Quinn was being held. I told her to spare no expense to get Quinn paroled.

It turned out that the two people she'd shot were Holly and Bonnie. My captors, my torturers. After releasing me, they'd tracked her to Owyhee, and she'd gotten the drop on them.

Her video had been the biggest in the history of Facebook Live, and every news station in the country was talking about it. Side-by-side, time-synced videos of the aerial footage and her video were already popping up on YouTube. Message boards were debating Quinn, her background, and her mental health.

But even more, people were discussing the shooting. The full audio, combined with Captain Payton's photos, had forced the LVMPD to admit its errors in the case. It had also gotten her fired because the crime scene photos had been copied illegally and displayed to the public even more illegally. I'd called to offer her a job as a crime consultant for *The Barker*, figuring we could launch a new crime blog and a YouTube channel discussing the big cases of the day. But she'd turned me down, saying that she was going to fight her firing through the police union. Once the whole thing quieted down, and assuming she was proven right, she thought she might be able to get reinstated.

Bird's listicle had gone more viral than anything we'd run at *The Barker*. As he'd predicted, the fan base of Star Wars responded loudly to his headline. Bird was pissed that we'd cost ourselves about $200,000 by running the story ad-free. But our app had been downloaded a half million times in the last day, which would more than make up for the loss.

IFMH itself was catching heat from all angles. Various petitions to boycott the company's media properties had sprung up online, and rumors were swirling in the business press that a combination of pressure from consumers and the Chinese government would derail Gunstott's deal. According to Tudayapi, *The Dissident Blog* had been shut down overnight, but the journalists involved had escaped and managed to remain anonymous, their data secure in her loft on the Duck Valley Indian Reservation.

By the time Greta and I reached the jail—a one-story brick building that looked like it belonged on a postcard for a Nevada ghost town—the press was swarming. They'd driven in from Las Vegas, Boise, and Salt Lake City, and flown in from California and New York. Rumor was that a handful of Chinese journalists were flying in as well.

I parked across the street from the jail and checked my phone. My lawyer had texted me.

Inside with the police. They will not let you see her. I tried. More when I know more.

Seconds later, a guy with a microphone recognized me and ran across the street, accompanied by a guy with a TV camera.

"Alex," Greta said. "Can we get out of here?"

I pulled away from the jail without another word, and we drove to the edge of town, stopping on a dusty side road surrounded by distant brown hills. Greta got out and sat on the hood of the rental. I followed and perched on the hood alongside her.

It was only ten in the morning, but already in the high-eighties. I was happy to be alive, and sitting with Greta.

"Do you want to tell me about what happened?" she asked.

I did. I wanted to tell her everything. To go through the last week and a half moment by moment, to cry about James and tell her about Quinn. I wanted to see the look on her face as I took her through Vegas, Duck Valley, and ARDS. I wanted to display my storytelling chops and weave the whole thing into a narrative that would make her love me.

And I wanted to apologize for the fact that she'd gotten wrapped up in it, and to ask for her help in undoing the damage done to me in that box. In that room. And, for the first time, I felt ready to talk about Rebecca.

I opened my mouth to tell her everything, but, instead, I

said, "Can we just sit in quiet for a minute? What I really want to tell you is...just thanks for coming. For coming with me."

My cellphone rang, but I didn't move to get it.

Greta smiled. "It could be your lawyer."

I slid off the hood of the car to grab it from inside.

"Alex, it's gonna be okay." It was my lawyer, calling from her car. "I'm on my way back to the airport."

"Wait, aren't we going to meet? We're just outside of town. Can you get me in to see Quinn?"

"Alex, listen. You're not going to get in to see Quinn. No one is getting in except her lawyer and direct family."

"But she doesn't have any—"

"Alex, I know, listen!" She was quiet until she was sure she'd shut me up. "Thank you. I was saying, it's going to be okay. I have *good* news. It's too early to know for sure, but I don't think they're even going to charge her with murder. The sheriff was a straight shooter, which I appreciated. He said they had security camera footage from outside the gas station. Said they had two witnesses saying it was self-defense. The people she shot weren't cops, and didn't identify themselves as such. It's still not clear who exactly they were, or who they were with."

"They're private security contractors, cleaning up a very big mess they made themselves."

"If that's true, they're operating illegally on U.S. soil, and self-defense is going to be a makeable case, if they even decide to prosecute. Other than that, Quinn's firearm wasn't registered, but in Nevada that's not as big a deal as it would have been elsewhere. I can likely get her probation for that. They have her on resisting arrest and trespassing, for driving off the highway. But with her mental health issues...I don't know. We might be able to get her off with a few slaps on the wrist."

"What about bail?"

"We'll know tomorrow. Just sit tight. Stay out of the press until we see what happens."

"How did she seem?"

"Better than expected with all she's been through." She paused, and I was about to hang up. "Oh, and there's one more thing. They're holding a dog at the local pound, under your name. Animals usually go to next of kin, but, since Quinn doesn't have any, she named you."

I thanked her and told her I'd pay any bail or do anything else necessary to get Quinn out. She was going to get in touch with the best defense attorneys in Nevada to try to bring a local partner onto the case by the end of the day. Given the profile of the story, and the amount of money I was willing to spend, it wouldn't be hard to get the very best.

***

Greta and I sat on the hood of the rental car for another hour, then drove south until we found a town big enough to have a hotel and a diner. We slid into a red leather booth and sat in silence until the waiter came from behind the counter. After we'd ordered, Greta excused herself to use the bathroom and I pulled my phone out of my pocket.

I'd been wanting to check it for a while, but Greta's presence was enough to stay my hand. I wanted to see if there had been any new developments on any front, to check how the networks were covering the Gunstott deal and the China situation, and to check in with Bird and Mia.

But when I opened my phone, I had a new text from a site called Text UR Buds Free. The message seemed to have no phone number associated with it and, when I swiped open the message, the official sender was listed as noreply@texturbuds.com.

But I knew who it was from.

If you're receiving this, I'm either dead or in jail. I set up this message to send automatically by installing a pretty basic script at a 24-7 Internet cafe in Boise. When I decided to drive back to Owyhee, I knew things might get ugly. I thought about Innerva and James. What they had.

And I thought about who I'd want to know if something happened. If I died. Don't get too full of yourself. I was drunk when I made that pass at you. But you're not as bad as I thought you were. Also, if you're getting this, take care of Smedley for us.

Greta eased into the booth and saw the smile on my face. "What?"

"Quinn. She set up a Dead Man's Switch for me."

"A what?"

"It's a thing where...never mind. Doesn't matter. Quinn's going to be okay. And we're getting a wrinkly-faced brown dog." I looked up, realizing I'd said "we're" instead of "I'm."

I felt encouraged that Greta didn't take her eyes off me. We both sipped our water awkwardly. It was one of those moments where there's so much to say that no one can speak.

When our food arrived, I said, "We have time, Greta. I want to tell you what happened, and I will. But I know you're not my therapist, and I'm going to need one." I paused, then said, "Things happened. I was tortured."

"Oh my God, I—"

"It's okay, I'm okay. Well, I'm not okay, but I will be."

"I'll help you find help."

"Thank you."

The food came a couple minutes later. Greta had ordered a half cantaloupe, filled with cottage cheese. Not her normal brunch. "I thought you didn't eat dairy," I said, just to break the silence.

"Usually don't, but I've actually relaxed a little since we separated." She managed a slight smile. "Everything in moderation, right?"

I nodded down at my plate. "You're okay with me ordering bacon?"

She smiled. "No, but I was thinking, maybe we should start meeting for coffee again."

All my ideas about saving my marriage were dissolving. What I wanted was to be with her, to spend time with her. To enjoy her at her best, with me at mine. I loved her enough in that moment not to care whether she was going to go through with the divorce. I just loved her. I said, "Sounds good. I'll have my people call your people in a couple days to set it up."

We looked at each other and laughed, all tensions between us resolved. It might have only been thirty seconds, but it felt like forever. Finally, I asked, "What does 'walk each other home' *mean*, anyway?"

"You've asked me that a hundred times."

"And you've never told me."

"How does it make you feel when you hear it?"

My eyes watered and I looked down, studying the bacon and toast and home fries on my plate as they went out of focus. I took a deep breath as Greta placed her warm hand softly on the side of my neck.

"It makes me feel like I *am* home," I said.

—The End—

ACKNOWLEDGEMENTS

As always, there are more people to thank than I can possibly remember. But I'm going to make a go at it anyway. For all their love and support along the way, and for playing roles large and small in the creation of this book, I'd like to thank:

Amanda Allen who, in addition to being my wife of fifteen years, is my first editor and greatest supporter. She deserves credit for many of the best lines in this book.

My dad, Robert Fuller, for his excellent editorial advice on this book.

My children, Arden and Charlie.

My extended family of Fullers, Johnsons, Allens, and Andersons.

All my wonderful guests on the WRITER 2.0 Podcast, who teach me so much.

The staff and students of Northwest Indian College and the Suquamish and Port Gamble S'Klallam Tribes.

My proofreader, Sue Currin.

My cover designer, Melissa Panio-Petersen.

The members of my Street Team and Advanced Reader Team, who offer support and feedback on early drafts. I can't thank them enough.

ABOUT THE AUTHOR

A.C. Fuller is the author of media thrillers and the creator and host of the WRITER 2.0 Podcast, a weekly interview show featuring award-winning writers and publishing experts. Once a journalist in New York, he now teaches writing around the country and internationally, including workshops for the Pacific Northwest Writers Association and the Royal City Literary Arts Society.

From 2006 to 2008 he was an adjunct professor of journalism at NYU, and he now teaches English at Northwest Indian College near Seattle. He lives with his wife, two children, and two dogs near Seattle. For a free sample of one of A.C.'s books, check out: www.acfuller.com/readerclub